FEARLESS

STEEL DEMONS MC BOOK THREE

CRYSTAL ASH

Prologue

RORY

AGE SIXTEEN

"My mom is going to fucking kill me."

"At least you'll be put out of your misery," Jandro grumbled next to me. He shifted uncomfortably, straining at the handcuffs holding his wrists behind his back. "Tia Ana is gonna make damn sure I suffer if I get home. And if not her, my sisters will."

"Hey!" The sheriff's deputy in the passenger seat of the van slammed his baton against the partition separating us from him. "Shut the fuck up back there, fucking delinquents!"

"Fuck you, mall cop," I shot back, straining against the bite of metal on my own wrists.

"Watch your damn mouth, son. You want to spend some time in the hole?"

"You busted us for smoking weed and skateboarding in an empty pool. Don't try to fucking scare me!"

"Rory," Jandro hissed under his breath.

"What?"

"Ever think shutting your damn mouth might be a good idea?"

"We're minors, Dro. They can't do shit to us."

"Unless they want to try us as adults," he kept whispering. "In case you haven't noticed, we're close to the border and I'm kinda brown."

I bit the inside of my cheek. Fuck, I hadn't even thought of that. Jandro was like a brother to me. It hadn't occurred to me that he might have a completely different experience when it came to cops. As lame as these stupid deputies were, they still had guns, batons, and pepper spray. Assuming the news reports weren't faked, law enforcement had been targeting Latinos and other minorities for decades. Especially since that law passed that officers of the law couldn't be charged with murder. That was some bullshit.

"You speak perfect English though," was all I could think of to reassure Jandro. "No one's gonna mistake you for an illegal."

He gave me a scathing look. "Maybe not, *if* I get the chance to open my mouth before they pop a hundred caps in my ass." He sighed as his head tipped back to lean on the van wall. "And if they raid my aunt and uncle's place? What then?"

I swallowed dryly. His aunt and uncle were kind, albeit simple people. They spoke only broken English but welcomed me into their home like a son. I liked hanging out there because it was more low-key than my house with my mom and three dads hovering all the time. Plus, Jandro's sister Angelica was pretty, and I wanted to kiss her next time I went over.

I'd never see any of them again if the cops raided Jandro's house.

"Sorry, dude," I muttered. "I'll shut the fuck up."

"Why thank you," he declared sarcastically. "I swear to God, you'll be the death of me one day."

"Noelle tells me the same thing, especially after I lit that firework right next to her face," I snickered. "She's started calling me Reaper."

"Huh," Jandro snorted. "You could make that your road name. It actually fucking fits."

The deputies pulled up to the county jail and hauled us out of the back of the van by our arms.

"Hey, wait a minute." I struggled to catch my footing with how hard these assholes were shoving me. "We're sixteen. Why aren't we at the juvie hall?"

"It's packed full of other lowlifes like you. You dicks are overflow." A hard push slammed into the center of my back. "Move."

We got stripped of all of our belongings, then our fingerprints and mugshots taken before being shoved into an iron-barred cell not much bigger than a bathroom. At least the handcuffs came off then.

"Hey, don't we get a phone call or something?" I asked the deputy locking our cell door.

The fat, bald dipshit lifted one shoulder in a shrug before grinning snidely at me. "Maybe. If I feel like it on my next shift."

"You piece of shit! We have rights!" I called after him as he left the room.

"No, we don't." Jandro was already making himself comfortable on the cot along the cell wall. "Not really, anyway."

"Yeah we do, bro. They gotta give us lawyers and trials and shit."

"Have you listened to the radio lately? People are disappearing and jack shit's being done about it. They'll keep us here as long as they damn well please."

"Dude, we'll be fine. I mean fuck, we didn't even *do* anything!"

"Exactly my point." Jandro raised his pointer finger to the ceiling. "We're sitting in a jail cell for what? Stealing? Assault? Running a traffic light? No, Rory. They had no reason to arrest us and therefore, no reason to let us out. That's the way the world's going."

The door down the hall opened before I could retort. Expecting to see the deputy, I called out, "Yeah, thought you'd come back, dickwad!" much to Jandro's chagrin.

Instead, some kid, no older than us, came swaggering up to our cell wearing a smug, punchable smile. I hated him instantly.

He wore some kind of prep school uniform, shirt untucked and navy tie loosened around his neck. His blonde hair was cut close to his scalp, not a single strand out of place. Add in his perfectly aligned, white teeth and baby blue eyes, it was clear this kid lived worlds apart from me and Jandro.

"See something you like, punk bitch?" I challenged, pressing up against the bars.

"Stop it, Rory," Jandro groaned from the cot.

I ignored him, naturally.

"You want some of this?" I squeezed my dick through my pants, not taking my eyes off of the preppy dipshit. "If I squint real hard and pretend, I might even mistake you for a girl."

"I don't want to suck your dick," the kid said. "Just wanted to see what all the chatter was about upstairs," he nodded toward the hallway leading out. "Seems you all pissed off the deputies."

"What, and someone let *you* come down here and risk getting your hands dirty?" I mocked.

"My uncle's the sheriff," the kid grinned. "And trust me, my hands are way dirtier than he knows."

"Don't think you can impress us with your slum tourism," Jandro piped up.

"Aw, don't let the uniform fool you, *hombré*." The kid ran a hand through his blonde hair, a few strands coming loose. "I got connections you guys can't even fathom."

"Please," Jandro muttered, rubbing his forehead. "Just stop talking and don't ever call me *hombré* again."

"Fair enough. I'll prove it. You two want outta here?" That got our interest and the kid's eyes sparkled with glee. "I'll post your bail. You can walk out of here in an hour, tops."

"In exchange for what?" I crossed my arms.

The kid paused, shoving his hands deep in the pockets of his pressed slacks.

"Can one of y'all fix a vintage motorcycle?"

"For real?" I coughed out a laugh.

"It has sentimental value, okay?" He glowered at me.

"It was my grandfather's before he passed. I've tried fixing it myself, watching videos and shit, but something's not clicking."

"Make, model and year?" Jandro asked, sitting up from the cot.

"Harley Road King, 2020."

Jandro let out a low whistle. "That was a damn good year. Hard to find parts nowadays, but I can probably scrounge 'em up."

"You can fix it?" The kid's blue eyes grew wide with hope.

"Depends on what's wrong, but yeah, most likely."

"That," I pointed over my shoulder at Jandro, "is the best damn bike mechanic you will ever fucking meet. We ride on weekends sometimes, and if you really can get us out of here," I leaned against the bars, "we might let you tag along once your granddad's steed is running again."

The kid smiled again, and it looked genuine this time rather than smug.

"I'll go talk to the bondsman," he said, walking backward away from our cell. "Back in a flash."

"Hey, hold up," I called after him. "What's your name?"

"Gunner," he answered. "Gunner Youngblood."

I stole a glance at Jandro. Maybe this preppy Gunner cat wasn't so bad after all.

ONE

MARIPOSA

PRESENT DAY

"**P**lease…"

The man let out another pathetic wheeze like he was dying. Like he could fool me, the one keeping him alive in order to receive justice from the Steel Demons, from the brotherhood he betrayed. I ignored his plea, and proceeded to stick him with a fresh IV bag for his bare minimum of nutrients.

"You're a healer," he tried again, reaching for my hand. "You're a good woman with a kind heart. Please, if you just set me up with a bag of food, and let me out of here so I can get my bike——"

"I may be a good woman with a kind heart, Python, but I'm not an idiot."

He tried yet again, from a different angle. "I could take you with me. You're miserable here. I saw it from that first day Reaper dragged you in. You don't have to be scared. I can protect——"

7

"Python," I sighed. "Even if I wanted to run away with you, you've got gunshot wounds in each leg, are still recovering from blood loss, and you've been on a liquid diet for three days. You might make it from your bed to the floor, but not much further than that. You're certainly in no shape to ride through the desert."

I cleaned up my supplies, snapped my gloves off, then rubbed a generous amount of hand sanitizer into my palms.

"Because I have such a kind heart," I stood up, "I won't tell Reaper you offered to take away his woman. He'd surely dish out something extra on you for that."

Python's face paled. "He's sharing you?"

"Yes."

"With who?"

I hesitated for a moment, unsure of how open these multi-person relationships were to the rest of the club. Then again, I kissed Reaper and Jandro in front of everyone at the party. I didn't recall anyone reacting weirdly to it, although I was only really focusing on two people at the time.

"Just Jandro for now," I answered.

The prisoner scowled and looked off to the corner of his cell. It was a comfortable room, as far as jail cells went. It reminded me of a cheap motel room, with a bed, bathroom, desk, and seating area. Only it had no windows or entertainment.

Reaper told me the cells had been quarantine rooms. Rich people had them installed in their neighborhoods about a decade before the Collapse, to isolate people who displayed symptoms of contagious diseases that had been on the rise, such as measles, polio, and deadly strains of flu. All the more reason to get the entire club vaccinated.

"Same time tomorrow," I told Python before nodding at Dallas, who stood guard in the room.

Dallas let me out and proceeded to stand just outside the door after locking it, weapon brandished. I knew they changed shifts every few hours and Gunner would take his post eventually. The only one not in rotation for guarding Python's cell was Bones, with whom he had been close. Python and Bones shared the same woman —Reaper's ex, Heather.

"Thank you again, Dallas." I didn't know him well, but he always struck me as one of the warmest Steel Demons. He had a kind face for a biker, with bushy eyebrows atop smiling blue eyes, a shaved head, and a dark beard reaching down to the top of his chest. Unlike one of the other guardsmen, Big G, Dallas seemed completely devoted to his wife, Andrea, which earned him points in my book.

"No need to thank me, Mari," he chuckled politely. "Just doin' my job."

I smiled in return. "Do you know when your captain's coming on guard duty?"

"Another hour, I think." He tilted his head in the direction of the conference room down the hall, where the club usually held church, and gave me a playful wink. "He's in there with Reaper now. I'm sure they wouldn't mind if you interrupted," he teased.

"Or Reaper will blow a head gasket and not speak to

me for the rest of the night," I returned, only half joking.

"That's always a risk," Dallas laughed. "But you have Jandro in case that happens."

Did I really? Have Jandro in the same way I had Reaper? Could I treat him like my man automatically? Did I have that right? Reaper encouraged us to spend time alone, to get to know each other. But the surly Steel Demons president was my safety net, and I didn't know how to navigate this thing with Jandro without Reaper there. In any case, I'd barely seen the charming VP since the party. He was buried in work at the shop with all the wrecked bikes from the Razor Wire ambush.

"Think I'll hang out with the guard dog to be safe." I tossed a small wave over my shoulder at Dallas, which he returned, before continuing down the hall.

Hades' big head lifted off of his paws, ears straight up in the air the moment he saw me turning the corner.

"How's my favorite boy?" I asked, quickening my pace toward him.

He let out a soft whine but didn't move a muscle from the closed door he guarded. I sat on the floor next to him and he immediately placed his head in my lap.

"Hades, I might love you more than your master," I said, massaging over his forehead and ears. "You are just the sweetest thing."

The affectionate, protective Doberman licked my hand and nuzzled into my pets, but his body remained alert and guarded. He took his job seriously, evidently, but who could resist pets? And Hades seemed especially partial to mine lately. Even Reaper started complaining that he liked me more.

The Steel Demons' president's low, murmuring voice floated to my ears through the door, though I couldn't make out the words. Gunner's voice answered him, whatever he said punctuated by an occasional chirp from Horus.

While I wasn't trying to eavesdrop, I still listened to their tones as I rested my head against the wall. They sounded tense. Not angry, but maybe a bit worried. Gunner just came back from a mission I still didn't know the full details of. All I knew was how pissed Reaper was about him going, but had allowed it anyway. And that it was some kind of last resort measure for the survival of the whole club. From how tense things were since Gun's return, the mission didn't appear to be a successful one.

He came upon Python, the imprisoned man I was just checking on, conspiring with a member of Razor Wire, the same club that ambushed us right on our doorstep. Finding the club traitor was the biggest Steel Demons victory, that and losing no one in the ambush.

But Python's punishment still had to be carried out. And I had a feeling the Steel Demons were wound up and tense because they felt like sitting ducks. Many of their bikes had been wrecked in the ambush.

Heavy footsteps approached the door and opened it before I could move. Hades lifted his head from my lap to look at his master with wide, innocent eyes.

"Some guard dog you are," Reaper huffed, reaching a hand down to pull me to my feet. He immediately braced a forearm against my lower back, anchoring my hip to his. "You didn't have to sit on the floor out here, sugar."

"I didn't mind." I scratched under Hades' chin. "And I didn't want to interrupt anything important."

"Nothing's too important for you," he murmured much lower and sexier than was necessary. "Just knock and I'll let you know what's up."

"Okay," I smiled, stroking a hand along his bicep.

He was being charming and sweet lately, all starry-eyed and smitten when he looked at me. This side of him was adorable, and I had to admit that I was surprised he kept it up for three days without totally putting his foot in his mouth. Not once did he take out club frustrations out on me. He snapped orders at his men, especially concerning the prisoner, then in the same breath, turned around and told me my ass looked nice in my scrubs.

Nothing but romance and poetry, being the president's old lady.

Even right then, his gaze softened from the pinched brow he wore coming out of his meeting with Gunner. He drew me close and kissed me full of depth and tongue, like we hadn't seen each other in days, much less a few hours ago.

"Done for the day?" he asked, dragging his lips to my cheek.

"Mm." I turned my head to catch sight of the tall, blonde captain of the guard, apparently trying to sneak out into the hall without saying anything. "Where you off to, Gunner?"

He whirled back around on the ball of his foot with

a sheepish grin, the falcon on his shoulder fluttering his wings at the sudden change in direction.

"Grabbing something to eat before I relieve Dallas on guard duty." He reached up to stroke the feathers on Horus' chest. "This little guy needs to catch some food too, before it gets dark."

"You owe me more swimming lessons, remember?"

Thanks to his gentle guidance and positive reinforcement, I was able to float on my back in the pool at the Sandia outpost. If any of the other guys had attempted to teach me, I'd probably end up looking like a drowned rat, and trust none of them near a body of water again.

His grin widened with a shy glance downward. "I sure do, baby girl. We'll get around to it, okay? Once all this other bullshit is taken care of."

"Sure." I returned a forced smile through the pang of rejection in my chest. "See you, Gun."

Reaper pressed a kiss to my temple with a chuckle as I watched the back of Gunner's cut float further down the hallway. "He'll be yours one day, sugar. Just give him time to come around."

"It's not even that," I said, turning into him. "We used to be able to talk like friends. And now he keeps blowing me off every time I say hello."

"Because he wants you as more than friends. And in his mind, you're off limits now that you're mine and Jandro's." His hand slid down to my ass where he took a gratuitous squeeze. "Speaking of, want to pay your Latin lover a visit?"

"Can you really call him that if there's been no loving going on?"

The question came out more grumbly than I intended. Jandro was busy. All the Steel Demons were, but it was up to Jandro and the two prospects to fix up the dozen or so wrecked bikes from the ambush. You'd think these men were caged animals with the way they acted with no motorcycles between their legs.

"Greedy girl," Reaper teased me. "Trust me, Mari, he wants to see you but it's a two-way street." He gave me a playful tap on the nose. "He knows you're new to this and doesn't want to overwhelm you. Now that the three of us are official, hiding out in the shop is a convenient way for you to come see *him*. Your comfort zone is sticking with me and he's not going to be the one to pull you out of that. That's on you, sugar."

He was right. Reaper repeatedly reminded me that I was the one in control of this three-way relationship. I was setting the pace and so far, I'd taken the easy route of just spending all my free time with him. Because I didn't know any other way. He and Jandro directed the kisses at the party, but they couldn't take charge like that all the time. I was an equal, contributing part of this relationship and I couldn't treat this the way I always had before. Not when I had the hearts of two men to care for.

My decision made, I removed Reaper's hand from my ass and laced my fingers with his. "Let's go see him."

TWO

GUNNER

"Do you have any good news to tell me?"

I wanted to drop my eyes to the table under the scrutinizing gaze of my president, but I wasn't a pussy. If I had to tell him I failed, I'd have the balls to look him in the eye as I did so.

"We have our snitch," I said. "Although that is some dumb fuckin' luck I rolled up at the exact moment I did, and nothing to do with my skills."

"I'm not even sure he's the only one," Reaper answered, rubbing his jaw. "If Bones and Heather knew about his scheming and didn't tell me, they have to answer for that too."

I nodded my agreement, drumming my fingers on the table while Horus adjusted the grip of his talons in my shoulder. Those sharp fuckers used to kill me. He dug in hard at first, and I had multiple scars on that one shoulder to prove it. Eventually, I got used to him always sitting there and he loosened his grip enough to hold on without piercing me.

"So you're holding him, then? Until you question the other two?"

"That's the plan. He's getting royal treatment for a prisoner, better than he fucking deserves, so he better not bitch." Reaper's lip curled. "If he does, I'm sure Mari will tell me about it."

Reaper's gaze softened as he uttered her name, and I fought the urge to snort derisively. He was utterly in love with our pretty medic and still passed her off to Jandro like some prized whore. I couldn't begin to understand it. If she were mine, any man that looked at her with desire would feel my knife at his throat. Women had to be cared for, protected. Especially in a world like this.

And fuck me, I did care for her. Maybe too much.

I could never bring myself to join the rotation of men who orbited her. I had to be content with my place on the outside. I was a guardian and provider for the Steel Demons. I'd guard her with my life and provide whatever supplies she needed for her medical practice. I knew what I was good at, and sharing a woman was not one of them.

"So your uncle really believes General Tash will sell part of his conquered land to him?" Reaper got back on topic, his expression hardening again. "He chose expanding his territory over paying a debt? Over his own family?"

"It was a long shot anyway," I sighed, propping my elbows on the table. "Tash has a way of making you feel like you're getting a good deal without being too generous. And he *will* honor his agreements, up to a point."

"Hindsight is 20/20, huh?" Reaper scoffed.

"Fucking tell me about it," I groaned. "I should have known a rising general wouldn't play ball with an MC forever. They all look down on us like scum."

"You couldn't have predicted this," Reaper said. "He didn't just cut us off, he worked to destroy us from the inside. Using another MC, no less."

"He probably pays Razor Wire a fraction of what he paid us," I realized. "We have standards and people to protect. They're just a bunch of dirty thugs on wheels."

"And he'll try to wipe them off the map too," Reaper added. "Once they've served their purpose for him. And good riddance to that, but," he tilted his head, "do you think he'll betray your uncle in the same way?"

I tented my fingers, idly tapping them together as I worked through all the likely scenarios in my head.

"Yes," I decided. "I don't believe for a second he's going to give part of the New Mexico territory to my uncle. Not after he obliterated the last governor's regime to take control of it. He's not a rebel anymore. He stormed the castle and now he's the new king. And he sure as shit wants to keep that crown on his head."

"That doesn't change a damn thing for us," Reaper growled. "He *will* be brought down. To keep using your metaphor, I want to throw his corpse over the castle walls wrapped in a Steel Demons flag."

"It'll be difficult," I warned him. "But easier with support, of course. The question is, are you willing to accept my uncle's help when he realizes the truth and crawls to us with his tail between his legs?"

"Hmm." Reaper lifted his gaze to stare at the wall, his jaw tense. "Maybe. Depends how badly he needs us.

I regret not making him dance like a monkey last time he begged us for protection."

"We will be in a position to negotiate to our advantage," I pointed out. "How much depends on if Tash simply goes back on his promise of land or actually moves to invade Colora—I mean, Jerriton. If my uncle's back is pushed against a wall, it could work out very well for us."

In all honesty, I actually hoped General Tash moved his army into Uncle Jerry's territory and set the whole fucking thing on fire. The vineyards on rolling hills, our gaudy Youngblood family crest engraved onto every gate and set of doors. The manicured topiaries, marble statues, and high-arching ceilings of his mansion—all built on the backs of slaves. I couldn't get that girl out of my head, the skinny blonde who'd been servicing him under his desk when I arrived. The poor thing was already dead inside. She'd probably willingly jump into the flames if an invading army came.

Uncle Jerry just couldn't be satisfied with the title of General. Like most others in my wretched family, he sought power and prestige at any cost. In his eyes, he saw a lavish lifestyle just like that of his ancestors before they left Hollywood. The price tag? Free labor, now that he didn't have pesky laws and concepts such as human rights to keep him in check.

"And he'll keep his word?" Reaper lifted a skeptical eyebrow.

"Honestly, I dunno," I sighed, leaning back in my chair. Horus hopped off my shoulder and fluttered to my leg to avoid smashing his tail feathers into the chair back. "He rose to power by being a fucking backstabber, just like Tash. He's manipulated his citizens and kept them prisoner. But if he's desperate enough, he might be forced to keep his word."

"So we should use him, but not trust him."

"That's what I suggest." I massaged the back of Horus's head with my thumb and forefinger. "After that gigantic waste of time of a visit, I don't think I can even pull the family card with him anymore. He'll always do what's in his own best interest."

"You didn't completely waste your time." Reaper slid off the table and headed for the door, indicating our meeting was over. "We're slightly less in the dark and learned valuable information because of you. And we did catch a snitch."

"Aw, shucks. Thanks, Reap," I laughed, rising from my chair. Horus returned to my shoulder and nipped at a lock of my hair, his signal that he was hungry and needed to get outside to hunt.

"I'm just stating a fact, not complimenting you." Reaper rolled his eyes. "But really, good work, Gun."

"Thank you, President," I said in a more formal tone, but couldn't help the smirk that followed. "I do think Mariposa is softening you up, though."

"Get the fuck out of here before I take it back," he snarled. But the hidden smile as he opened the door said he didn't disagree.

Hades was in his spot just over the threshold, but rather than sitting guarded and alert, he laid on his belly with his head in Mariposa's lap. She looked up at us with a smile, and I resisted the impulse to grin back. She wasn't mine and never would be.

"Some guard dog you are." Reaper reached down to pull Mariposa to her feet, his hand immediately transferring to around her waist. "You didn't have to sit on the floor out here, sugar."

"I didn't mind." She looked at my president like the sun rose and set on him. "And I didn't want to interrupt anything important."

"Nothing's too important for you," he murmured, lowering his face to hers.

I tried to slip out behind him into the hall. Not that I was trying to avoid Mari, but just keep a respectful distance. I didn't want to give anyone the idea that I wanted to join their weird harem arrangement. Plus, it was just too fucking awkward to stand around while those two sucked face.

But of course, I wasn't fast enough.

"Where you off to, Gunner?"

Plastering a smile on my face, I whipped back around on my foot. Horus flapped at the sudden change in direction and puffed up with annoyance. He was hungry and hated flying indoors.

"Grabbing something to eat before I relieve Dallas on guard duty." I stroked the feathers on Horus's chest to calm him. "This little guy needs to catch some food too before it gets dark."

Mari gave me a challenging, playful look that made my heart skip a beat. "You owe me more swimming lessons, remember?"

Of course I did. It was all I could think about. The

way she held onto me in that pool. The fear in her eyes, but her determination to overcome it. Not only was it sexy, I found it brave and admirable as hell. I'd be lying if I said I didn't consider making a move then. A wayward touch or a kiss would have been easy.

But she trusted me. And right after that shitty church session where Big G all but straight out accused *me* of being a traitor, I wasn't about to stomp all over that trust. Hell, it felt like she was the only person in the world in that moment who didn't look at me with suspicion and accusation. That swim lesson allowed me to calm the hell down.

She had no idea, but she'd already started talking me out of seeing red after making sure I didn't break my hand on the pool wall. It was just what I needed after feeling like I'd just been punched in the gut. Once she started floating on her back all by herself, I felt like myself again. More than that—she made me feel like I was needed and valued.

Mariposa needed to learn how to swim. It was an important skill. But I couldn't be the one to teach her. Because the next time we were alone in a pool, I might not be able to stop myself.

There was no way I could tell her all that. So I grinned sheepishly down at the floor, unable to look her in the eye. "I sure do, baby girl. We'll get around to it, okay? Once all this other bullshit is taken care of."

"Sure. See you, Gun."

I tried to ignore how sad she sounded as my motorcycle boots stomped down the hall, putting as much distance between me and her as possible.

MARIPOSA

"Have you seen the shop yet?" Reaper's hand remained clasped in mine as we walked through a quiet side street crossing the main road from the clubhouse.

"No. Was it already here or did you guys build it?" I asked.

It was fascinating to me how the Steel Demons and their families weren't only squatting in this once affluent gated community, they transformed it and made it into their home.

"It started out as one of the ugliest homes here," Reaper chuckled. "A two-story duplex, just this ugly-ass tall, rectangular building with no character. But the garages were spacious and really nice. They took up almost the entire first floor, so we opened up the ceiling, broke down the walls between the two duplexes, moved in some tools and equipment, and there you fuckin' have it."

He waved an arm as we turned a corner and there it

was. The building was grey and stuck out like a sore thumb among the other nice houses on the block. But it had that masculine, old-school mechanic's charm with both garage doors open, tools and motorcycle guts strewn all over the place, and hip-hop music playing on an ancient looking CD-player.

"Jandrooooo," Reaper called as we walked up the driveway. "Where the fuck are ya?"

A man popped his head out from behind a wall. I recognized him as Larkan, the guard from the Sandia outpost who gave the Steel Demons information about the general who attacked them. And the guy Reaper's sister seemed to have an instant-connection with.

"Hi, Reaper. Mariposa," he greeted us with a friendly smile, wiping his hands on a rag.

"You can call me *president*, prospect," Reaper hissed. "I'm not Reaper to you until you've earned it."

I stifled a groan, but otherwise didn't comment. These men and their ridiculous pecking order.

"Sorry, president." Larkin's smile faded. "Jandro's inside. I'll let him know you're here."

While he left, I turned around slowly to observe the place some more. Motorcycles in various states of assembly were everywhere. Against one wall, piles of tires in various sizes were stacked up nearly floor-to-ceiling. A few posters of bikini-clad women leaning over bikes in suggestive poses decorated the walls.

"There's my baby." Reaper came up next to me, pointing to a bike next to a work-bench. "Looks like Jandro's been trying to realign her frame."

"It doesn't even look like the same bike," I mused. "Last I saw, it was pretty much folded in half."

"Mm. That's why Jandro's the best at what he does."

I playfully nudged him in the ribs. "You realize I've never ridden on the back of your bike? At least, not willingly anyway."

"That's true, huh?" A mischievous spark lit up the president's green eyes. "Wanna go for a ride tomorrow, sugar?"

"Tomorrow?" I repeated, surprised. "Jandro's gonna be done by then?"

"I have other bikes, you know." He pinched my waist until I squirmed and swatted him away. "What kind of MC president would I be if I didn't have at least three?"

"So maybe I can ride my own." I lifted my chin at him.

"Not a chance," he laughed. "Not until I feel you all snug and sexy on my back at least once."

"I guess that's fair," I said, but jokingly pouted anyway.

He ran his thumb down my plump bottom lip. "We'll start you on a little dirt bike like Noelle's. The fat boys like we ride are bigger and harder to control. Don't worry, sugar," he grinned at me. "We'll make a Steel Demon out of you yet."

"Que quieres, chingado?"

The voice made us both turn around to see Jandro wearing a white fitted tank top that made his arms and shoulders look even bigger than normal, and accentuated his warm, caramel skin tone. His hands were clean, but he missed a grease stain on his forehead, which did nothing to detract from his looks. If anything, it made him even cuter.

His hazel eyes widened the moment he saw me.

"Shit. Sorry, Mari. I didn't know you were here too."

"It's okay," I smiled. "It was this *chingado's* idea to stop by and see you."

Both guys snorted with laughter. Movement from behind Jandro in the house's kitchen, which looked like a converted break room, made me look past him.

"Stephan!" I called with a wave. "Hey! How are you?"

"Oh! Mariposa." His pale cheeks flushed a shade of pink. "Hi. Nice to see you."

I originally met Stephan at Fight Night, the monthly event where the Steel Demons settled conflicts between each other with their fists. As a prospect, Stephan was not an official SDMC member yet and wore no patches. He apprenticed for Jandro at the shop, and was subjected to his hazing. Fight Night gave him a chance to unleash his frustrations back onto Jandro.

Unfortunately for him, Jandro was a better fighter.

"Nice to see you too," I smiled. "That lip is looking much better."

"Yes, ma'am." He reached up to touch his bottom lip, which had nearly returned to normal size. "Thanks to you."

"So it looks like you," I turned my gaze to Jandro, "haven't been abusing him?"

"No, ma'am." Jandro mimicked Stephan. "Been too busy putting him to work, honestly."

"Speaking of." Reaper pulled his cigarettes from his

pocket and stuck one in his mouth. "Let's take five, prospects. Out back."

Larkan and Stephan exchanged a nervous glance. Reaper just winked at me as he walked through the shop to the outside smoking area in the back. The prospects were quick to follow him, although clearly uneasy about having the president's undivided attention on them.

"That's one way to get us alone," Jandro chuckled, looking down as he arranged some tools in a metal box. He almost seemed nervous too.

"I just hope he's not a total dick to Larkan," I glanced toward the plumes of cigarette smoke already filling the air from the back patio.

"He won't be," Jandro grinned. "But I'll bet you every bike in here, he will use Fight Night as an excuse to beat his ass."

"Ugh. Is that coming up again?" I groaned.

"Next week," he confirmed with a nod.

"And are you going to use it as another excuse to humiliate Stephan?"

Jandro paused in his steadfast tool rearranging, pinning me with an intense look before answering. "Nah. I'm not fighting anyone this month. Honestly," he rubbed his jaw, glancing over his shoulder toward the others outside, "I'm really proud of Stephan. I'm gonna advocate for getting him patched in at our next church meeting."

"Wow," I breathed. "That's a big deal, isn't it?"

"He'll be a true Steel Demon." Jandro's eyes brightened. "He'll need a better road name than Stephan, that's for sure."

"How does that work? Do you guys give him a name or does he pick his own?"

"Depends. If something funny happens to him that warrants a nickname, we'll give him one. Or if all of his own ideas are dumb as hell."

"Why don't you have one?" I asked.

"'Cause there ain't no other Jandro," he grinned.

"You're right about that."

I slowly drifted closer to him as we talked. First my upper body swayed, leaning toward him as if carried by gentle breeze, and then my feet followed until I stood right next to him. He watched me with calm, measured interest, staying rooted to his spot.

"So how've you been?" My cheeks heated with the question. Reaper and I never really had the awkward small-talk phase in our relationship. But with Jandro, I wasn't sure how to act.

"Too fucking busy fixing all this shit," he grumbled, rubbing a hand down his face. "I've missed you."

My heart jumped into my throat at hearing that. When he reached across the short distance between us to rest his fingers on my waist, I had a momentary sensation of floating.

"I've missed you too," I answered, resting my hand on his bicep.

The touch barrier now crossed and miles behind us, he solidified his contact on me, pulling me closer as his other hand joined the first. The muscle under my hand flexed, his skin soothing and warm. This close, I picked up the scent of his soap, something citrusy mixed with a hint of motor oil.

"What have you been up to while I've been holed up in here?" His warm breath fanned across my lips. I could see my reflection in his green-brown shifting eye color.

"Babysitting Python. Monitoring Tessa's pregnancy. Some vaccine and check-up appointments." My hands drifted across his broad shoulders to rest around the back of his neck. "Nothing too exciting."

"Rory still being good?" He gave me a playfully stern look, lacing his hands at the small of my back.

"Yes," I giggled at his use of Reaper's real name. It became like an inside joke between us to tease the surly president. "He's been really good."

"Well, you know where to come if that changes." His voice grew lower, huskier as he pulled me closer still, widening his legs so I could stand between them.

"I won't just come to you for that." My torso now against his, I craned my neck to look up at him. "I've been wanting to see you. I just didn't want to bother you while you were working."

"Please come bother me." His forehead lowered to nearly brushing with mine as one hand slid up my back. "Your gorgeous face will be a welcome sight among all this fucking grease and metal and testosterone."

My lips pulled back into a smile. If this multi-partner thing worked out, I wondered if Jandro would keep the charm turned on or if he would stop eventually. It felt nice to be flattered by him, as much as I tried to resist it at first.

"Yeah, that's the smile I missed." One hand came up

to cup my chin, his gaze flicking from my lips to my eyes in a silent ask for permission.

I answered by lifting onto my toes and pressing my mouth to his. He sucked in a sharp breath of surprise before crushing me to his chest. His lips parted, returning the pressure of mine with pillowy softness. The last time I kissed him was a whole three days ago at the party, and I almost forgot how much I loved it. His lips were thick and succulent, his kisses slow, drawn-out and sensual.

He turned me into a puddle with that mouth while somehow keeping me together with his broad, strong arms around my back. My fingers curled into the dark hair on his head, dragging my nails across his scalp as he elicited soft moans. Our tongues danced erotically, but he always met me in the middle—never dominating the kiss like a certain president.

I didn't even realize how much I needed to breathe until he broke away with slow reluctance.

"Thanks for coming to see me," he whispered, stroking his thumb along my jaw. "I'd love to keep you and do this all night, but..." His eyes drifted to our surroundings of unrideable bikes and their guts strewn everywhere.

"You have to keep working," I finished for him.

He nodded, but didn't release his hold on me. "It doesn't look like it, but the biggest repairs are done. In another couple of days, my workload should be back to normal again."

"How long will you be at it tonight?"

He shrugged. "'Til I can't keep my eyes open."

I pressed my palms to his cheeks and looked straight at him. "You need to sleep. And make sure you drink enough water. Medic's orders."

"Hmm, not sure I can remember all that," he teased. "I'm just a dumb gearhead."

"Shut up," I rolled my eyes. Like Reaper, I had a feeling he was far more intelligent than he let on. When it came to bikes, I was all but certain he was a genius.

"You should come see me again, Mariposita," he grinned. "To remind me of those orders."

"I will if I have to," I said in a playful warning tone.

"Hell, I'll let a fat boy fall on me if that's what it takes to get you out here."

"That won't be necessary." I re-wrapped my arms around his neck and hovered my lips a hair-breath away from his. "As long as you keep kissing me like that."

FOUR

SHADOW

S unsets.

They were one of the few things I liked to take in and just appreciate. And from what Jandro and Reaper told me, the ones here in the Arizona territory were among the best in the world.

I liked to sit on the clubhouse rooftop balcony in the evenings and just watch the sky explode into colors. Some of which I didn't know existed until I was nearly ten years old. With a trusted bottle of liquor in my hand, it felt like I was swallowing the sun's fire from that sky. A death I would welcome, but whoever ruled the underworld these days didn't seem ready for me yet.

Soft laughter floated up from somewhere down below me, bringing my gaze from the sky to the streets.

Reaper and Mariposa walked together, looking like toy figures from my vantage point. Their hands clasped together, swinging between them. Hades walked a few feet in front of them, sniffing along the ground. They remained like that, their shadows long on the street until he wrapped an arm around her shoulders, drawing her into him as she laughed again.

I still wasn't all too familiar with what happiness looked like, or felt like, for that matter. But her smile at him appeared unrestrained. It reached her eyes, which remained glued to him. He looked and smiled at her in a similar way. Was that what happiness looked like? Or being in love? Did one automatically assume the other?

I took a pensive swig of my liquor bottle. Navigating the world in search of love or happiness seemed to be more trouble than it was worth. Especially for me, always trying to keep up with what was normal and accepted or not. Being brought into the club was the closest thing to happiness I would reach. It was better than anyone else born in my position could hope for. A connection with a woman, or anything beyond the brotherhood between my fellow Steel Demons and I, was simply out of the cards.

A door opened and shut behind me, but I didn't turn to look. The weight of the footfalls and the space between each step told me that Gunner had joined me on the balcony.

"Evening, Shadow," he mumbled as he fished a cigarette from his cut pocket and lit it.

I grunted out a wordless reply before taking another swig of liquid sunfire. Curiosity slid my gaze over in his direction. He didn't usually come up here during this time. The harsh exhale of smoke from his lungs indicated some proverbial weight sat on his chest. But I wasn't about to ask. We could drink and smoke, talk bikes, weapons, and hunting, but I couldn't offer deeper conversation than that.

I chalked it up to the ongoing conflict with General Tash, and how the club would be supplied with food and basic necessities now that our biggest trade partner was gone.

"Horus hunting?" I asked, noticing the absence of the bird usually perched on his shoulder.

Gunner nodded. "Yeah," he said with another harsh exhale. "He can't see that well once it starts getting dark, so thought I'd come up here so he can find me."

"Oh." I absently scratched at the scar cutting through my eyebrow and eyelid.

"He's a daytime hunter usually, but we've been meeting with Reap all day," Gunner continued, stretching his long arms above his head.

"Riding out tomorrow?"

"Yeah. Nowhere far, though. Just some local contacts for basic necessities." He looked at me with a smirk. Smiling came easily to him, whether he was with a woman or not. "I tell ya what, Shadow. I love riding as much as the next Demon, but I am not about to sit my ass on that thing for three straight days again. Gotta save some of my future children, you feel me?"

He cupped his crotch with a lewd chuckle. I understood what he meant, but couldn't relate to the feeling. So I just nodded and drank some more.

Returning my gaze to the sunset, a dark speck against the dark oranges and yellows of the sky slowly grew bigger. After a few seconds passed, I could make out wings stretched to the sides.

"There's my boy," Gunner muttered.

Horus approached us quickly. Gunner mentioned before that peregrine falcons were the fastest predators on earth. After seeing the crow-sized bird dive-bomb some Razor Wire members, I had to agree.

"What the—"

Surprising both of us, Horus's outstretched talons grabbed the balcony railing right in front of me, instead of his master. The falcon's beak and talons smeared with bits of fur and blood from his kill, he began to preen himself as if nothing was amiss.

"I guess he likes you," Gunner chuckled, lighting another cigarette.

I found that hard to believe, even for an animal. Nobody liked me, except maybe Jandro. And even then, I often felt like he tolerated me more than truly *liked* me.

Still, the close-up view of the curved beak and dark feathers on Horus's head pulled up a memory in my mind. My heart began to pound like a drum. Oddly enough, it was one of my last memories of being able to feel pain, but was one of the few positive, if even miraculous, occurrences in my life.

It had been years since I thought of that day, but I remembered it clearly. Drawing my blood had not been enough. The women were particularly ornery that day. When kept in darkness for most of my existence, bright light was an especially painful experience, and she had been eager to exploit that.

The cut over my eye still hadn't finished healing. She peeled back my shredded eyelid and shone a flashlight directly into my eye. It might as well have been a knife blade directly through my eye socket to my brain. My entire world was nothing but pain and darkness, and right then I had never experienced such pain in my life.

After she was done, there was more darkness and not the usual kind. I was almost certainly blinded. Whenever the mood struck her again, she'd surely do the same to my other eye. I'd never screamed like that before, and while I had a decent understanding of my bleak circumstances, I knew with absolute certainty then, that no one would help me. No one would ever stop them.

My sunset view back then was a mere crack in the wall of the prison I called home. I saw how the sky changed color throughout the transition from day to night. Sometimes I thought I saw slivers of clouds, but I could never be sure. The crack was only about an inch wide at the most.

The day after the light torture, I tried to look at the outside world with my one remaining good eye. But a fucking bird blocked my view.

Its dark eyes blessed with binocular vision taunted me. Small chunks of raw meat clung to its sharp beak, reminding me that I hadn't eaten anything in two days. I cursed out that bird and tore at the crack in the wall with my already weakened, bloody hands. I must have looked insane, scratching at a wall and yelling at a bird to get the fuck out of the way. But it was blocking the only view of the world I had from this cold, cruel prison.

I'd never forget the way that bird looked at me, with the wisdom of humanity and so much more, through an animal's eyes. Never would I forget what happened afterward.

My vision didn't just return to my blinded eye, but I saw what I never could before. While my occasional cell mates fumbled in the darkness, I could see everything as if it were broad daylight. When my torturers came down with flashlights and had to blink to adjust to the darkness, I saw every movement and expression.

That bird gave me the first, and one of the most precious, gifts I had ever received in my miserable life. I saw colors and details like I never imagined before. It was the first and only time I cried.

And that bird looked exactly like the one that rode around on Gunner's shoulder all day.

"Go ahead. He might peck at you as a warning if he doesn't like it, but he won't hurt you."

While lost in my memory, my hand reached out to touch Horus without realizing it. I knew Gunner and his falcon had some kind of otherworldly bond, just as Hades and Reaper did. But was it really the same bird that healed and enhanced my vision? I wondered ever since I first saw Horus with his talons curled into Gunner's shoulder. But it never felt right to ask. And the falcon had never flown so close to me before.

I stroked the back of my fingers against Horus's chest feathers a few times. When I put my hand down, the bird pecked at me.

"He doesn't want you to stop!" Gunner laughed. "Damn, look at you two all chummy."

"I feel like I've met this bird before." I looked at the blonde, smiling man with an uneasy glance, trying to gauge his reaction. Gunner was my brother by the Steel Demon code, but we weren't particularly close.

"Yeah, when?" His tone was curious, which came to me as a relief.

"Years ago," I confessed. "Way before I joined the club. When I was a kid."

"Not possible," Gunner shook his head. "Horus is just about two years old. I found him as a chick."

"Ah, okay."

He continued to look at me curiously. "What makes you think it was Horus?"

My heart rate sped up by half a beat. Despite knowing he could see through Horus at will, the gift of sight from my childhood felt deeply personal. I wanted to keep that knowledge under lock and key. Some of the guys figured out I could see well in the dark, but no one paid it any special attention. And I intended to keep it that way. No one could take anything away from me if they didn't know about it.

"I just knew the bird I met was different," I said.

A brush-off and he knew it, but he didn't bother prying.

"Interesting." Gunner flicked away his second cigarette. "Maybe there's more like him out there, who knows?"

Another question nagged at me. I almost couldn't bring myself to ask it, but not knowing the answer would torture me if I didn't.

"Does Horus ever…talk to you?"

Gunner's brow pinched. "What do you mean?"

"Like you can hear a voice in your head. But it's not your thoughts. It's like another person is talking to you, directly into your mind."

He took a long moment to answer.

"No, Horus doesn't talk to me like that."

"Oh. I was just curious."

The bird in question blinked his large, brown eyes at me before hopping a short flight across the railing to perch on his human's shoulder.

FIVE

REAPER

"You're wearing that?"

"What?" Mari stared down at her clothes before looking back up at me. "Should I change?"

She had on a long skirt with some bright tribal pattern, black ankle boots, and a simple black tank top. It was the skirt that concerned me. Not for riding, but for me. She'd have to hike that thing up, spread her legs open and press her bare thighs against me as we rode. Just the thought of it sent my cock twitching.

The fabric wasn't too form-fitting. She'd be comfortable, but the garment still outlined her hip and thigh in a way that drove me wild with wanting her. I had her every morning and night since after the party when Gunner returned, and it still wasn't enough. Oh, I *thought* I was sated after her sweet body drained my balls empty. But after a few hours of sleep, just a look, a wandering touch, or a kiss had me craving to get inside her again.

I've wanted women, but not like this. I never

continued to want them once they were well and truly mine.

"Just be careful," I told her, hitting the button to open the garage door. "Don't want you burning those legs on hot metal." I grabbed one of Noelle's helmets off the shelf and handed it to her.

"Where's your helmet?" she asked, securing the strap under her chin.

"Inside my head," I smirked at her. "It's called my skull."

"Rory," she whined. "Don't play like that. I've seen what head injuries can do, and it's not pretty."

"Relax, sugar." I approached my vintage Triumph Bonneville and stuck the key in the ignition. It wasn't my favorite bike, but it was one of the best for carrying passengers comfortably. "To keep you safe, I need to be in top shape. Trust me," I turned the key and the engine roared to life, "I know what I'm doing."

Her eyes narrowed at me through the helmet visor, but she didn't argue. "Where are we going?"

"You'll see."

"Kidnapping me again?" she teased, grabbing the edges of my cut.

"I'm glad you see my daring rescue of you as such a lighthearted joke now." I leaned in and kissed the bridge of her nose, the one part of her face I could reach through the helmet. It felt like an eternity since I rode off from the Old Phoenix service center with a bound, frightened medic in tow.

Mari's eyes darkened at my mention of her kidnapping-slash-rescue. "I hope the other girls back there are okay," she mused softly. "Especially Gretchen."

"The ones exploiting them are dead," I reminded her. "Those girls can take that building, those supplies, and turn it into whatever they want. We warned other MCs of Tom's untrustworthiness, so no one will be coming around there any time soon."

She nodded, still looking off in thought when I shut the visor down over her eyes. "Hop on, sugar. It's about an hour's ride."

I sat astride the bike and felt her climb on behind me. Sure enough, bare legs pressed against the back of my thighs. My pants grew uncomfortably tight at the thought of no barrier between me and her spread open center, except for her panties. Only God knew if I'd be able to hold off from pulling over and fucking her right on this seat before we reached our destination. Her hands sliding under my cut, caressing over my abs and chest through the thin material of my shirt, did nothing to help my resolve.

And we hadn't even left the garage yet. Fuck.

I wet my lips with my tongue and let out a loud, high pitched whistle. Hades howled a reply and immediately ran from where he waited on the front porch out to the street, heading straight for the gate.

"Hold on," I yelled to Mari over the engine as I hit the throttle.

She tightened around me at every point of contact —legs, arms, and chest against my back. How Jandro and Gunner were able to concentrate with her holding onto them like this, I had no fucking clue.

We peeled out of the garage like a bat out of hell, following after my dog running on all fours. The guard at the gate waved as we passed through, leaving behind the safety of our home into a world constantly at its own throat.

My body remained rigid even as we hit the open road at a comfortable cruising speed. Only Mari's hands smoothing over my chest again relaxed me a little. I couldn't let myself kick back completely, because I wasn't just taking her to any place.

Today, I was showing the woman I loved what I'd never shown anyone.

My past.

———

"OH MY GOD, REAPER!" Mari hopped off my bike and fiddled with the helmet before I even came to a complete stop. Normally I would've chewed her ass out for being unsafe, but her enthusiasm was so fucking cute, I could only smile.

"Ever been here before?" I asked, shutting off the engine.

"Never! Is this really…?"

"The Grand Canyon," I finished for her. "This lookout used to be called Yavapai Point."

I'd seen it hundreds of times. The vastness of the canyon stretching out like it went on forever, the stripes of color on the jagged rock formations, the sheer size of everything making you feel like an ant on an edge of the world. And it never ceased to amaze me.

While Mari remained entranced with the view, I got to setting up our picnic. A tree offered shade from the sun, so I spread the blanket underneath it. From the other saddlebags, I grabbed our other essentials—aged cheese, olives, grapes, homemade crusty bread, and a bottle of wine.

She turned around just as I spread everything out on the blanket and lowered to the ground. "What is this?" Her eyes widened at the sight of the containers.

"It's food." I popped an olive into my mouth. "And me."

"You mean this is you being romantic." She lowered onto the blanket next to me and leaned over to plant a kiss on my lips. "Thank you, handsome. I love this."

That was partially true. I wanted to show her I wasn't just a brute who liked fucking and violence. Warmth filled my chest as I returned her kiss, holding the back of her head to keep her there for more. I was happy she was pleased. I always wanted to show her the canyon, but I had to give Noelle credit for the picnic idea.

The other part however, was that I wanted to ease her in to what I was about to show her. The view wasn't going to be nearly as nice as this. For me it might be downright unsettling, as difficult as it was to admit that.

"I love you," I murmured, finally releasing her so she could nibble and drink. "I would have brought glasses, but didn't want to risk broken glass in the saddlebags," I explained as she took a pull of wine straight from the bottle.

"Oh no. How will we ever survive?" she chuckled

before passing the bottle to me. "This is perfect, and I love you too."

Her kiss landed on my cheekbone as I took small sips. I didn't like to drink a ton while riding, less so with a passenger I actually gave a fuck about, so I drank just enough to take the edge off.

"Something on your mind?" Mari asked, laying down with her head in my lap once she had her fill of food. "You seem a little distracted."

"Python," I answered, stroking her long, silky hair. On top of everything else, that certainly was one of the things occupying my mind.

"What about him?"

I took a few moments to think before answering. "I've executed and tortured men before. It's nothing to me at this point. But I always knew they were the enemy from the start. It just felt right to feel them die by my hands, like the natural order of things. With him...I know it must be done, but it doesn't feel right."

"Because you trusted him before?"

"Yeah." I stroked my fingers along her neck and shoulders. "He rode by my side. Proudly got the demon tattooed on him. He swore his life and loyalty to me and the club. Shit, I was happy he started fucking Heather 'cause then she left me alone."

Dappled sunlight through the tree made shifting patterns of light and shadow on Mari's face. Once again, I was awed at how naturally beautiful she was compared to the trash I'd woken up next to before.

"Are you worried you won't be able to do it?" She ran her hands up my forearms.

"No, I will. I'm just not sure how I'll be affected afterward." My fingers curled around hers, feeling the small, fragile bones in her hands compared to my heavy mitts. "I've never killed someone I considered a friend before."

She lifted her head from my lap, scooting over my legs to lean her head on my shoulder.

"And you have to do this? You can't just banish him?"

"Our code is very clearly spelled out. It was drafted by me, Jandro, and Gunner. If I go against something I helped make into law, that would put the whole club in turmoil. My leadership would be questioned, and rightly so." I cupped the back of her neck as my lips brushed across her forehead. "I might as well hand over the club to General Tash at that point. A club that's not unified and doesn't trust its president is already dust in the wind."

Her arms went around my neck with a deep sigh. "You carry so much on your shoulders for these people, and I don't think they even know half of it."

"It's better that way," I assured her. "They deserve a relatively secure life. Not everyone can handle this shit. I can."

"Trauma and heavy mental loads affect even the strongest of men," Mari said. "Just look at Shadow."

"Funny you say that," I chuckled. "He'd be able to end Python quickly, without a second thought. But every time you say good morning to him, he looks like he's gonna shit his pants."

"He's getting better." She drummed her fingers on my neck. "But he can't do this for you, huh?"

"No. It has to be me."

Her hands pressed to my cheeks, making me face her. "You know I'm here for you, right?"

I looked at my woman, wrapping tighter around her. I knew she was, and I'd never let her go. She had too much of what little remained of my heart for me to do that.

"You don't have to be the Steel Demons president with me," she whispered, thumb tracing my jaw. "You can just be Rory. And I'll be here no matter what."

She leaned in to press kisses to my neck, each pass of those soft lips a loving, sweet promise. But were they promises she could keep?

My eyes lifted to look over her shoulder at the dog watching us with more wisdom that any animal should have. How would Mari react if she knew I was just the instrument? I didn't choose who I killed, but followed the orders of someone else.

I didn't hear them often but when I did, it was unmistakable. I heard the same words when I learned Tom had been abusing Mari's friend in Old Phoenix, and when Gunner dragged Python's ass to me. I didn't know if my goofy, protective dog was saying them. Even that seemed far-fetched to me. But I never heard voices in my head until I found Hades. And it was always a variation of the same sentence.

His life is yours to take.

Their lives are yours. Reap what has been sown.

MARIPOSA

"Come on, sugar." Reaper patted the side of my hip. "I want to show you something."

"More surprises?" I was content to stay snuggled up against him on the picnic blanket, but he was practically shoving me off his lap.

"Yes, but unfortunately the view isn't as nice."

He corked the wine and gathered up the food containers while I shook out the blanket and folded it up carefully. Once everything was packed away, he grabbed my hand and led me wordlessly toward a barely-marked trail I didn't notice before.

"Watch your step," he murmured, pausing to wait for me as the trail became steep, like we were hiking down into the canyon itself.

I kept a firm hold on his hand as I carefully maneuvered my feet over rocks and areas of loose sand. My mind buzzed with questions, but I kept quiet. He was showing me something for a reason, and his own quiet demeanor today told me that seeing with my own eyes would explain better than words ever could.

The ground finally leveled out again as we came to a small valley. All around us, the striped ridges of the canyon decorated the horizon. I spun around in a slow circle, still awed by the view. Texas had nothing like this, and I never ventured outside of my home state until after I began my adventures as a medic.

"Are we *in* the canyon?" I asked, my breath still stolen.

"Sort of," Reaper answered. "Not at the very bottom or anything. That's still another ten-mile trek."

When I finally tore my eyes away from the breath-taking cliffs, I realized we appeared to be in some kind of campground. Broken-down RVs, pop-up campers, and every kind of travel trailer imaginable laid out alongside a wider path in organized rows. Further back, I could see cabins and what looked like more permanent structures.

"What is this place?" I took a few steps forward, the silence and stillness of everything but us gave me an unnerved chill.

Reaper took a few moments to answer, his footsteps following me on the dirt path between the trailers. "This is where I grew up."

I turned to look at him, stunned. "You *lived* here?"

He nodded in a way that was almost defiant. "Me, Noelle, Daren, our mom, dads, and about twenty others."

I continued walking through at a snail's pace, taking in every detail of the now-abandoned miniature ghost town. So this was the matriarchal community where women were in charge and had multiple male partners.

I noticed one area had three trailers arranged in a semicircle, like each family member had their own space. Near the door of the biggest RV, a large bin still had toy buckets and shovels for building sandcastles. Their once-bright colors of pinks, purples, and greens were now bleached out and faded by years of sun exposure.

In the middle of the three RVs, a central fire pit still had grey ashes in the circle of stones. The rusted out frame of a folding chair had been knocked over and was halfway buried in the sand.

"What happened?" The question tore out of me painfully. I didn't know if I'd be prepared for the answer. Children and families once lived here and from the looks of it, they all vanished.

"I wish I knew." The ache in my voice was nothing compared to the pain in his.

"Reaper." I turned to him, my arms reaching, but he was already there.

Strong arms pulled me close, enveloping me in security. I stood to the side so we could keep walking through together as his head bent low to tell me.

"I first moved out when I was seventeen," he began. "For the usual shit, you know? I was tired of being around my parents and neighbors all the time. I took Daren with me and we got a shitty place together with Jandro, who was also sick of being around his family all the time."

"No Noelle?" I asked with a tiny smile.

"Nah, we were tired of being bossed around by women. That was the whole point. She was kind of being set up to become the new head of our family here, anyway."

"Really? At what, sixteen?"

"Fifteen. Other communities like ours had been raided by rogue cops and military, so no one really knew what the future held. Anyway, Jandro, Daren, and I worked odd jobs to pay rent and buy weed, then rode motorcycles every free chance we got. We wanted to play at being adults, but had no idea what that really meant."

My hands wrapped tighter around the back of his neck, rubbing into the tight knots there as his body tensed.

"My brother, Daren, he—" His voice cut off abruptly as he cleared his throat.

"Your brother that passed away?"

"Yeah, he…saw things, sometimes." Reaper's brow furrowed as he looked at me, as if gauging my reaction. "He had bad seizures as a kid, and had like, visions."

"Visions?" I repeated. "You mean, like he saw the future?"

"Yeah, but it was weird. He would have dreams of random, mundane shit. Like one day I blew out both tires in my bike and had to wait three hours for Jandro to pick me up in his uncle's truck. Before it happened, Daren told me I'd taste a clove cigarette for the first time that day. It was because Jandro's uncle had a pack of cloves in his glove box."

The explanation tumbled out of him, rushed and

unfiltered. I could tell he hardly believed it himself, but was just explaining it as best as he knew how. He didn't understand his brother's ability any more than the fast healing and endurance of his dog. It was just a part of his life.

"Anyway," Reaper scrubbed a hand down his face. "Daren told me one day that I had to come back here and get Mom's stuff. That was all he told me. But he kept repeating it over and over, like it was really impor-tant, like I had to do *right then*. I kept trying to blow it off like, 'Okay, I'll go this weekend.' And he told me, 'No, now.'" I asked if they were moving or if anything was wrong, and he kept saying, 'I don't know, but you need to get her stuff right now.'"

His fingers curled into my waist, making a fist as he grabbed the fabric of my top. I pressed a hand to his chest and felt his heart racing underneath my palm.

"When I got here," he went on, "the place looked pretty much like this." He gestured to the scene before us. "Completely empty. Everyone was gone and left everything behind. I went home," he nodded up ahead to one of the cabins, "and found Mom's journal, her clothes, and a few pieces of jewelry she made but hadn't sold yet." The silence in his pause permeated deeply, wrapping around us like a cage. "A box of her things are all I have left of her."

Now my fingers curled into his cut, clinging to him as I willed myself not to cry.

"She could still be alive," I whispered. "Maybe they got word early that a raid was coming."

"No," he shook his head. "Everyone would have

packed their belongings if they got word ahead of time. Trust me, sugar. I've considered all the possibilities."

"What about your dads?"

"One died when I was fourteen. Another was drafted to fight at the border. The other had to have been with her." He licked his lips and sighed. "I can't imagine him ever leaving her side."

"I'm sorry." The words sounded so hollow but I didn't know what else to say.

"What I think most likely happened was," he went on, "they stormed the place, but didn't kill anyone. From the looks of it, everyone went willingly, probably fearing for their lives. Once they rounded everyone up, people got sorted according to their skill. Men probably drafted into the military. Women sold to be used. Kids sent to camps to be further indoctrinated."

"What about Noelle?"

Reaper smiled for the first time since stepping foot in his former home. "That crafty bitch," he chuckled. "She hid. Mom had dug out a cellar in the floor of the cabin and Noelle stayed down there, dead quiet for two straight days. She didn't even say a word when I came poking through until I went down there myself. Then she fought me, nearly scratched my fucking eyes out, 'til she realized who I was."

"Oh my God." I brought a hand to my mouth. "That must have been awful for her."

"What she told me adds to my theory," he said. "She heard voices threatening to shoot, but no actual gunshots or sounds of struggle. Then footsteps walking away, and then nothing."

"It's weird that no one would come back here and loot," I observed.

"We were a bit hidden and tricky to get to, despite being so close to a tourist spot," he nodded up the hill to the lookout point where we had our picnic. "But people also thought we were a witch's coven, so that might have had something to do with it."

"Witches?" I repeated. "Why, because this place was run by women?"

"Exactly," Reaper nodded. "There could be no other explanation for women running an independent community, completely self-sufficient and off the grid."

"I bet that was why they were attacked so often," I mused sadly. "The people in charge are always afraid of what they can't control."

"Correct again." He loosened his hold on me to resume walking through the central path. "Looking back, I'm honestly surprised they lasted as long as they did. I think ours was among those who hung on the longest. It was about five years before the Collapse."

"I'm so sorry," I repeated, hating that there was nothing else I could say or do. Healing was my specialty, but I couldn't do anything to alleviate the guilt he must have felt, the helplessness of not knowing what happened to his family.

"This was why I started the Steel Demons." Reaper kneeled to pick up something half-buried in the dirt. When he stood again, I saw it was a small toy motorcycle. "So the community I called home wouldn't be left undefended."

The toy was only a few inches long, cast from metal

and encrusted with dirt. I touched it as he held it out for me to see, and the wheels still spun freely.

"Your mom would be proud of you, I'm sure."

"I looked at the cover of her journal every day for about a year." Reaper ran the tiny motorcycle across his palm before setting it back down on the ground. "But I could never bring myself to open it and read what was inside. I still can't."

I slid my arm through his, wrapping my hand around his bicep. "At least you kept it with you. Maybe one day you will."

He looked at me, green eyes dark. "You wanted to know about me, how I grew up. I've never brought anyone here. So," he tilted his head to indicate our surroundings, "what do you think?"

My head rested on his shoulder as I wrapped tighter around his upper arm. "I think your past made you the best MC president this world has ever seen. It made you strong enough to be ruthless when necessary, but you care enough to protect those that need it most." A smile pulled at my lips. "Thank you for showing me this. It even makes me love you a little more."

He mirrored my smile and leaned down to place a very un-Reaper-like soft kiss on my lips. "My parents would have adored you. They'd be trying to convince you to have a harem of ten guys."

"Yeah, right," I laughed. "Who knows?" I added, with a kiss to his shoulder. "I might still be able to meet them one day."

Reaper sighed and gave a slight shake of his head,

but still humored me with a smile. "You might be right, sugar. In times like these, who knows what'll happen."

SEVEN

MARIPOSA

We continued walking around the abandoned settlement for the rest of the afternoon. Reaper told me stories of his neighbors and childhood friends. However, we never went inside any of the homes, and kept a respectful distance away from the personal belongings that remained. Hades gave some things a curious sniff or two, but otherwise stayed near us and left things alone. It felt like we were visiting a cemetery, and had come to pay our respects.

I was moved that he brought me here, and felt like I got a glimpse into a part of him he kept locked away inside. The more I got to know Reaper, the more I saw how big his heart was. He just kept it protected, wrapped in steel.

The mood shifted throughout the day, from our flirty, sensual ride, to the lighthearted picnic, to the dark melancholy of uncovering his past. And he remained calm and even-tempered throughout it all. It made me realize the volatile temper was part of his armor to keep people out. Now that he had let me in, I found the calm within the storm.

We hiked back up to the picnic spot a few hours before dark. We'd have one hell of a sunset view on the ride home and I couldn't wait to take it all in, flying across the landscape while wrapped around my man.

"Hold on there, sugar." Reaper stopped me with a wily smirk before I could put my helmet on. "Hop in the driver's seat for me, but face backwards."

"What?" I stared at him.

"Just do it." His smile grew. "For me."

I straddled the bike, my back toward the handlebars. He climbed on facing me, and my pulse spiked when his fingers skimmed up my calf where my skirt hiked up.

"Scoot toward me." His voice took on a low, husky tone. "Come closer."

I did as he instructed, my eyes glued to his heated gaze as my legs went wider to drape over his thighs. My skirt crept up inch by inch as I moved toward him.

His touch ventured under the fabric, still lightly caressing me as his fingertips moved up my thighs.

"I swear you wore this to torture me," he said with a soft growl. "To see how long I would last without touching you like this."

My tongue darted out to wet my parched lips. All the moisture in my body seemed to surge to one place, mere inches away from his hands.

"I might have picked it with the idea that we might want to be…discreet."

He leaned forward, eyes already dilated and hooded with desire. "Is that so?" He sounded pleased as his forehead rested on mine. "My sweet little medic had some naughty ideas of what we'd be doing on our outing?"

"I didn't think it'd be happening on your bike," I admitted, leaning up for a taste of that mouth hovering over mine.

"Mmm." He kissed me in a rough claiming of teeth and tongue, his usual style that never failed to leave me breathless. "I've never been inside a woman on my bike before."

His hands continued to venture under my skirt, kneading my thighs in a possessive grip as they moved closer to my center. I dipped my head back, letting his kisses trail over my neck and jaw as my body continued scooting toward him in its eagerness. With my knees glued to the sides of his hips, he was moments away from finding out what else I'd been thinking when I picked the skirt.

When his touch reached my pelvis and felt bare flesh, he inhaled sharply and I physically saw his cock swell in his jeans.

"No panties?" His expression morphed as he stared at me. "You've been without panties all day?"

"They get in the way of things," I shrugged. "It would've been pointless to wear a skirt if I still wore something I had to take off."

"Oh, I'm sure I would've managed, but *fuck*." His thumb stroked through my lips, eliciting a grin at my wetness as he circled that digit all around my sensitive, aching vulva. "You're fucking dirty, sugar, and I love it."

"Show me how much you love it," I moaned, reaching for the bulge in his pants.

He gave me another deep kiss as I unzipped him, supporting my back gently with one hand as I reclined on the bike. As I stroked him from root to tip, he shoved all the fabric of my skirt up to my waist, baring me to the world of only us.

"Look at you, getting my seat all wet," he groaned, returning his hand to my drenched core. "I'm never washing this bike again."

"Don't tell me that." I licked my hand and squeezed my palm around him again, rendering him speechless enough with wordless moans.

When he leaned down to kiss me again, both arms stretched above me. The next thing I heard was a deafening roar, and then felt the rumbling of the bike's engine beneath me.

"Reaper, what are you—"

"Did you like the ride over here?" he asked in my ear, nudging his cock against my thigh. "Feeling the whole bike vibrating under your bare pussy?"

"Yes," I breathed, sliding my hand under his shirt and up his taut chest hovering above me. "But I loved holding onto you more."

"You wanna know something?" He pulled back to look at me, and those green eyes shone with a new kind of mischief. "I've never ridden a bike and a woman at the same time."

My eyes widened and I immediately pulled my hands away. "Reaper, no."

"It'll be fine. I'll go slow." He reached up for one of the grips. "On the bike, not on you."

"What if I fall?"

"I won't let you. Just hold onto me with your legs. Please?" He looked like a child begging to do a flip off of a high diving board. "We can try it for this straight stretch of road. I promise I'll go super slow."

"I don't know—"

He kissed me sweetly, nuzzling my face. "I won't let anything happen to you. I just want to know what it feels like."

I sighed, leaning my head back to look at the sky above us both. "Why am I actually entertaining this crazy fucking idea?"

"Because you know it'll be fun." His hips rolled forward, the head of his cock caressing my clit as he kissed my neck. "Because you trust me."

I did trust him. Only weeks ago I questioned everything about him. I couldn't believe that a man like him was capable of caring for me, of loving me. It never occurred to me that wanting to share me was an expression of that care, but now it made total sense. Over the past few days, all those questions dissipated like evaporating puddles in the sun. I still didn't understand some things, but I found myself happier since admitting I was completely in love with the Steel Demons president.

"Slow," I contended. "Like a grandma using a walker slow."

"Mmm." His mouth moved to my chest, pulling my top and bra aside to reach my nipples with that devilish tongue. "We'll start without riding first. Then add it in. Slow."

"Very slow," I repeated, letting my eyelids fall closed at his hands and mouth doing what they did best.

"I love you," he moaned deliriously when his mouth found his way to mine again. "You let me be who I am. I love you so much for that."

"I love who you are—ohh!"

He slid into me in one deep stroke, swallowing my cry as his tongue dominated mine. His legs adjusted under mine, assumedly to set his feet on the footrests, and my legs wrapped tighter around his hips. We built into a steady rhythm, rocking into each other like our bodies were made for this connection.

"Comfortable, sugar?" He crashed into me solidly with each thrust, arms stretched out on either side of me on the grips.

My legs around his waist and my fingers curled into the worn leather of his cut, I was about as steady as I was going to be.

"I'm good," I breathed, trying not to squirm on the narrow seat as he fucked me.

"Here we go," he grunted, pausing while sheathed fully inside me to begin a gentle acceleration forward.

"That's good, that's good! No faster!" I pleaded, the sensation of forward movement already making me regret agreeing to this.

"No? How about harder?"

He resumed his thrusts, putting more force into his hips as his eyes kept looking straight forward at the road in front of us. His jaw tightened. He sucked his lower lip into his mouth. He wanted so badly to look at me.

And he looked so fucking hot, pounding into me while the muscles in his arms flexed and the landscape moved past us. I thought I'd be too scared and distracted to actually enjoy this, but holy hell, I did. The angle of him crashing into me sent my clit buzzing at each impact. He penetrated me deeply, knowing how much I loved to be filled by him and not skimping on any thrust.

His eyes still glued to the road, he brought one hand down to hold my hip. His palm added an anchor of stability to my position on the bike, while his thumb reached over to tease my clit.

"Put your hand back," I yelled over the engine.

"I'm good, sugar," he bellowed in return, grinning at me like a madman. "She's steady. You're steady. There's just one thing missing."

He pressed harder with his thumb, closing in on that bundle of nerves already sparking with tension like a live wire. Then he upped the ante by leaning down and sucking my nipple into his mouth.

"Stop that!" I cried. "Eyes on the road!"

He laughed wildly as he sat back up. "Goddamn, I'm in fucking heaven."

"How fast are we going?" I only then noticed how the landscape whipped past us, when earlier I was sure we were going slow enough to take in every detail.

"Don't worry about it," he smirked with a shift of his hips that lifted us both from the seat.

I whimpered and clutched desperately at him with the sudden change of movement, knowing the road running just a few feet below me would skin me alive.

"It's all right, I've got you." His eyes flicked down to me for a moment of warm reassurance. "I won't let you fall."

"How much longer do you want to do this?"

That grin filled with maniacal glee returned. "Until you come."

"That's not gonna happen! I'm too fucking scared."

"And I'm telling you not to be scared. You love riding. You love it when I'm inside you. So just combine the two of them in your mind."

"Easy for you to fucking say," I groaned, leaning my head back in defeat.

Looking straight up at the sky felt way too much like I was in freefall. And leaning my head to either side, watching the world zip by at speeds unknown freaked me out too much. So I looked at Reaper, calm and in control. The fucking daredevil would probably embrace death from a fiery crash, his dick still lodged inside of someone.

He was fascinating to watch, his hips rolling as he slid in and out of me. His left hand occasionally resting on me when it wasn't on the grip. The pressure of his palm on my hip intensified the vibrating of the motor-cycle throughout my whole body. As minutes passed and we continued to be alive, I was able to feel less afraid and really feel the sensations coursing through me. From him. From the machine carrying us. And from the thrill of the ride.

"That's it, sugar," he rasped, sliding a free hand under my askew top to cup my breast. "I can feel you getting wetter. Just enjoy this for how good it feels."

The wind steadily grew colder, erecting goosebumps on my skin and turning my nipples into tight, aching buds. But his hands were so warm, soothing the bite of the cold, as they moved over me. I didn't even protest when he leaned down again to caress my other nipple with his tongue.

We took a few winding turns that required both his hands to steer, while he pressed into me with a new depth and fullness. A gasp stole my breath as my fingers dug into his muscular thighs. The force of gravity molded us into a single three-part unit—me, him, and the motorcycle.

"Reaper," I whimpered, each lean of the bike through the turns setting off a new mini-explosion within me. "I'm gonna…"

"God, yes, I can feel you," he growled back, jaw tight and his eyes staring straight ahead. "I always want to see your face when you come, but I'm not tryin' to run us off the road."

The crashing of him against me grew desperate, hurried. He barely left me at all before he filled me up again and again, until I overflowed with a crash of my own.

"Jesus, fuck!" The motorcycle wobbled for one tiny, heart-stopping second.

He quickly regained control, but barely. My orgasm closed hard around his thick shaft, pulling him in deeper and holding on almost as tightly as my hands and legs did. The shockwaves continued to roll over me, so much that I didn't realize the bike had slowed down until we nearly stopped.

"What are we…"

Reaper hauled me up, still fully sheathed inside me as he kissed me roughly. His arms clasped around my back, holding my chest to his as he swung a leg over the bike to dismount. As he stood, he shifted his grip to under my thighs and bounced me once on his cock. I moaned a whimper into his mouth as I wrapped my arms and shaky legs around him like a tree.

"Grab the blanket," he growled against my lips. "In the saddle bag."

"Mmph…" I leaned toward the bike, reaching with one arm and fumbled with the buckle for all of about five seconds.

"Nevermind. Fuck the blanket." He turned us away from the bike and looked over my shoulder. "There's some grass here. It looks soft enough."

In the next moment my back was laid gently onto solid ground, and the only movement came from the man hovering above me. Our bodies never disconnected once as he laid me down, then draped over me to kiss me deeply.

He shoved my top and bra up to my neck to maul the sensitive flesh of my breasts with both hands. I yanked his shirt up to the top of his chest because I was desperate to feel his skin on mine. The ride had been terrifying, exhilarating, and hot as hell, but it didn't give me a chance to touch him like I wanted to.

Our skin, cooled by the early evening air quickly heated up as our bodies seared together. He fucked me with his whole body, groaning like a beast mad with lust as he slid into me and against me.

Another orgasm began building deep within my core, still feeding off the thrill of the first one. From his ragged breathing, the wild, frenzied way he touched me, and how incredibly rigid he felt inside me, I knew he was close too.

"Come with me," I breathed against his ear. "Fill me up, you fucking daredevil."

His moan was animalistic, fingers curling into a fist at the base of my skull. The pull of hair on my scalp intensified the electric jolts shooting through my clit.

"Mariposa," he rasped, his voice tight as he swelled within me. "You fucking ruined me. I'm yours—"

His words choked off as his warmth spilled, flexing hard inside me as he took me over the edge with him. Our pleasure fed off of each other in an endless feedback loop, shooting off through the atmosphere before we returned on a gentle descent down to earth.

"Can I tell you something?" he murmured softly over our matched, thundering pulses.

"Always." I slid my hands up his abs and chest to cup the sides of his neck.

"It's weird, but," he paused, turning his head to kiss my palm, "I think this was the best day of my life."

I tried to think of some sarcastic remark about him almost killing us both on his bike, but no words broke through this heady, elated feeling. And I couldn't bring him down with how blissed out, sexy, and sated he looked.

"I think it was mine, too."

EIGHT

JANDRO

"**F**uck!" I spat, throwing the ill-fitting spark plugs on the concrete floor. *"Que chingon estes..."*

Naturally, all of the Razor Wire bikes we acquired after the ambush fit different-sized plugs than what the majority of our bikes had. And Gunner just told me the fantastic news that none of his current suppliers had the right ones. Just fucking great. I could tweak some things here and there, but it was just more work that I wasn't expecting to do.

In nearly the past whole week, I spent every waking hour in the shop. The last two nights I didn't even go home, opting to shower and crash here instead. We gutted most of the duplex to make room for all the bike shit, but kept the kitchen, a full bathroom, and one room that functioned as my office, or crash pad, depending on what I needed.

I slept on a futon against the wall. Other than that, the only pieces of furniture in there was a desk and a bookshelf filled with old manuals and random motorcycle books. Crashing here wasn't nearly as inviting as my house, but the lack of comforts didn't bother me. After spending so many nights on the road, sleeping under the stars and in all kinds of sketchy lodgings, crashing where I landed was second nature to me.

Besides, Shadow probably appreciated the alone time at home. Although, for being such a loner, he did seem to appreciate my company as a roommate. He was perfectly capable of living in his own place and had plenty of empty houses to choose from. But whenever I brought it up, he said he was fine to stay as long as I was okay with him being there. Sure, I might've picked living with a beautiful woman over a hulking giant of a man, but I was more than fine sharing a large house with someone else. He promised to feed my chickens, and while he'd never admit it, I had a feeling Shadow enjoyed having animals.

Right then, I would have happily been covered in chicken shit or dealt with another one of Shadow's nightmares than look at another fucking spark plug. Bikes were my passion, but after several days of little sleep or food, I was reaching my fucking limit.

"Piece of pig shit," I grumbled, rising to my feet.

My foot swung forward and kicked the tailpipe of the gutted Razor Wire bike. I was frustrated, exhausted, and not thinking straight. To add insult to injury, the metal dented cleanly where my foot connected. I barked out a defeated laugh. I wasn't even wearing steel toes! These bikes were so shitty and low quality, they weren't even worth parting out. Few things pissed me off more than a so-called MC that took no pride in their steeds and just bought the cheapest shit.

"What did that bike ever do to you?"

I turned in the direction of the playful, feminine voice. Mariposa looked like a mirage standing under the open garage door, an illusion of something too good to be true. Her dark hair was up in a loose bun and her lavender medic scrubs were on, indicating she'd just been working, or was heading that way.

"It existed," I answered her. "That's what it did to me. This piece of shit is a personal insult to any good mechanic."

A smile lit up her face as she adjusted the canvas bag on her shoulder. "Well I'm sure it's sorry after that kick."

A chuckle escaped me as I strode toward her. Not many women, or people in general for that matter, entertained my sense of humor. It felt like something unique and special between us and no one else.

Her eyes heated, lips parting just slightly when I stopped in front of her. A rush of need went straight to my dick and it was all I could do to not grab her and pull her into me.

Keeping my hands at my sides, knowing I was covered in filth and grime, I leaned down and smacked a peck to those pouty lips instead.

"You heading to work or leaving?" I asked her.

"Both." She laughed at my bewildered face. "I have a couple hours free before I check on Tess and Python this afternoon. Thought you might like some lunch." She patted the bag at her side. "Have you eaten today?"

It took me a few long seconds to answer. First, I had

to come down from the high of realizing she came to see me, because she *wanted* to. She thought of me and brought me food because she was concerned about me.

It was such a simple gesture for a basic biological need, and yet I couldn't begin to express how much it meant to me. So many women thought they had to jump through hoops to impress a man—wearing tons of makeup, staying thin while having gigantic tits, sucking dick like a porn star, but *this* was all I ever wanted. Someone sweet and thoughtful enough to take care of me.

"That depends," I said skeptically. "Are you having lunch with me?"

"I will if I'm not getting in the way of your work."

"Oh, you are. And I'm so grateful for it, you have no idea." I kissed her again, longer this time, like she was the appetizer I was savoring before the main course. My fists curled at my sides, fighting the urge to touch more of her. "Come in. We can eat in the kitchen." Her lips were flushed and swollen as I reluctantly pulled away. "Give me a minute to wash up."

When I returned from the restroom with clean hands, Mari's simple lunch spread out on the table looked like a feast for a king to my half-starved body.

Rice, beans, salsa, grilled onions and bell peppers, and strips of well-done steak were arranged neatly in their own containers. The only things missing were tortillas, which Mari heated on the cast-iron griddle in the wood-pellet stove.

"Damn, we still got steaks, huh?" My mouth watered as I took a seat.

"We're down to the last pallet according to the club-house kitchen." Mari dropped a stack of freshly warmed tortillas on the table. "These were cooked a bit too long the other day at the party. So they said I could have the leftovers, and I sliced 'em thin, *carne asada* style. A bit tough but they're edible."

"I love a resourceful woman," I said, piling fajita fixings into a tortilla, then immediately bit my tongue.

It was way too soon to be throwing the L-word around. Mari was still figuring out how to be with two men, for shit's sake.

She took no apparent notice of the word I used and smiled sweetly, the apples of her cheeks flushing with color. "I just wanted to make sure you were eating enough. I know you've been putting long hours in here."

"And I feel every single one of them," I sighed, scrubbing a hand down my face. "But bikes are no good to a crew if they're unrideable."

"Not everyone has extras, I take it?" She took a delicate bite out of her own fajita.

"Nah. Reaper has a few. I got one spare and I think Gunner does too. But most of the guys only have the one ride. It's just hard to find good parts. Everything's been scrapped and scavenged."

"And you have an eye for quality, I assume?"

"I do," I said with a nod, appreciating that she seemed to take interest in my passion. At least enough to have a conversation about it. "Quality parts make all the difference, especially in the desert. With all the sand, wind, and changes in elevation, you need machinery you can rely on."

"I feel the same way about medical supplies." Mari paused in her eating, resting her chin on her hand. "Cheaply-made scalpels pose a higher risk of infection for the patient. Good quality materials help me do my job better."

"You'll hear no argument from me." I helped myself to a second tortilla. "So I saw you and Reap ride back in last night. Where did you two go off to?"

The pale pink in her cheeks immediately deepened to a bright red, the color spreading to her neck and the rest of her face.

"Um, we had a picnic at a lookout point at the Grand Canyon. Then he showed me where he grew up."

"That sounds nice. Well the picnic does, at least. I bet it was tough to see the ruins of his old home."

"It was. But it was good too, I think." She swallowed. "I think it was kind of like closure for him. And it seemed to mean a lot that he took me there and told me what happened."

"Yeah, that's huge. I don't think he's been back there since the last time, when Daren told him to get his mom's things." As I responded, Mari stared intently at the table, avoiding my eye. "What's wrong, *Mariposita?* You look uncomfortable all of a sudden."

"Is this weird?" She returned my gaze hesitantly. "Talking to you about what I did with him?"

"Why would it be weird?"

"Because I'm used to being with one guy at a time. A guy I'm seeing wouldn't normally be thrilled to hear about my date with someone else."

"Nothing about our situation is normal."

"I know, I just," she sighed, "I don't want to upset either of you. I care about you both and I don't want to like, rub in your face that I spent all day with him."

"Hey, you're not upsetting me." I leaned forward and grabbed her slender fingers. "And I asked the question, so of course I don't mind hearing the answer. Now, I'm not gonna ask about all the ways he fucked you yesterday because yeah, I might get a little jealous of that." Her eyes widened slightly and her neck flushed even redder. Damn, he must have turned her inside out.

"Only because I wasn't there to join in on the fun," I added with a smirk. "But don't forget, I care about Reaper too. He's the brother I never had. You're making him happy. And a happy president means less bullshit for the VP to deal with."

Her fingers curled around mine as she humored me with a giggle. "I suppose that's true."

"It is. And hey." I nudged my foot around the back of her chair leg to pull her closer. Lowering our clasped hands to her lap, I hovered my lips over her ear. "You have no idea what coming here with food means to me. Not saying you should be slaving in a kitchen all the time, but it's little things like this that make me feel cared for. So thank you, *Mariposita*. You're rocking this two-men thing."

I kissed the shell of her ear, dragging my lips down to the quickening pulse in her neck. Our hands untangled as if they had minds of their own. Mine nestled into the luscious curves of her waist while hers wrapped around my shoulders.

"You deserve it," she breathed, her voice warm against my cheek. "You take care of everyone here. Especially Shadow, Reaper, me…someone ought to take care of you too."

An involuntary groan of longing rose in my chest. She had no idea at all how perfect she was for me. This woman understood me, from my sense of humor and appreciation of fine machinery to the deepest, basic needs of a full belly and a cozy home—which was right here at this shitty table pulled from a dumpster. *She* was my home.

I did not fall in love easily. I could flirt and charm the panties off of any woman in my sleep, but that was a game. It was meaningless. This was real, and I was free falling into the Grand Canyon itself.

"Come home with me tonight." It was all I could do to not sound like I was begging. "I'll be done for the day in about four hours. Meet me back here after you see Tessa and everything else you gotta do."

"Jandro, I—"

"I'll make you dinner for bringing me lunch. We can just watch old TV shows, hang out with the chickens, and not do anything else. Shadow will be there, but he won't bother us. I'll walk you back to Reaper's if you're not up for spending the night. I don't care what we do, I just want to spend more time with you, Mari."

"Okay!" she laughed, planting a kiss on me like she was trying to shut me up. "I was about to tell you I'd love to, silly, if you'd let me get a word in."

"Oh." I grinned sheepishly, our smiles touching in a

not-quite kiss. "I was expecting more resistance, but all right!"

"Yeah?" she challenged playfully. "I figured you knew exactly how irresistible you are."

"I do know, but a certain type of girl, called a Mariposa, has a knack for holding out on me."

She chuckled, but her smile was more cautious this time. "I guess I'll just have to let Reaper know where I'll be."

"You do that." I reluctantly pulled away from her, sliding my palms down her thighs. "And if he gives you shit for it, let him know I'm coming for him at Fight Night."

"Ugh, that again," she groaned, dropping her forehead into her palm. "I almost forgot."

"Yes, that again." I smacked a kiss on her cheek before standing to clear the table. "At the end of the day, we're just animals after all."

NINE

MARIPOSA

My feet touched the ground, but it felt like I was floating on air after leaving Jandro's shop. I was really doing this—seeing two men. And feeling intense, vastly different things for both of them.

Even so, this floaty feeling, the smile I couldn't erase, and the fluttering in my stomach, it was all familiar. Every person felt this at some point in their lives, when someone stood out as special to them. My brain and body were processing all the chemical reactions of an intense crush.

And the crazy part was, I couldn't tell if it was over Reaper, or Jandro.

I still felt the physical, sweet ache of the green-eyed president on top of me, inside of me, and all over me. Yesterday consisted of the most thrilling, scariest sex I ever had, but the day was so much more than that. He took me to a painful place, trusting me, and himself, enough to open up and share a side of him that few others knew.

Everything seemed to change between us since then for the better, like we reached a new appreciation and understanding of each other. He couldn't keep his hands off me when we got home, and not for more sex. But from the door to the shower to the bed, those rough hands maintained some form of contact on me and he never stopped kissing me. Only this morning did we peel apart reluctantly to attend our separate duties.

Reaper was a deeply emotional man, but a man of actions more than words. On some level I knew every caress and kiss after that trip was a silent thank-you. A wordless whisper of appreciation for accepting him, loving him, despite what he perceived as flaws.

And every time I touched him and kissed him back, I hoped he understood that I didn't see his past as flawed. The fact that he missed his family, that he wasn't there in time to save them and it ate him up with guilt— it all just made him human. And seeing that side of him made me love him even more.

Jandro, on the other hand.

He talked endlessly compared to Reaper and still, I felt like I barely knew him. I couldn't always tell what was his flirty banter and what was the real him. Today, I was certain I got a glimpse of the real Jandro. But what would tonight at his house bring? A smooth-talking man trying to charm me into his bed or a deeper look at who he really was?

Rather than wrapping his heart in steel, he seemed to hide behind jokes, banter, and charm. The life of the party and a mind for mechanics. But the way he advised Reaper and helped Shadow was anything but attention-seeking. Helping others came so naturally to him, his most selfless actions seemed to slip by without notice.

Not to me, though.

I noticed. And I knew what it felt like, giving so much of yourself to help someone without a word of gratitude or appreciation. Jandro wouldn't be taken for granted, not by me.

My floating feet carried me to the clubhouse, stopping first at my medic office for some IV bags before heading down the hall to where Python was being kept. Dallas saw me coming from the far end.

"I take it you're having a good day," he teased me gently.

I laughed lightly, looking down at my feet. Not even tending to the prisoner could put me back into a work-mode mindset after the lunch I just had with Jandro. I was excited to see his house and spend more time with him.

"I am, Dallas. How's your day?"

"Oh, can't complain. Counting down the minutes until Drea's done schooling the kids so we can ride around on the mini-bikes I made them." He turned to unlock Python's cell door as he spoke.

"That sounds like fun."

"Sure is! My daughter's popping wheelies already. Scares me half to death, but I'm still proud as fuck."

I grinned at the mental image. Dallas seemed like such a sweet family man under the beard, the tattoos, and the leather cut. Andrea was lucky to have him. A passing thought of what kind of father Reaper or Jandro would be made my chest flutter.

Dallas opened the door to the quarantine room and stepped aside to let me through. I should have been more aware as I walked in, but I was looking down, fiddling with the IV bag when two hands grabbed my shoulders in a painful grip.

"Mariposa!" Python rasped, his rank breath in my face.

He startled me so badly, I dropped the bags and froze up. Thankfully, Dallas was right there.

"What the fuck d'you think you're doing?!" the gentle family man bellowed as he shoved Python away from me. "You don't put your hands on *anyone* coming in here, much less a woman!"

Still weak from his wounds and bare minimum care, the prisoner stumbled backward across the small room until he hit the frame of his bed. Dallas turned to me, concern and anger in his large blue eyes.

"You okay, Mari?"

"Yeah, thank you." I picked up the IV bag with a shaky hand. "I just wasn't expecting that."

He turned back to Python with a growl. "You have no right to be touching her and getting up in her face, shitbag. You bet your sorry ass the president is going to hear about this." He crossed his broad, tattooed forearms and widened his feet. "I'm not leaving you alone with him, Mari."

"Look, I'm sorry," Python groaned, moving to sit painstakingly back in his bed. "I didn't mean to scare you, just wanted to grab your attention before you stuck me and left."

"What for?" Dallas demanded. "You don't need to grab her attention for shit!"

"I have a…medical issue." Python's sunken eyes darted at me. "And I'd like to talk to the medic about it in private."

"Absolutely not!"

"He does have a right to privacy," I said, looking at Dallas. "Regarding medical information."

"Mari, I am not leaving this room. Least of all because Reaper would kill me if I left you in danger."

"I'll stay right here. I won't touch her again, Jesus fuck." Python laid back against his pillows, arms flopped defeatedly down to his sides. "I just have questions about…issues I'm having."

I placed a hand on Dallas's forearm and looked up at the big, protective man's frown. "Don't worry about me. Maybe keep the door cracked and just stay on the other side? If you hear anything except for normal conversation, come back in."

"This is not a good idea, Mari." His eyes shifted over to Python. "That sneaky fucker's up to something. He'll do whatever he can to escape Reaper's punishment."

"So watch us through the crack in the door, but I'll be talking quietly to keep the conversation private." I gave a gentle squeeze of his arm. "He might be scum, but he does have a right to medical knowledge about his own body. And that information is only his to share, if he so chooses."

Dallas sighed heavily, stroking his beard. "The door stays open. I'm not taking eyes off either of you, but I'll stay far enough to not hear the conversation. Deal?"

"That's fine. Thank you."

"If he so much as breathes at you in a way I don't like, I'm coming back in."

"Works for me."

Sucking in a deep breath to steady the shaking of my hands, I approached Python's bedside and set to switching out his IV bags.

"Okay, so what do you need?"

"Come closer," he whispered, leaning over to look at Dallas watching us from the doorway.

"No. He can't hear us, so just ask me what you need to know." Python flinched as I took his arm and and re-stuck the IV syringe where he had ripped it out. "Better start talking before I leave."

"Okay look. I just said that shit to make him go away." He covered his mouth as he spoke. "But I figured out a way to get out of here and take you with me. You'll have to steal a bike for me, though. Can you ride?"

"Are you fucking kidding me?" I raised my voice so Dallas would definitely hear.

"Shush!" Python hissed. "Look, you don't have to be my chick or nothing, but you're a prisoner here too. You can be free!"

"You're delusional." Finished with him, I stepped away and crossed my arms. Footsteps behind me indicated Dallas had re-entered the room, which helped me feel a little braver. "I was being nice the first time you tried talking me into escaping, when I said I wouldn't tell Reaper. Now? I'm all out of reasons to be nice. You have no one to blame but yourself for what happens."

"Please!" He was shamelessly begging now, tears rolling down his face. "You've got to get me out! He's going to feed my balls to his fucking dog!"

I turned to the door, Dallas following after me.

"I hope Hades finds them delicious."

———

THE CONFRONTATION with Python had me so on edge, I blinked in confusion upon stepping back in my office to find Tessa waiting for me.

"Tess, honey. What are you doing here?"

She laughed darkly, running a hand over her 33-week-plus baby bump. "I had an appointment with you, silly. Did you forget?"

"Of course not! But I could've come to your house. You didn't have to walk all the way here."

"It's four blocks. I'm pregnant, not an invalid," she teased. Her smile began to fade as she looked down at her belly, still rubbing it protectively. "Besides, I wanted to get out of the house. I'm sick of being cooped up in there with endless messes to clean, and not just from my *little* boys."

"Well, you're welcome to come see me anytime." I grabbed my stethoscope off the wall and quickly cleaned it off with alcohol wipes. "And not just at work. We should have a girl's night with Noelle and Andrea soon."

"Good luck coordinating that with all we've got going on," she chuckled. "I've barely seen Noelle since she and Larkan have been all gaga for each other."

"She'll come around. It's just exciting being with a new man. Lean back a bit for me?"

We rolled up some blankets behind her so she could recline comfortably on the exam table. After sticking the eartips in, I lifted her shirt and placed the chestpiece next to her navel to begin listening to the baby's vitals.

"I'm sure you know that well," she teased, her voice distorted while I had the stethoscope on. "It's been so long, I can't even remember what the start of a new relationship feels like."

"Honestly, it's overrated." I moved the diaphragm over her belly. "Sure it's exciting, but you're also second-guessing yourself all the time. You don't want to be too eager or too aloof. It's hard to tell if your feelings are real or just infatuation that will fade. You over-analyze every little thing they do. It's exhausting really. I can't wait to get to where you are, knowing each other so well with years of memories together." I closed my lips, choosing not to voice the next thought floating through my brain, but Tessa went there anyway.

"It's not all it's cracked up to be," she whispered. "Years of being with the same person makes men bored. They start looking for what's newer, prettier, younger."

"Tessa!" I pulled the eartips out and let the stethoscope hang around my neck as I grabbed for her hand. "You are still young and *so* beautiful! No matter what Big G does, it doesn't reflect on who *you* are."

"I know what he does when they go on rides," she said flatly. "Everyone just looks the other way and doesn't say anything, but it's so obvious. His clothes smell like cheap hooker and he's a shitty liar."

"Tess…" I sat on the table next to her, squeezing her hands as if that would prevent her heart from breaking any further. "Honey, I'm so sorry. I wish I could do more, but I don't know what to say," I sighed. "I can heal cuts and fix broken bones, but there's no fixing men being idiots."

She huffed out a dry laugh. "It's all right, Mari. I knew what I signed up for, even though I hoped for better. Every other man in his family was the same way." She leaned her head back with a sigh. "If he wasn't so good with the kids, if they didn't idolize him as much as they do, there would be no question of what I'd do."

We sat together in silence for a minute, while I tried to figure out how to broach a solution for her.

"You can still let him be their father without being with him yourself," I said cautiously. "What if you moved out and agreed to split time with the kids?"

She shook her head. "He'd never allow that. For a woman to leave *him*? He's too prideful for that."

"What, is he going to physically prevent you from leaving? Keep you trapped in the house?"

"He might, I don't know."

"The other guys wouldn't allow that." I looked intently into her eyes. "Reaper wouldn't allow one of his men to mistreat his woman."

"We see it as mistreatment, they see it as keeping a family together," she whispered sadly. "That sums up why the Collapse happened in the first place, Mari. Men have never been able to see things from our perspective."

I opened my mouth to argue, but no sound came out. I never thought of it from that perspective before, but realized she was right.

TEN

REAPER

What a fucking day.

I needed to find Heather and Bones, and find out if they were in on Python's scheme. But the two of them had mysteriously disappeared. They didn't leave Sheol, of course. Gunner with his people at every exit made sure of that. After wasting a day of trying to find them at their usual haunts, I sent a team of envoys to search for them more diligently.

They weren't guilty of anything. Yet. But hiding from me wasn't doing anything to help them. I didn't give a shit that Heather was a woman, or that I fucked her. If she was in on this, she deserved to be punished just as much as Python.

The day dragged on until I finally had enough, and broke out the cigars, whiskey and deck of cards by the pool. Some of the off-duty guys joined me, along with Hades, of course.

He laid at my feet like normal, facing the clubhouse door with his chin on his paws. He didn't start doing that until Mariposa came into our lives, like he was waiting for her.

Me too, boy, I thought, leaning down to scratch him. After the difficult, but amazing, time we had yesterday, I couldn't get enough of her. Never in a million years would I have imagined going back to that place, nor taken a woman with me. But I was serious about this and I wanted her to know that.

Telling her I loved her was easy. Almost too easy. Easy enough that those words didn't seem very meaningful at all. I never was much of a poetic, wordsy guy anyway. I had to show her what she meant to me. And fuck me, it felt like she actually understood and felt the same way.

Halfway through the second card game, as dusk began swallowing the landscape in darkness, Hades lifted his head. His nose pointing stiffly at the door, I followed his gaze, waiting.

The door opened and he was off running, not even giving Mari a chance to poke her head through before jumping on her with excited whines and yips.

"Ha-*des*," I called, adding a high-pitched whistle. "Don't knock her over, you big oaf."

"Ohh, it's okay!" She laughed as she came toward us, walking my big mutt backward on his hind legs with her arms around him. "He's my favorite boy. Aren't you, Hades?"

He gave her a slobbery kiss, nuzzling and sniffing her as his stubby tail went nuts. Jesus, standing upright, he was almost as tall as she was.

"What am I, chopped liver?" I grunted around my cigar.

"That's what you get for having a dog, Pres," Benji, one of Gunner's younger guards, chuckled. "They seem like a chick magnet until you get the girl. Then you realize she loves the dog more than you."

"Unfortunately, I think you're right, kid," I sighed.

Gunner himself had been oddly silent at the table. Usually he talked the most shit during our card games as he tried to swindle us out of our chips. Now that Mari was here, he studied his hand like he wanted to disappear into the cards themselves.

"You know that's not true," Mari scolded, finally bringing Hades' front paws down to the ground.

I pulled the cigar from my mouth and leaned back in my chair. "Then get over here and show me how untrue it is."

She gave me a sultry look that made me so fucking hard before striding over. Sliding a hand along the back of my shoulders, she leaned down to kiss me. I knew she meant it to be a quick, sweet peck designed to be appropriate in the company of others right in front of us.

Naturally, I couldn't allow that.

I grabbed the back of her neck to prevent her escape before molding my mouth to hers. Soft and pliant, her lips opened for my invading tongue. My other hand grabbed the back of her thigh, pulling her around my leg so her sweet ass could take a seat in my lap.

She stopped resisting before ever sitting down, wrapping both hands around my neck to tongue-fuck my mouth with the same intense passion. This woman got me hotter than metal pipes in the sun and I didn't give a fuck who was in the front row audience. To be completely honest, I hoped Gunner got a sense of what he was missing now, and would think twice about blowing her off.

I smiled woozily as we came up for air. The booze, her lips, and the wild fucking realization that this woman loved me, hit me all at once in a heady rush.

"Now I hope to whatever fucking god that still listens that you don't kiss my dog like that," I teased, circling my arms around her waist.

"Only right before I'm about to see you," she dished back with a swat to my chest.

"That must be why you taste so good," I laughed.

"Hey." Her arms tightened around my neck as her lips brushed my ear. "I came to tell you something serious actually."

"Something wrong, sugar?" I cupped the side of her neck, pulling back to look at her.

"No, it's just," she bit her lip, visibly nervous, "Jandro asked me to come over tonight and I said yes."

"Really?" I squeezed around her tighter, a grin spreading on my face. "Finally getting some alone time, huh?"

"I guess." Her gorgeous eyes twinkled and a smile pulled at her lips. She was excited about this, which just made my heart fucking soar.

"You spending the night there?"

"I'm not sure, maybe. We'll see how it goes first."

"I won't wait up for you," I said with a kiss to her nose. "If you're in bed with me in the morning, great. If not, that's good too. It means you're in a safe place with someone I trust."

"You're sure?"

"Of course I'm sure, beautiful. Hell, you've already spent the night in a tent with him."

"Nothing happened back then."

"I know. Even if it did, I was being an ass and we all know it. You would've been entitled to a revenge-fuck."

"Reaper!"

"It's true. Anyway," I patted my fingers on her hip, "I'm glad you two are progressing, sugar. I know he'll make you happy, but in the event he fucks up, his ass is mine at Fight Night."

"He said the same thing about you," she groaned, rolling her eyes.

"See? You have good taste in men."

"Or the worst," she grumbled, but was unable to hide her smile as her fingers played with the hair on the back of my neck. "So I'll see you tomorrow?"

"You better." I closed my fist in her hair and pulled her mouth to mine again, sinking my teeth into her plump lip just enough to make her gasp. The territorial part of me wanted her to feel my bite when she kissed Jandro. "Have fun, sugar. I love you."

"Love you, *Rory*," she snickered against my neck and bounced away before I could spank her for calling me that.

With a final head scratch and kiss for Hades, she left through the pool gate and headed down the street toward Jandro's shop.

"Man, I dunno how you can do that." Benji broke

the silence that had fallen over the table. "Knowing my girl was spending the night with another man? I'd wanna punch through walls."

"That's 'cause you just grew hair on your balls last week and don't understand shit." I stuck the cigar back in my mouth and picked up my hand of cards, trying to remember what my strategy was while the blood drained from my dick and returned to my brain.

When my gaze slid over to Gunner, he was just as entranced with his five-card hand as the whole time Mari was here. I saw her stealing glances at him, but he stayed mum like a coward and didn't so much as look at her. She was only hoping for a hello from her friend, even my caveman ass could see that. And for him to ignore her was just rude as hell.

No one was a dick to my woman besides me, and that was only accidentally. Especially not my captain of the guard.

"You're awfully quiet there, Gun." I couldn't help but goad him. "Couldn't even say hello to our medic?"

"I'm not in the mood, Reap." He bit the phrase out with an edge of warning. The falcon on his shoulder turned its sharp gaze on me.

"Not in the mood?" I repeated. "For what, to not be a dick? You two were all buddy-buddy up until you got back from Colorado, now you're acting like she has the plague."

"Just stop. Can we play this fucking game or what?"

Nah, fuck that. He kept hurting my girl's feelings and I wasn't about to let him blow me off like he did her. I snatched the cards from his hands and tossed them over my shoulder, letting them flutter across the patio while he stared at me with an incredulous face.

"What the fuck, Reaper?"

"I asked you a question, captain," I growled. "I expect an answer."

Benji and the other kid mumbled excuses as they set their cards down and slunk away from the table. I wasn't entirely sure what was about to happen, but they were smart not to stick around.

"I didn't hear any question that warranted an answer." Gunner pushed his chair back noisily as he stood. "Just a bunch of chest-thumping bullshit from some asshole who doesn't know how to treat a woman."

"Ah, now we're fuckin' getting somewhere." I stood and blocked his path, Hades alert and ready at my side. "Was that not a happy woman at my side just now? What makes you think I'm not treating her right?"

"Reaper, come on," Gunner sighed. "I don't want to have beef with you. Just leave me out of it."

"Oh no. You're in it, golden boy, whether you like it or not." I stepped closer, my boots nearly touching his. He was a few inches taller than me, but skinnier. I didn't particularly want to come to blows either, but I could hold my own if it came to that. "You accuse me of mistreating my woman, you better give me a good fucking reason."

"What the fuck is wrong with you?" His laidback, sunny demeanor finally burst into flames. "You're pimping Mari out to Jandro, now you're trying to throw her at me too? She deserves better than that, you fucking pig!"

My hands shot out and shoved against his shoulders faster than I could think. He stumbled backward a few steps, eyes wide and mouth agape in surprise. I stepped in again, closing the distance quickly. Whether out of shock or restraint, he didn't try to hit me back, but I could see how much he wanted to.

"You don't understand the first fucking thing you're talking about," I hissed close to his face. "Remember how hurt she was when I didn't talk to her? Well, you're doing that right fucking now, and I'm calling you out on it *because* I love her. I'm putting my ego aside and trusting her with everything I am. I'm expanding her options for love and pleasure, and *I'm* the asshole?" I shook my head at him in disappointment. "You think you know what she deserves? Well, it's a hell of a lot better than you."

I stubbed out my cigar and walked off, Hades trotting at my side.

MARIPOSA

I walked up the driveway to Jandro's shop just as he was pulling the garage door closed.

"Hey *Mariposita*," he grinned at me. "I was starting to wonder if you changed your mind."

"Why?" I asked. "I didn't keep you waiting, did I?"

"Nah, just, you know." He gave a sheepish shrug. "I know you've got options."

"Oh, stop that," I scolded. "I told you I'd come over, so that's what I'm doing."

"That might be common sense to you and me." He towered over me, grabbing both of my hands in his. "But it's not so common these days."

"That's a damn shame." I looked up at him, resisting the urge to kiss those pillowy lips of his. "And still, it's not just that. I've been *wanting* to see you outside the shop."

In the fading daylight I couldn't tell if he was blushing, but he looked adorably speechless all the same. A rarity for the quick-tongued vice president.

"Shall we?" He released one of my hands to walk me back down the driveway, lacing his fingers through mine in a tighter grip on the other hand.

I followed his lead down the quiet street, rubbing my thumb over the back of his palm. The only sounds I heard were excited voices of children and the rumbles of bikes a few blocks over. I imagined it was Dallas and his family playing around on their mini bikes.

"So you and Shadow live together?" I swung our hands between us like we were a pair of innocent kids ourselves.

"Yeah. At first it was out of necessity for him. He didn't know how to live on his own, and kind of just stuck by me so he could figure shit out. Now he's a lot more independent and also a great roommate, as it turns out. We leave each other be, for the most part, but even a loner like him doesn't like to be alone all the time."

More questions turned over in my head, but like usual, I sensed that Jandro purposely omitted details about Shadow's life out of respect for his privacy, and I couldn't violate that.

He led me up a wide, gently sloping driveway to a house with a similar floor plan as Reaper's, but a smaller version. It had the same central entryway with two wings on either side. I had a hunch that he and Shadow each had half of the house to themselves. When he pushed open the heavy wooden door and led me inside, I saw my instinct was right.

A central staircase greeted us upon entry, leading up to walkways branching off to the left and right at the second level. The first floor was clearly the common area, with a large TV surrounded by comfortable but mismatched furniture, and an open concept kitchen and dining area toward the back. I spotted Jandro's chickens pecking at the ground through the sliding glass door at the back of the house, and a large, dark figure leaning over a desk across from the living room.

"Shadow, don't be fuckin' rude," Jandro muttered under his breath after closing the front door behind us and leading me inside.

"Hi, Shadow," I chirpily greeted the large man hunched over the desk before he could say anything.

"Hi, Mariposa." A desk lamp pointed down at an open book in front of him, casting half his face in shadow as he glanced up at me.

"How are you today?"

I felt elated that he said hi to me without any apparent distress. After greeting him at least once per day since he donated blood at my office, he seemed to become less abrasive to small, social interactions with me. Now that we had established that as a comfort zone, I couldn't resist pushing the envelope just a tiny bit further.

"I'm fine." He moved his forearm to rest on the page of what I now realized was a sketchbook. A pencil spun absently over his thumb and forefinger. "How are you?" he remembered to ask after a long pause.

I smiled wider at him, immensely proud at his progress. "I'm great, thank you."

Jandro cleared his throat, pulling me toward the

kitchen as Shadow's attention returned to his sketchbook.

"You're brave," he murmured, brushing a kiss against my ear. "Want anything to drink?"

"For saying hi, how are you?" I asked in a low voice. Then louder, "What do you got?"

"I know you're trying to push him to be more social, and he doesn't usually react well to that." Jandro grabbed a lime from a small basket on the counter and tossed it in the air before catching it again. "I can make a mean margarita."

Forgetting about Shadow for the moment, my mouth dropped open. "You have tequila?"

"Do I have tequila," he scoffed, reaching under the counter to produce a large, unlabeled glass bottle. A pale amber liquid swirled in the lower third of the vessel.

"Is that an añejo?" Nostalgic memories of my father sneaking me shots of his "good stuff" as he called it, filled my brain. Tequila aged for at least one year was smoother than younger spirits and best for sipping.

"Ah, my girl knows her stuff." Jandro's eyes sparkled with glee while I tried to ignore my stomach flip-flopping at him calling me *his*. "It is an añejo. I've been savoring this since Gunner scored it about a year ago."

"It would be a shame to dilute it down in a margarita," I said. "I used to drink añejo with my dad with just salt and lime."

"Then that's what we'll do." He brought down two shot glasses and a salt shaker from a cabinet, then dug out a cutting board and a knife from a drawer. "You make those how you like 'em while I get the food started."

"What's for dinner?" I slid into a stool across the elegant, granite countertop and started cutting the limes.

"Breakfast," he grinned, opening a small, wooden crate to show me rows of eggs in various shades of brown to off-white. "Huevos rancheros, to be precise. My girls have been good to me."

I smiled back as I untwisted the cap of the añejo and began to pour. "That means they're happy with you."

"I like to think I know a few things about keeping ladies happy."

While the eggs fried and he prepped the sides, I poured the shots and dumped a few good shakes of salt onto the lime wedges.

"Bite the lime and then take a sip," I said, sliding his glass toward him across the counter. "Savor it in your mouth for a few seconds, like a good whiskey."

He took the filled shot glass and raised it carefully. "A toast first."

"To what?"

We pondered together in silence for a few moments. "To your dad," he said quietly. "For raising one hell of an amazing woman who knows her tequila."

That was so utterly sweet and unexpected of him to say. My throat closed up with emotion, but I gave a shaky, appreciative smile.

"To Javier Luis de los Angeles," I whispered, gently touching my glass to Jandro's.

"*Salut,*" he murmured.

Our eyes remained locked on each other as we each

bit the flesh of our lime wedges. Citrus and salt coated my tongue as I brought the drink to my lips. Jandro copied my movements like a mirror, sipping gently at the rim of his glass. The burn of the alcohol evaporated into a sweet, refreshing flavor as it mixed with the acid and salt on my tongue.

"Damn, that's good." Jandro turned away briefly to check on the eggs.

With the intensity of his gaze gone, I found it easier to talk again. "Do you need any help?"

"Absolutely not." He turned back toward me and flipped a knife in the air with a smirk before returning to chopping bell peppers. "Is your old man still around?" he asked in a softer voice as he worked.

"No. At least I'm pretty sure he's not." I took another small sip of añejo. "He was drafted for the border war between our county and Texahoma. Every two weeks or so, they gave him leave to come home for a weekend. Eventually, he just never came home again."

"Fuck. I'm sorry, Mari."

"Don't be," I told him. "The last few weekends he came, he was different. I was a year away from graduating school then, so I recognized the symptoms of PTSD, but it still hurt. Just violent outbursts out of nowhere, treating my mom and I like we were the enemy."

"How about her, she still around?"

"I certainly hope so," I sighed, taking another sip of tequila. "When he didn't come back for months, she decided to go out and find him."

"You're fucking kidding me," Jandro breathed. "She went out to find him and left you?"

"It wasn't like that. I was almost done with school and pretty independent. I was more worried that she was out there alone and unprotected. And even if she did find out what happened to him, who knew if she'd be able to handle the news."

"Did you ever hear back from her?"

"I got a 'congratulations on graduating' card from somewhere in Montana, but other than that?" I shook my head.

"I get that you were an adult and all, but it's still messed up." Jandro's hand clenched on the counter. "She left *you*, her daughter, a fellow woman alone in the middle of a war zone."

"I think she knew I'd be fine," I replied. "She figured I'd be valued with my medical skills, and that it was my dad that needed her most." I smile down at my tequila glass, circling a finger around the rim. "He was the love of her life. I can't say that I blame her."

"Well, I hope they're together," Jandro offered. "Wherever they are."

I took another nibble of my lime flesh. "How about you? Your folks still around?"

"Nah." His voice softened. "I only really know them from the stories my sisters told me. The oldest two and my parents trekked up through Mexico from Guatemala to escape the dictatorship there. My mom found out she was pregnant again by the time she reached Arizona. She had me and the two youngest of my sisters, almost back-to-back, while we all stayed with my aunt and uncle. They were deported shortly after I was born, even though they were granted political asylum. Some glitch in the system that never got corrected."

"I'm sorry," I told him sincerely. "You never saw them again?"

"No. They sent letters with my sisters back and forth for a few years, but then the postal service got really unreliable and…" He lifted a shoulder in a shrug. "Kind of like with your dad. We just never heard from them again."

"I had family on his side too that got deported despite having green cards and work visas," I sighed. "Cousins, aunts, and uncles I've never met. It's so fucked up."

"And look where we are now." He huffed out a dry laugh. "Funny how no one wants to come here now that this place is a fucking free for all."

"The people we trusted to protect us failed us," I sighed. "Now we're on our own."

"You know what this conversation needs?" Jandro spread his hands wide on the counter, lifting his eyebrows suggestively at me.

"A less depressing topic?" I asked.

"Yes. And also more tequila." He leaned across the counter and placed a surprise peck on my lips. "Food's ready. I'll plate it up while you pour us another round."

———

A HALF-HOUR LATER, I was scooping up the last of my delicious egg-yolk and salsa mixture with a tortilla. If

Jandro hadn't provided any, I would have licked my plate clean.

"Holy shit," I leaned back in my chair. "I don't think I've ever had huevos rancheros that good." Placing a hand on his shoulder, I leaned over to kiss his cheek. "Thank you. Breakfast-dinner was delicious."

"My pleasure, *Mariposita*." His hand slid along my back, resting with gentle pressure just above my ass as he leaned in to kiss me properly.

He tasted spicy, citrusy, hot and cool all at once. The tequila, now like liquid fire in my veins, burned away my shyness about exploring him through touch. My palm skimmed over his large, broad shoulder, fingertips trailing over his neck and collarbone as he turned in his chair to face me.

Grabbing one of my chair legs, he pulled me closer to secure both arms around me. I braced two hands on his chest to combat the falling sensation in the pit of my stomach. He stayed there the whole time, broad and solid. His kisses were the perfect dessert—smooth, buttery, and warm. Even as he kissed deeper, his hold on me growing tighter, nothing was rushed or rough.

Jandro was incredibly responsive in his affection, gauging my reactions with movements of his hands and soft flicks of his tongue. He took the lead, but never swept me away. I began to see taking full control wasn't his style—he gave just as much as he took. With every gentle pull back, he led me on a chase. And when I caught up, he matched me on every beat.

"This is the part where I either take you home, or you come upstairs with me." His voice grew lower, gravelly and sexy. "Because I can't keep my hands off you unless there are multiple walls and doors between us."

We both panted slightly, out of breath like we really did chase each other around. My whole body was a vessel of pulsing, liquid heat and there was no question of what I wanted to do. He was a decadent dessert, too delicious to be good for me, but I didn't care.

"What's it gonna be, Mari?" Impatience roughened his voice and I liked it.

"Take me upstairs," I breathed against his lips, eager for another taste.

He needed no further invitation. The moment our mouths clashed together, he released a deep, sensual moan. Large hand slid under my thighs to scoop me up and deposit me in his lap. I straddled his waist, my heartbeat spiking at the brush of a hard bulge against the inside of my thigh.

"Who knows if we'll make it to the stairs," he murmured, dragging that hot, luscious mouth over the pulse in my neck.

Just then I got hit with the memory of the first time he kissed me there—at the first Fight Night I witnessed where he split Stephan's lip open. He asked me for a good luck kiss and pointed to his cheek. I did, just to make him leave me alone, and got his lips on my neck in return.

"What're you giggling at?" he muttered, pulling my hair in a gentle tilt back so he could kiss my throat. "Am I tickling you?"

"I was just remembering the first time I saw you fight, and when you tricked me into kissing you."

"That feels like so long ago," he chuckled, grazing a kiss along my collarbone. "I was hoping to take you upstairs *that* night, after impressing you with my fighting skills. Before all that other shit went down."

"Hah, sorry that getting the shit beat out of me and being carried to the medic's office cockblocked you."

"I'm not. I mean—fuck." He leaned back, slapping a hand over his mouth. "That came out wrong."

"Uh-huh." I remained seated in his lap, but crossed my arms as I pulled away. "How was it supposed to come out?"

"Don't be mad at me, *Mariposita*. Come here." He wrestled one of my hands away from my cross-armed position and pressed a kiss to my palm. "I'm sorry you got hurt that night. Of course I'd never want that. What I meant was, I'm glad I didn't sleep with you then. Because if I had, we probably wouldn't be here right now." He laced his fingers with mine. "Like this."

Here it was. He pulled the curtain aside and gave me a glimpse at the real Jandro. But I wanted more than just a hint at what was underneath the charm and the swagger. I wanted him laid out bare for me.

"Why do you say that?"

"Because," his eyes closed for a moment with a sigh, "I didn't care about you then like I do now. I thought you were pretty and I wanted you on my dick. Nothing else mattered to me. I would've used you and discarded you. But *everything* matters now. When I don't see you, I miss you. I want us to laugh together until we make Reaper's head explode. I want to *always* feel like I did when you brought me lunch, and I want to keep showing you how much I appreciate that." His voice lowered to a near-whisper. "I want to be one of the reasons that you feel happy."

I was stunned. Speechless. I didn't just get him laid bare. I got a confession, atonement, and declarations of *always*. That free falling sensation came over me again— a rushing, thrilling mix of emotions, but with absolutely no fear. It was almost jarring how I *wasn't* afraid of diving headfirst into my feelings for two completely different men.

I wrapped both arms around Jandro's neck, bringing my lips down on his to kiss the tension away. He took a risk in showing his heart to me and I would treasure it.

Skimming my lips across his cheek to his ear, I whispered, "Try again for the stairs?"

He made a noise somewhere between a chuckle and a groan, then cupped my ass before lifting us effortlessly up from the chair.

TWELVE

JANDRO

"Strong legs," Mari remarked with a soft giggle as I took the stairs two at a time. Her body bounced against mine, wrapped around me with her arms and legs.

"Nah, you're a light little thing." I set her down gently when we reached the second floor landing.

Her feet touched the floor but her hands remained solidly on my arms. "Oh, just take a compliment. You're strong as an ox."

"Nope, you're thinking of the guy down the hall." I wanted compliments and so much more from her. Reaper was the rough one, but I wanted to leave my own kind of mark on her. Right in that moment however, something else distracted me.

"My bedroom's the door at the very end." I turned her away from me and gave her a light swat on the ass. "Go on ahead. I've got to do something real quick."

She looked back at me, confusion furrowing her brow. "What do you have to do?"

"I'm just checking on something with Shadow. I'll be right in after you." I grabbed her arm and planted a quick kiss on her lips before letting her go. "Don't get naked yet. I want to do that to you myself."

The answer seemed to satisfy her and I waited until she disappeared behind the bedroom door. Honestly, she'd probably understand what I had to do if I explained to her. I just didn't want to right then. I wanted to get it over with and enjoy her for the rest of the night properly. Chances were, if she kept coming over, she'd see every facet of my and Shadow's living arrangement anyway.

I went to the opposite end of the landing, pausing just outside of his bedroom door. When Mari and I first went up the stairs, I noticed he wasn't drawing at his desk anymore. Usually he told me when he was going to bed, but this time was considerate enough to not interrupt our dinner and make out session.

"Maybe you really *are* getting better, man," I muttered to myself as I approached the heavy wooden door. The third one we had to install in as many years.

Eager to get back to the gorgeous woman in my bedroom at the other end of the hall, I moved quickly. First I slid all the deadbolts into place on the knob side of the door. Originally I installed three, then it became clear I needed more. I went from bottom to top, starting with the one at waist-height, then reaching the eighth one on my tiptoes near the top of the door. I wasn't a short guy by any means, Shadow was just *that* huge.

Once those were in place, I grabbed the handful of padlocks from the side table. Moving to the hinged side of the door, I closed the eight latches installed there before slapping the locks in place. It would take a group of men with a battering ram to knock this door down. Better than Shadow's shoulder or forehead.

I hated doing this, locking him in like he was some dangerous animal. But truthfully, he was. He couldn't control what happened in his sleep, but that didn't make me or our furniture any safer. I found some small comfort in knowing the extra locks were his idea. And so far, it was the only thing that worked.

Once everything was secure and I gave the door a few cursory pushes to check for any weak spots, I hurried down the hall in the opposite direction. Despite the necessity of it, locking him in always made me feel weird. Something was wrong about it. We did this nightly ritual for a month and a half now, and I had yet to get used to it.

It reminded me of my days as a prison guard, when I had to hide our friendship, cuff him, and lock him in his cell. When we left that hellhole together, I never wanted to lock another human being in a cage again.

So much for that.

Mari was standing next to the floor-to-ceiling panoramic window in my bedroom when I arrived. She looked over her shoulder at me with a sweet smile. "Everything okay?"

"It is now," I sighed, crossing the room toward her. My arms came around her from behind, hugging her back to my chest as I placed a kiss on her shoulder. "You like the window?"

"I do. The sunrise must be amazing. Did you make this yourself?"

"Yeah, I don't know construction like I do bikes, but I used to do some odd jobs."

She pressed her head back against my chest, looking straight up at me. "Is there anything you can't do?"

"Well, so far I haven't been able to get you in bed with me. Maybe you should prove me wrong."

"Smartass," she laughed, spinning in my arms before shoving me playfully back toward the bed. "You can do anything you put your mind to," she joked, sounding like an old teacher Reaper and I used to have.

"I like where this is going." I bit my lip, pulling her with me as I walked backward. "And you can do anything to my body that comes to mind. Is that what you're saying?" The mattress hit the backs of my knees and I sat down.

"No," she laughed again, climbing on to straddle me. "I have no idea what you're saying."

"I should probably stop talking, then."

"Yeah, maybe."

Our mouths crashed together. My palms slid under the hem of her shirt and found a slender waist and warm skin. Lifting higher, a bra blocked me from finding more of her. Her shirt went first, then mine, and then that pesky bra.

Her skin erupted in goosebumps as she became free from clothing, her nipples tight little buds that I wanted to soothe and soften with my tongue.

"You okay?" It came out a hoarse, lusty whisper.

She leaned against me, arms braced between my

chest and hers while my hands did their best to warm up her long, curving back.

"Do you ever worry about someone seeing you?" She glanced behind her at the window.

Only the midnight blue of the sky dotted with billions of stars looked back at us. Underneath, the landscape was dark, murky and unknown.

"Nah," I told her. "This side of the house faces the desert outside Sheol. It's the main reason why I picked it." I brought my lips to her ear. "Only gods and stars can see us, but we can see everything."

I sucked her earlobe, eliciting a soft gasp and bringing her arms around my neck. She went wild every time I kissed this area of her body and I intended to fully take advantage of it. Her thighs squeezed around my hips as my mouth found the tender spot between her neck and shoulder. My hands came forward, running up her ribs to graze the undersides of her breasts, my thumbs sweeping over her nipples.

"Jandro…" She rolled her core over my dick, which was fighting like hell to get free of boxers and jeans. Her small hands went everywhere as if wanting to touch me all at once.

"Mari," I answered, my mouth now against her sternum as I lifted us and turned.

I held her by the waist, lowering her back to the bed while our lower bodies refused to separate. Her thighs remained glued to my hips, the friction of all our movement inching my jeans down too fucking slowly.

I pulled away from her just to get out of my damn pants, while she took the opportunity to do the same.

"Ha, I'm faster," she joked, flinging away her pants while mine were still around my calves.

"Fuck, I hope so," I said in a tight whisper, kicking them away as I lowered to hover above her again. "You got me feeling like I'm going to explode already."

"Well, we've got all night, don't we?" She curled one leg around my waist, running her foot down the back of my thigh. The same movement drew my cock to rub against her hot core. Fuck, her panties were already slick. I couldn't tell what was her wetness and what was my pre-come.

"That's certainly what I was hoping for." I palmed her breasts while I kissed the valley between them. "Is my bed comfortable?"

"Mm-hmm," she hummed, massaging down the back of my neck and shoulders. "I wouldn't mind a sleepover."

"Good." I dragged my tongue to a nipple, rolling over the tight little peak before grazing it ever so slightly with my teeth.

With a soft gasp, she dug harder into my back. Her fingers brushed over the still-healing scar she stitched up last week—the gunshot wound I took to protect her during the Razor Wire ambush. The tenderness of the wound made me flinch a little, bringing my eyes up to hers.

"I'm sorry," she pulled her hand back, "did I hurt you?"

Did she ask me a question? I couldn't say.

"Fucking Christ, you're beautiful."

All I wanted to do was look at her, and just marvel at

the warmth, care, inner, and outer beauty of this woman. But I couldn't kiss and please her if I was too busy staring. Damn the choices a man had to make.

"You're not too bad yourself," she giggled sweetly. "And this has been a beautiful day with you—"

"Shh, it's not over yet." I moved lower, gliding the tip of my tongue just under her breasts now. "Not even close, *Mariposita*."

Her curves could make a grown man cry and I wanted to make sure she knew that. My hands ran up and down her sides, taking in every dip and swell from her perfect teardrop breasts to the edge of her panties at her luscious hips. All the while I kissed a trail down her belly, slow enough to torture myself as well as her.

She tried to wriggle and writhe underneath me but I kept her still. And when I finally gripped the edges of that flimsy fabric and peeled them away, my mouth followed right after. Hot and delicious, her freshly uncovered skin was soon covered again by my lips and tongue, reaching lower until my kiss reached her clit.

Her legs sealed shut, she tried to buck against my mouth, but it was no use against me holding her down. I allowed her legs to stay closed only to slide those panties down and away, then opened her up again like a Christmas present.

"Jan—ah!"

Whatever she was going to say cut off as I sealed my whole mouth against her center, sucking on her lips and dragging my tongue up and down her slit. I wasn't even completely concerned with her pleasure at that moment, I just wanted to get drunk on her taste.

She was absolutely delicious and I could not get enough.

I hummed and moaned against her sensitive skin as I lapped and sucked at her pussy, knowing the vibrations would drive her wild. Her nails dug into my scalp in a way that urged me on, tingling with a pleasure that bordered on pain. She was probably moaning but I couldn't be certain—her thighs made great earmuffs.

Bringing one hand in, I kneaded the inside of her thigh as I dragged my mouth away, kissing the crease between her leg and hip.

"Why are you stopping?" she panted.

"Because I need to breathe." I shot her a teasing grin. "I'm no good to you if I suffocate, am I?"

"But I'm so close."

"Fuck yeah, you are." I gazed in awe at her stretched out on my bed, quivering and breathing hard. My hand on her thigh pressed to her hot, drenched core. "You want to be filled, beautiful?"

"Yesss…" she dragged the word out into a sexy hiss as my finger pressed inside her. "I want you so bad, Jandro."

"Do you want *me* or just my dick?"

The question came somewhat out of nowhere. It rattled around in my brain sometimes as a random thought, often without any words attached to it. Just a worry. I knew how to bring women to bed, but wasn't the best at keeping them. Her, I desperately wanted to keep. But it was a two-way street, and my mouth ran before my brain.

"I want *you*, Jandro all of you." She sat up, pulling

me toward her. My finger slipped out from between her legs, foreplay momentarily forgotten. "I want your smiles, your jokes, your cooking, your kisses." Her hands pressed to my cheeks and she kissed me languidly, apparently not caring that my lips and tongue were still coated in her sex. "I want your dick too, but that's far from the most important thing. I want everything that is *you*."

No one had said anything remotely like that to me before. Not even close. This adorable, sexy, kind, incredible woman reached a place deep inside me no one else had ever occupied. And I never wanted her to leave.

My next kiss pressed her back down into the pillows. My hands left her body only to take off my boxer briefs in a hurry. The next thing I felt were her slender fingers wrapped around my length. I sucked in a breath with a hiss. Just the contact of her gliding up and down my rigid shaft was enough to start unraveling my control.

"Damn it, Mariposa. I told you I was close to exploding already," I reminded her in a harsh whisper.

"And I told you we have all night." She released my cock, her hand traveling down to my balls. Her massaging and gentle tugging took me away from the edge just enough to think straight again.

I grabbed her thighs, kneading the sensitive flesh as I maneuvered between them. All the while, I made it a goal never to stop tasting her. From her lips, her earlobes, and her neck to her pert nipples and the sexy curves of her waist, my mouth needed to be on her at all times.

Her legs around my hips as they were meant to be, I

pressed forward to sheath myself in the hot, slick center of her. She clutched my shoulders with a soft gasp upon entry. I covered her mouth with mine, and she opened up for my tongue just as she did my cock.

"You okay?" I murmured into her neck once fully seated inside.

"So, so much more than that…" Her arms and legs wound even tighter around me, nails scratching deliciously across my back. "Please, Jandro."

How could I say no to that? I could only pull back so much with the grip she had on me with those gorgeous thighs. Still, I made every movement count. I angled my thrusts to maximize her pleasure, listening to the shifts in her moans and breaths. Her clit felt harder with every impact from the base of my cock, which was the clearest sign she was getting close.

The soft whimpers and moans from her throat were the sexiest music to my ears, growing louder and uncontrolled as she neared release. Her thighs around me started to tremble and that was when I slowed down.

"Don't stop. Why'd you stop?" she panted.

"What's the fun in that?" I massaged her breasts in my hands. "We've got all night, don't we?" I pulled her nipples into my mouth, grazing them with just enough teeth to distract her. "God, I can't get over how beautiful you are."

"I'll look even better once you let me come."

She had the gall to wink and I burst out laughing. "Nah, I want you burned into my memory just like this. On the edge, flushed, and wrapped around me. Just putty in my hands."

"I can't imagine why," she teased. "Control freak."

"Because I never want this moment to end." I started moving in her again, but slowly, with her face cupped in my hands. "I'm sure we'll make love plenty more times, but we'll never have another first time. I want to savor exploring you, uncovering you, for as long as I can—mm! And thanks to you squeezing my dick like that, it won't be for much longer."

"Kegel exercises are important," she informed me with a devilish smile. "A nice side effect is they contribute to much stronger orgasms."

"And just like that," I sighed into her neck, "I'm done for."

Her walls contracted around me rhythmically as I picked up speed and intensity. Our sex was violent now, a relentless crashing of flesh on flesh—not to mention my headboard against the wall. My dick felt like iron as she became even tighter, wetter, and hotter. Mari bit her fist to hold back her screams, but I grabbed her wrist and pinned it down next to her head. I needed to hear how I was making her feel.

"Do you still want all of me?" I demanded, never missing a beat as I kept fucking her. "Do you want all of this and more?"

"Yes!" she cried out as her release closed around me like a vice, holding me inside her like she'd never let go. "I need you, Jandro…"

Her convulsions and her words were too much for me to handle. My release came just as violently with a final crash , her orgasm wringing me out and milking me for all I was worth. All the strength and rigidity in my body vanished, now turning me to putty in her hands.

Mari seemed to already be falling asleep as I withdrew from her, slid up next to her, and pulled the sheet over us. But she flipped over, curling into a little ball and nuzzling into the center of my chest. If the sex turned me to jello, I melted into straight-up liquid butter at that point.

I rested my chin on her head and slid an arm around her back as I listened to her deep breathing.

"You're stuck with me, little butterfly," I mumbled, sleep and relaxed bliss settling into my limbs. "You just had to go and make me fall in love with you."

THIRTEEN

MARIPOSA

I awoke so slowly, I temporarily forgot where I was.

This bed didn't feel like Reaper's. The large bicep serving as my pillow wasn't his, nor was the arm draped over my waist. But a familiar weight pressed down on the foot of the bed like Hades was here, watching over us.

Hades? How...?

I had to be more asleep than awake. I remembered I was at Jandro's house, in his bed. There was no way Hades could be here. His presence was just what my subconscious craved as a familiar comfort while I slept.

And yet I swore if my toes stretched out just a few inches, they would touch whatever solid body weighed down the mattress at the end of the bed.

Maybe not Hades, but *someone* was in here with us.

I tried to force my eyes open but sleep still clung to me, pulling me back into unconsciousness like an anchor. I didn't know if my eyes were showing me or my brain was creating an illusion, but I saw someone sitting at the edge of the bed.

It looked roughly like a man facing the direction of Jandro's wall-sized window. No matter how badly I tried, I couldn't force myself to awaken, to see details of this person who snuck into the bedroom.

Looking at him, if I could even call it that, was like trying to stare into the bottom of a murky lake. Every time I almost made out some detail, like a nose, ear, or length of his hair, it would become obscured by some kind of fog or darkness. It seemed impossible to get a sense of his clothing or even how big he was. His weight on the bed felt solid, yet he seemed completely ethereal, like he could evaporate into thin air like a ghost. Was Jandro's place haunted?

I never believed in ghosts, and I didn't get a haunted vibe from this person. As I kept staring at him, I realized I never felt afraid for a moment. Whoever he was, he wasn't there to hurt me. He was just sitting, looking at the stars out the window.

"Hello, Mariposa."

It *was* a man. That voice was deep, rich and masculine. It was impossible for me to tell if I heard it with my ears or if it came from my own head. But I heard him say my name, unmistakably.

"I'm dreaming." That had to be the only explanation. I was in some kind of state between awake and asleep, and my mind was just playing out dreams that made them seem like hallucinations.

"Yes, you are." The voice sounded amused, but the

figure remained completely still. "But that does not negate the fact that I'm here."

Again, I felt no fear. No sense of alarm of this strange man sitting on my lover's bed and talking to me in a voice just as dark and deep as the earth. I never knew my grandparents but he spoke in a way I imagined a grandfather would—full of wisdom and experience of time passed.

"Who are you?" I murmured groggily.

"I'm Hades."

———

I WOKE up the second time with a start, now fully awake.

Rubbing my eyes, then blinking rapidly in the dim light, I stared at the empty air just above the foot of the bed. No one was there, not even a wrinkle in the sheets to indicate someone had been.

Crazy-ass dream, I thought, flipping over and snuggling into Jandro's warm chest.

"Mm," he groaned adorably in his sleep, wrapping around me tighter.

I tucked my head under his chin and let out a contented sigh, closing my eyes. If I was still asleep during that wild dream, what had startled me awake?

The answer came a few seconds later, when a loud thump made me gasp and freeze with fear. Next I heard voices coming from one of the rooms in Jandro's house. I couldn't make out the words, but then I heard a scream and another loud thump like someone was punching a door.

"Jandro," I whispered, shaking him desperately. "Jandro, wake up!"

"Hmm? You okay, Mari?" He rubbed at his eyes, his voice gravelly with sleep.

"Someone's broken in! I can hear them talking and banging on stuff in the house." Another yell and the loudest thump yet, like a body slamming into a wall, made me curl into him for protection.

But Jandro didn't seem fazed. He rubbed down my back and kissed my forehead with a sigh. "I was afraid this would happen tonight. Don't worry though, Mari. It'll be over soon."

I stared at him, bewildered. "What the fuck is going on?"

"It's just Shadow having his nightmares. It sounds worse than it is, but yeah. This is what I have to deal with a few times a week."

"Nightmares?" Another scream and unintelligible yelling made me flinch. "*Those* are nightmares?"

"Mm-hm." His fingers moved over my skin, caressing and soothing. "When I told you to wait here for me, I went to close up over a dozen locks on his door. He's not a violent guy when he's awake, unless he's doing his job. But when he sleeps, he's uncontrollable. He's destroyed so much shit in the house, dislocated my shoulder, given me black eyes. I fucking hate locking him in there, but we don't see any other options."

"Are so many locks necessary?"

"He's ripped the door off the hinges. Twice."

"Holy shit."

"Yeah." Jandro kissed my hair as he ran his fingers through the long strands. "He's my friend. I hate seeing him suffer, but he's strong as fuck and dangerous when he's like this. I just don't know what else to do."

Not a single brain cell was asleep in my head anymore. I mentally filed through everything I read about PTSD and the procession of trauma. God knew I researched the shit out of it, thanks to my dad.

"It isn't nightmares," I said after the thumping and yelling began to subside. "His brain is trying to process trauma from his past, probably from childhood. I'm only speculating, but from his screams…it sounds horribly abusive."

Jandro didn't speak for a long moment, his warm hands pausing their movements on my skin. "You're right," was all he said.

"Jandro." I slid out of his warm embrace, propping my head up on my arm to look at him in the dark room. "What happened to him? I don't specialize in this kind of thing but I might be able to help—"

"*Mariposita,*" he sighed. "I know you mean well, and I love that you're so caring and patient with him. But you can't help. His trauma runs *deep*. It's not just from his childhood, it's all he's known since the day he was born. And," he hesitated, "your gender is an intrinsic part of that."

"So he was abused by women," I said matter-of-factly. "Since he was an infant?"

"Yes."

"Family members, I assume?"

"Look, even I don't know all the details," he said. "I'll tell you what I can, but please, Mari, you can't push him. He's come such a long way, but avoiding women is a safety thing for him. I know you have the best of intentions, but I can't let him regress."

"Trust me, I get it." I snuggled back closer to him, realizing he'd much rather sleep than talk, but I was dying to know more. Maybe I'd have to be creative around helping Shadow, but there had to be some kind of way. "So what happened?"

"I don't know specific methods of what they did to him, and don't really care to," Jandro murmured against my forehead. His fingers began a hypnotic, circular pattern on my back. "So, you saw where Reaper grew up, right?"

"Mm-hm." I rested my lips on his warm shoulder.

"Well, his was one of maybe a dozen female-run communities that said 'fuck the patriarchy' for a number of reasons and decided to live their own way. Most of them were based here in Arizona, some stretched up to Utah."

"Okay." His voice vibrated in his chest as he spoke. I curled into him as I listened.

"So, as with all types of people, you have normal folks in the middle of a spectrum, then you have people at extreme ends. Reaper's was considered pretty normal despite the polyandry thing, since they allowed men to live there too. Some communities didn't allow men at all. And others were just fucking psychotic."

I felt his heartbeat pick up speed, and I was certain mine did too.

"Psychotic in what way?"

"Like these women were fucking violent and deranged. I met Shadow when I worked in a prison, but those vile bitches should have been the ones locked up." His tone deepened to one of anger. "They hated men and everything to do with us. They ran their communes like cults out of a horror movie."

"So they would hurt men," I realized. "And abuse them."

"Even before I met Shadow, I heard rumors," Jandro went on. "That they seduced men, drugged them, and sacrificed them to their culty goddess. I heard that if a woman got pregnant and the baby was a boy, they'd kill it on the spot."

"Oh my god," I blinked away tears. "Poor Shadow."

"Local authorities said the same kind of shit about Reaper's community, so who knows what details are true and what's made up. But Shadow knew nothing but literal Hell his whole life until I brought him into the Demons. He's never said a peep about what the cult did but," he moved my hand up and over his shoulder, touching my fingers down on the gunshot wound I closed, "you can see the scars."

I didn't want to change the subject entirely, but the overwhelming sadness of Shadow's upbringing had me craving a happier topic to fixate on.

"Tell me how the Steel Demons formed." I scratched lightly over his scalp. "And how you brought Shadow into the fold."

"You mean Reap hasn't told you already?" he chuckled with a kiss to my temple.

"Maybe he has and I just want to see if your stories line up."

"You suck at lying and it's adorable," he teased, kissing my neck. "Well Reap and I knew each other since we were kids, you knew that already. We met Gunner when we were about sixteen, when he bailed us out of jail by flashing his family's money around."

"I can see him doing that," I giggled. "But why would he help you two?"

"He had a vintage motorcycle that was precious to him, a family heirloom of sorts. But he couldn't get it running. I promised I'd fix it for him and, surprise for us, the preppy little punk actually held up his end of the bargain and got us out. We got along remarkably well for being from such different backgrounds. He was always kind of an outcast among his rich, snobby family, and I think we gave him a sense of freedom he never had."

"So SDMC was just you three for a while?"

"Daren and Noelle were with us too. But yeah, the five of us were the OGs." He sat up halfway in bed, propping pillows against the headboard. Apparently he was fully awake now too, and getting into storytelling mode. His arm fell around my shoulders and I nestled into his side.

"I keep forgetting about Reaper's brother," I admitted. "He's only talked to me about him a few times."

"Daren was kind of like that," Jandro nodded. "Quiet kid, always kind of in his own head. My loudmouthed ass would forget he was around too, until he had something really important to say. Then he'd usually grab one of his siblings. But anyway," he rubbed his jaw, "the five of us lived in a tiny-ass apartment after Reaper's home got swept. He and I were twenty-one, the others a little younger. But you know, we partied, revved our engines loud in the streets, got into bar fights, went on longer rides together on weekends. That was SDMC in its infancy, just a bunch of dumbass hooligans."

Jandro's voice softened as he stared blankly at a random wrinkle in the sheet. "When Reap went back home for a visit and found everyone all gone, it was like a switch flipped. He left as Rory and came back home as Reaper, the SDMC president we know."

I recalled how Reaper told me the story, standing in the middle of empty homes and artifacts buried in the sand. I wondered if that was the most emotion he allowed himself to show regarding the loss of his family.

"He said everyone had been taken away, and we couldn't afford to fuck around anymore," Jandro continued. "We had to become a club, a real one with a hierarchy, rules, and a reputation. At first, it was to shape up so we could find his family. After some years passed without so much as a clue about them, it was so we could form and protect our own."

I drifted my fingertips over his chest and abs like how he was caressing me earlier. "How did Shadow get involved?"

"That was a whole other ordeal," he sighed. "I was working in a prison at the time, and he was in the mental health building, for reasons I'm sure you can guess."

"Nightmares, talking to himself, and erratic violence?"

"Yup. You wouldn't even recognize him, Mari. Same height but skinny as a rail. A shaved head, no facial hair. I don't think he ever got a proper meal in his life."

"Jesus. Poor Shadow."

"Yeah. I could tell he wasn't mentally impaired in any way, so I felt bad that he got placed in that unit. One night, I snuck him a flask of my boss's hidden stash of liquor. He slept like a baby, but now he's dependent on booze to sleep at all. And he's developed a hell of a tolerance over the years so he always needs more."

"I understand why you did that, but that kind of drinking is poisoning him. I'm amazed he's still alive and functioning as well as he is. How old is he?"

"No idea. There was no record of his birth, only a rough estimate of his age. He was never even given a name before coming to the prison. I told him we could share the same age and he could pick a birthday. But yeah, you seen that white eye of his? Sometimes I wonder if he's a mutant."

I drummed my fingers on Jandro's ribs. "So how'd he join the club?"

"The Collapse ensured that for us," he laughed dryly. "The prison shut down three years later. It was a federal facility so when the Fed went tits up, so did everything it funded. Retirement accounts and pensions became worthless in a matter of days. Nobody was getting a paycheck anymore, so everyone threw their middle fingers up and went, fuck it! At some point, someone unlocked all the cells. One of my coworkers who had finally snapped started shooting at inmates."

"Oh my God." My hand flew to my mouth. His words were a poignant reminder that the impoverished and disadvantaged suffered most from the Collapse.

"It's okay, though. No one got hurt because someone shot that motherfucker from a hundred yards away with a pistol. I'm talking clear across the building! Guess who that was?"

"You?"

"Nope. Shadow. He took another guard's pistol and honestly saved everyone. Anyway," his hand gesticulated wildly, engrossed in his storytelling, "obviously, he had nowhere to go after that happened. I couldn't just leave him, so I invited him back home with me and," his fist closed and pressed to his lips as he tried to stifle a laugh, "you think he's awkward now? You should have seen him standing in our dumpy-ass apartment living room, Reaper and Noelle staring at him like he's an alien and asking me what the hell this guy was doing here. So that was fun, especially with Noelle, because just being in the same room as a woman freaked him the hell out."

"As opposed to now, where he just looks mildly uncomfortable?"

"Yes, exactly. So it took some work convincing the siblings to bring him into the fold. He was a hell of a shot, but never rode on a motorcycle before. Eventually, I think it was Daren who convinced Reaper having him was a good idea. There were learning curves, but eventually it all worked out. Gunner taught him about different kinds of weapons. He understood Reaper was our leader. He and Noelle just avoided each other."

"And you were his friend," I concluded, pressing a kiss to his chest.

"And his father, mother, life coach, riding instructor, you name it."

"You're amazing for that, you know?" I reached up to wrap an arm around his neck. "He's so lucky to have found you."

Jandro fell silent, one of the rare moments he was speechless. Then his arm curled around me tighter as he dropped a kiss to my head. "Thanks, beautiful. He really is a good friend to have. I wouldn't have done so much for him if he hadn't saved my ass on numerous occasions."

I slid lower into the bed, satisfied with the conclusion of the story. "Well, then I'm grateful for him too. For keeping you around for me."

"Yeah?" His mouth nudged closer to my ear. "Show me how grateful."

"Come here." I pulled him down with me, wriggled my body into position underneath him.

He followed my lead with a salacious grin, nestling between my thighs so I could do just as he asked.

REAPER

"Well, ain't this a peachy fuckin' turn of events."

Bones regarded me with a guilty look from my front stoop. He ran a hand over his shaved head, growing fuzzy from lack of upkeep.

"I wasn't hiding from you, Reaper. I just wanted to lay low for a bit. Until things calmed down, you know?"

"You can make your excuses inside." I turned and left the door open so he could follow.

His feet shuffled nervously over my marble tile floors, trailing after me to my study. Once I passed through the door, Hades looked up at me from his massive dog bed next to the fireplace.

"Have a seat." I waved a hand toward the chair across from my desk as I lowered into my own seat. "Was Heather *laying low* with you?"

"Um, yeah." He rubbed his hands together, leaning forward in the chair. "She'll be coming to talk to you later. She didn't want to, but I convinced her." He swallowed. "She's pretty upset about this whole thing."

"Tell that to someone who cares." I stuck a cigarette in my mouth and fished around for my lighter. "The only reason you're here is to tell me if you knew anything about Python's scheming."

"Absolutely not," he insisted. "He didn't breathe a word of it to me."

"Yeah?" I remarked, not buying it at all. "The three of you looked pretty tight to me."

"Maybe out in the open, among everyone else but," he shifted uncomfortably in his seat, "it wasn't really like that behind closed doors."

I narrowed my eyes. "What do you mean?"

"If I'm being completely honest, Reap," he sighed. "I was kinda their third wheel."

"How so?"

"Like, I've always had a thing for Heather. But she was with you, then Python, so I left it alone. But I got shitfaced one night and she came onto me pretty hard. We had a great time, in my opinion, and she talked up the whole sharing thing like it was so great. I was stoked 'cause it felt like this was finally my chance to be with her, you know? So I rolled with it."

"And?" I pressed.

"And it turned into her pretty much using me for threesomes. Which was fun, don't get me wrong, but I thought I'd have more time with her myself, you know? But she pretty much ignored me except for when she and Python wanted some extra fun in the bedroom. And of course, having two men on her arms at the parties."

"That fuckin' bitch," I groaned, leaning my head back.

It didn't surprise me at all that Heather would use a man so selfishly, but Bones's testimony just made me appreciate having Mari even more. She didn't have to let me know she was going to be with Jandro. It was her right to spend time with whoever she wanted. But she did anyway, because she cared. She wouldn't dream of manipulating a man's feelings to get what she wanted. That was why I shared her, and no other woman I met ever came close.

"So yeah," Bones concluded. "If Python was letting Heather in on it, I wasn't in that club. And if I was," he straightened his spine, "I swear I would've told you, Reaper."

"Would you?" I questioned. "Even if the woman you still clearly have feelings for begged you not to?"

He slapped a hand to his chest, where I knew the grinning, horned Steel Demon skull was embedded into his skin. "I might've been a doormat to her and that was my bad, president. But I live my life every day to do right by you and this club. I was a homeless nobody before you found me and I'll never forget that. The Steel Demons gave me a home and a life. I'm your man, Reaper. Yours, and no one else's."

"So why'd you hide?"

"Because I was afraid Python would throw me under the bus to save himself. I pussed out, but I should have come straight to you, Reaper."

His life is not yours to take.

My head snapped over to Hades, still in his dog bed. Those black eyes, filled with an unfathomable depth, bore straight through me. The voice felt like it echoed all over the room, but Bones made no indication that he heard it. No one but me ever did.

You will not reap. His life is not yours to take.

"Thank you, Bones," I mumbled distractedly, putting my cigarette out. "You can go now."

―――――

I NEARLY WORE a hole in the rug of my study, pacing back and forth as I waited for Heather. In reality, I was waiting for my dog, the god who possessed him, or whatever the fuck he was, to say anything else. But he just looked at me, curled up in his bed. I watched him lick his paws until the silence became too much.

"Why me?"

He paused in his licking, looked at me, but didn't answer.

"Why? *Me?*" I repeated, grinding out each word between my teeth. "I'm some kind of…servant to you. I understand that much. You chose me when you, this dog, whatever, was born. But why?"

I got a head tilt and a lick of his lips.

"Can you even fucking hear me?" I demanded, my frustration rising. "Or is this a one-way line? Just you giving orders and I'm supposed to obey? To what end? Why do you decide who lives and who dies?"

He yawned and lowered his head back down to his paws.

"Just my fuckin' luck." I shook my head in defeat and headed back toward my desk.

I chose you, because you are the perfect instrument.

The voice nearly knocked me off my feet. My skin broke out in a cold sweat as I braced my hands on the desk. The whole room felt like it was tilting, sliding away from me.

You know loss. You know death as intimately as a lover, yet you do not fear it. Reap for me, and I will protect those you hold dear.

"Mariposa…" Her name left my mouth in a ragged, desperate gasp. I was going insane. I had to be. She was the thread tying me to reality.

"Reaper?"

All at once, everything stopped. The heaviness of that voice, the room sliding out from under my feet. Like a snap of someone's godly fingers, everything returned to as it was.

I looked up to see Heather standing in the doorway of my study, her eyes puffy and red. She wrung her hands nervously in front of her.

"Ah, Heather," I cleared my throat, composed myself quickly, and gestured to the chair across from my desk. "About time you finally showed up. Have a seat."

She moved stiffly toward the chair. Her gaze felt heavy on me, but I fiddled with my cigarette case rather than make eye contact with her. Hades lifted his head, ears pricked forward with a low growl already rumbling in his throat. He never was fond of her.

Anything you'd like to say, now would be a swell time, I thought, my eyes locked on the dog. When no words came, I released a deep breath to clear my head. I had to focus on the matter at hand.

"Were you aware of Python's schemings with Razor Wire?"

"Reaper," she sniffed. "Why are you treating me like this?"

"Because you associate with a proven traitor." I wasn't raising my voice. Not yet. But my knuckles were white on the armrests of my chair. What did I ever see in her? Even as just a casual fuck.

"He made a mistake."

"Excuse me?" I couldn't believe what I was hearing. Was this woman really that dense? "Meeting with an enemy club outside the gates in secret, plotting behind my back for weeks, if not months, does not happen by fucking *accident*."

"Reaper, I know you're not heartless," she sniffed, trying to give me that sad doe-eyed look that worked on more desperate men. "You're a good man, even if the way you left me was cruel."

"I didn't leave you. We had nothing to begin with," I corrected her. "And you can stop trying to butter me up til I'm a soggy piece of toast. It ain't gonna work."

"I know, deep down, you don't want to do this to him," she went on like I hadn't said anything. That was another thing I hated. Even when I just tried to have a normal conversation with her, she never fucking listened. "He's one of your men."

"You're wasting your breath, Heather. My dog's morning shit means more to me than him."

"You don't mean that. Reaper, please." She leaned forward. If my desk wasn't between us, I knew she would've tried to reach out and touch me. "Please spare him."

"No. And I think you missed the whole point of you being here." I crossed my arms. "Python's fate is not up for negotiation. What I need to know is if he was operating alone or had allies in his little scheme."

"But he was the only man who would share me!" she whimpered, a large sob wracking her chest. Now that she saw her crocodile tears and doe eyes wouldn't work on me, she had no options left.

"Jesus Christ…" I set my elbow on the desk and rubbed my forehead.

"You've locked up the only man who cares about me, now you're interrogating *me* like I've done something wrong?"

"If you knew about what he was doing, you should have told me," I ground out. "So did you or not?"

She let out a dramatic sigh and carefully dabbed at the corners of her eyes with a tissue. "He bitched about you a lot. We both did, to be honest. He wants to run his own club one day. He'd be good at it, you know?"

"Absolutely none of that fucking matters to me," I said. "Did you know he was conspiring with an enemy to kill me and my men?"

"No," she finally said. "For all his complaining, he left that part out."

"If you're lying, I *will* find out," I warned her. "And I won't be merciful just because you're a woman."

Her life is not yours to take.

I nearly pulled a muscle whipping my head so fast. The voice was unmistakable, but Hades' demeanor hadn't changed. His ears were pulled back in annoyance at the sound of Heather's voice. His lips curled in the start of a growl, but she wasn't a threat, so he didn't react to her presence aggressively.

Do not reap. Her life is not yours to take.

She must have been telling the truth, then. It was the only conclusion I could reach.

Oblivious to my internal freaking out, Heather's lips wobbled as she continued trying to work me over. "Reaper, please let him go. Brand him, keep him imprisoned, do whatever you need to punish him, but he deserves—"

"He deserves what I *say* he deserves." I leaned back in my chair, itching for silence and a cigarette. "You can go now."

"But—"

"You're dismissed," I snarled. "Must I remind you how much I hate repeating myself?"

Heather stood from the chair, defeated. I fished out a cigarette as she made her way to the door, then glowered when she paused in the doorway.

"Is she really so much better than me?" she asked without turning to face me.

Despite myself, I huffed out a harsh laugh as I lit my cigarette, then sucked in the first drag and savored it before I exhaled. Hades said he would protect Mari, so I felt zero guilt at the words that left my mouth.

"In every way imaginable."

FIFTEEN

MARIPOSA

This is a bad idea. You told Jandro you wouldn't get involved.

I ignored the dissenting voice in my head as I marched up to Jandro's house. I promised I wouldn't *push* Shadow, but I had to help in some way. If there were more baby steps between a cordial conversation in my office and this, I would take them. But some progress had to be made and I knew for certain Shadow would not step out of his comfort zone. Not without someone there to guide him.

I've slept with him and I have to talk myself up to having a conversation with him. How backward is that?

My throat closed up with nervousness. I hadn't talked about it again since that night with Reaper, and neither did the guys. No one treated it like an elephant in the room, but I thought about it more than I liked to admit. Shadow was attractive. Sexy even. Maybe not in a conventional way, but surely I couldn't be the only woman who thought that?

I didn't know if I was fixated on helping because of what happened between us, or just that I tried to fix everything in general. Shadow deserved healing more than anyone, not to mention a peaceful night of sleep. I couldn't help being female, but I could only hope that he was getting comfortable with me enough to not hold my gender against me.

I raised my fist and knocked softly at the front door. When no answer came after about thirty seconds, I turned the knob and pushed it open.

No one in Sheol locked their front doors, I noticed early on. It was the ultimate safe neighborhood.

"Hello?" I called, stepping inside cautiously.

Just then I realized Jandro didn't give me much of a house tour last night. We'd been so starry-eyed for each other and he pretty much led me straight into the kitchen.

In the daylight, I noticed all the smaller details and personal touches I missed last time. I didn't realize it last night, but Jandro and Shadow's sides of the house were like a night and day difference.

Jandro's side was brighter, both from the open windows letting light pour in and the metallic bike parts set out on his work table. He kept tools of every sort organized in a case nearby, several five-gallon buckets stacked within each other, and neatly folded rags next to degreasers and other cleaning products.

It was an organized clutter, one that showed care and respect for every piece and component of his work. Jandro was a man who brought work home with him, not out of obligation but because motorcycles were his passion.

Shadow's side on the other hand, was the complete opposite.

Blackout curtains over the windows didn't allow a crack of light to slip through. His area was dark and completely devoid of clutter. Compared to Jandro's side, the lack of any personal touch almost seemed sterile.

Only a desk lamp gave any touch of warmth to the dark living space. The bulb illuminated an open sketchbook on the desk. It must have been the same one he'd been drawing last night. Curiosity got the better of me, and I leaned over to take a look.

The page was open to a highly detailed pencil drawing of some kind of cactus flower. A circle of long, sharp spines grew out from behind the base of the slender, white petals and surrounded the flower like a crown. The actual cactus plant looked to be some kind of vine species, spreading out in long elegant tendrils across the page. I'd never seen anything like it. The squat, round cacti around here didn't even compare.

I skimmed my fingers over the page, convinced the flower would jump to life had it been colored in. Did Shadow really draw this?

Pulling myself away before I started flipping through pages, I headed toward the back of the quiet house. Jandro's chickens pecked at the ground just on the other side of the sliding glass door leading to the backyard. I paused to watch them with a smile, never realizing before what cute and funny birds they were. Movement at the corner of my eye caused me to turn, and I nearly had to pick my jaw up from the floor.

A shirtless Shadow was doing pull-ups on a horizontal bar. His back was to me and unsurprisingly, more scars covered the wide wall of muscle. Overlapping and reaching every corner of his body, whoever gave him those didn't want to leave any piece of skin without the touch of pain.

But his muscles moving underneath the skin were a sight to behold. He pulled himself up and lowered himself down with such control and precision, making it look effortless. It took me a moment to realize he held a large weight between his legs.

I knew he was big, muscular, and a skilled fighter. But it only hit me in that moment how utterly fucking *strong* he was.

Chill out, Mari. Be cool. You and Shadow are friendly now, like two peas in a pod. Okay, bad example. But seriously, be cool!

I pushed the sliding door open just as Shadow released the pull-up bar.

"Hey," I greeted when he glanced over his shoulder.

I'd never seen a man move so fast until just then. He pulled on his shirt in the same time it took for me to blink. In another fraction of a second, he loosened his hair which had been tied back. With his back still turned to me, he seemed to rake his hair forward to cover his face.

"Mariposa!" he barked, panting slightly when he finally whirled around to face me.

"Sorry, I didn't mean to interrupt your workout," I

stammered out, my pulse elevating slightly at how he scowled at me.

But his gaze softened after I spoke. "It's okay. I just wasn't expecting anyone." He looked down and rubbed at the tape wrapped around his hands. "Jandro's not here. He's probably at the shop."

I swallowed. *Be cool.* "I actually stopped by to see you."

"Me?" His dark eye widened, brow lifting. "Why?"

I pulled the orange bottle from my pocket and held it at my side. "If you don't want this, just tell me and I won't bother you with it again."

"What is that?" he growled, eyes on the bottle of pills in my hands.

"They're sleep aids." I rattled the pills inside once. "I uh, heard you the other night, when I was with Jandro—"

"I'm sorry about the noise," he interjected sharply, "but there isn't much I can do about it. It doesn't happen every night and Jandro tells me it never lasts more than fifteen minutes. If you just ignore me, it won't affect you."

An ache gripped my chest and refused to let go. It killed me that he saw his nightmares as nothing more than a nuisance to other people. How long had they been happening for him to accept as completely normal?

"Well, it clearly affects *you*." I held the pills out to him. "And these might help. You'll develop a tolerance over time if you keep taking them, but there are no major side effects." I lowered them to my side again.

"But the choice is completely yours. If you don't want them, just let me know."

His gaze lingered thoughtfully on my hand before flicking back up to my face. "They'll stop the nightmares?"

"Maybe. I'd have to do a full sleep study on you to know more, but that's not my area of expertise. But I have seen cases of people having fewer trauma-related nightmares after taking these."

He took a few cautious steps toward me and I had to steel myself not to step back. Not that I was afraid of him really, just that his presence was so big and overwhelming.

"You said no side effects?" he repeated in a softer voice.

"Nothing major," I said. "Dry mouth is a possibility so make sure you stay hydrated. Heightened blood pressure is another. I can always check that for you if you're concerned. Other than that," I shrugged, "not much."

"And if they don't work?"

"Bring them back to me and we can discuss other options if you'd like. Or not. It's completely up to you, Shadow. I'd," I chewed my lip and swallowed, "I'd rather not see you suffer if it can be prevented."

He gave me a long look that I couldn't read. So many seconds ticked by without him saying a word, I was just about to say my goodbyes when he mumbled, "I'll try them."

I tried not to smile too wide, knowing what a milestone it was for him to trust me with something like this.

"Okay, great. I'll leave these inside and let you finish your workout."

"No! That's okay, I'll uh," he paused, looking off to the side as if trying to remember something. "I'll walk you to the door."

"Oh, sure. Thanks. Here you go, then."

I held the bottle out closer to him, watching the large man step closer toward me until he was within reach. When he took it from me, I noticed he took care not to touch my hand.

I turned to go back inside, his presence behind me like a solid wall against my back despite him keeping a respectful distance away. As we walked through the house, I had a small urge to stop suddenly, just to feel him a bit closer. Jandro once described him as feral, and it sure seemed that way. The tortured, haunted beast named Shadow was still skittish, but slowly trusting me more.

I had to remember not to push for too much too fast, or else risk sending him straight back into his shell. Stopping suddenly to force touch between us was definitely too far. That or he'd see it coming and dodge me with his assassin reflexes.

He gave me an inch, probably more than he'd allowed any woman into his life. And still I couldn't resist asking for a centimeter more.

"Did you draw that?" I asked, turning my head to nod at the sketchbook as we passed by his desk. "It's beautiful."

He leaned over and slammed the book shut with so

much force, the desk and lamp shook under the weight of his hand.

"No," he growled. "It's nothing."

And like that, I learned one more centimeter was also too far.

SIXTEEN

MARIPOSA

The bloodlust hung thick and cloying in the air, just like the sweat and motor oil permeating my senses. It turned my stomach. I'd been dreading this night since the first time I saw it.

Fight Night. Where friends and family settled their disputes with their fists. Just like last time, a crowd gathered in the cul-de-sac in front of Reaper's house. Two guys rode around in figure eight patterns, revving their engines loudly while everyone else drank, smoked and talked excitedly. Men began peeling off their cuts and then their T-shirts. They took off their silver rings, necklaces, and leather bracelets. Because fists were the only weapons allowed.

I leaned against a retaining wall off to the side of the action, a small first aid kit next to me. There was no sign of Heather, the skanky woman who slept with Reaper before me, and who turned out to be sleeping with Python, our prisoner. She challenged me last month and beat my face pretty badly, but it turned out to be for nothing. Reaper didn't want her back. He cleaned the blood off of my face and kissed me for the first time that night.

Now, I was happy to stand aside and clean up anyone else who would need it. Being the club medic gave me immunity to the violence that was about to break out in this otherwise caring community.

From my outside view, I spotted all the usual suspects. Like last time, Shadow was nowhere to be seen. I wondered if he ever attended the fights or just preferred not dealing with the crowd. I couldn't see him picking a fight with someone over some petty argument, nor could I imagine anyone having the balls to challenge him.

Jandro's cut and shirt remained on as he talked to people, indicating he wasn't planning on fighting anyone tonight. Whether or not someone else challenged him was another matter. I sucked my bottom lip between my teeth, thighs rubbing together as I remembered his sexy beefcake body sprawled out on the sheets.

In another small group of people, Reaper and Gunner had their heads bent low toward each other. Gunner was saying something into Reaper's ear, who nodded as he listened. Both of them were dressed too, but my relief was short-lived as Reaper slid off his cut, handed it to someone, and peeled off his shirt.

He was glorious to look at, as always. The contrast of his body to Jandro's couldn't be stronger, and yet they were both utterly sexy. But my pulse shot up, knowing what the removal of his shirt meant. I rose from the curb and cut through the crowd straight to him. Gunner pulled away from his ear and slid his tall, lean body away through the throng of people. At that moment though, his ignoring me was the last thing I cared about.

"There she is." Reaper grinned wickedly as I approached him. He took hold of my upper arm the moment I was in reach and pulled me into him. He dropped a crushing kiss to my mouth before I could speak, sending my head spinning.

"You'll have to tell me all about the fun you had," he growled against my mouth. "I want you home with me tonight." He stroked a knuckle against my cheekbone, green eyes alight with love for a moment instead of bloodlust. "I missed you."

"I missed you too. Of course I'll be with you tonight," I said in the rushed breath that filled my lungs. "Who are you fighting?"

"Don't worry, sugar." He cupped my chin and kissed me again. "I just have something to settle. He won't land a scratch on me."

"I'm more worried about what you'll do to *him*."

His laugh was throaty, dangerous, sexy, and accompanied by a gratuitous grab of my ass. "I'll just pop him a few times to teach him a lesson. Get my blood pumping for what I'm gonna do to you later."

My thighs clenched at his words, my core already hollowing from the inside out. Even after a passionate, sensual night with Jandro, I craved the rough touch of my president. And still, I wanted many, many more nights of talking, laughing, and lovemaking with the VP. The feelings didn't necessarily conflict with each other, I just wanted it all. Maybe I was finally getting the hang of this two-men thing.

With a final bruising kiss, and double-handed squeezes and slaps of my ass, Reaper slid past me into the open circle the crowd created. Engines lowered to a dull roar and people's conversations faded away until the crickets were the loudest noise. All eyes were on the shirtless Steel Demons president.

"My challenge is for Larkan," Reaper announced, turning around slowly until his eyes fell upon the blue-eyed newest prospect, who had his arm around Noelle.

Shit. Jandro was right.

Larkan said nothing and didn't look especially surprised as he slid off his patchless cut, but Noelle was wide-eyed and pale as a sheet. I watched her throat work as she swallowed her nerves, offering Larkan a tight, but encouraging smile as she took his cut and shirt. In a bold move, Larkan murmured something and kissed her before walking out to meet Reaper.

"On what grounds do you challenge me?" He pitched his voice so everyone could hear, lifting his chin bravely at Reaper.

"On the grounds that you have the fucking balls to put your mouth on my sister without my approval. The club is grateful for your information regarding General Tash, but this is a separate matter. As the president of this club and head of my family, your behavior with my sister is out of line."

"I disagree." Larkan's tone was remarkably calm and even. "I haven't done anything to disrespect you or Noelle. We are two consenting adults with a strong connection. I haven't forced or coerced her into anything. You care deeply about her wellbeing, which I admire. But I do too, president. You're challenging me out of overprotectiveness, and the need to control everything around you."

Reaper's fists clenched at his sides as he and Larkan walked a slow circle around each other like two predatory animals. I met Noelle's eyes across the crowd, but couldn't place what she was feeling or thinking. She knew better than me that there was no stopping this. Gunner's men would stop the fight before it got too bloody, but who knew what kind of damage would be done before then?

Noelle's hand moved at her side and my heart swelled when I saw that she was petting Hades. He probably knew she needed more comfort than me in that moment. The memory of my dream flashed briefly through my mind before I shoved it away. Maybe I'd tell Reaper about it tonight, but I had to focus. A bad injury could happen quickly, and I needed to be ready.

Like a flipped switch, Reaper suddenly relaxed. He smiled at Larkan, then swept his arms out to the sides with his hands open.

"Let's settle this, boy."

And then he moved like lightning.

I had never seen Reaper fight before. Even though it was happening right in front of me, I barely saw anything. I blinked and Larkan's head snapped to the side, spitting out blood. He recovered quickly, moving in to land a punch on Reaper, who dodged with fluid agility. It almost looked inhumanly fast.

Every one of Larkan's attempts did absolutely nothing, cutting through air. Reaper dodged and weaved while staying close enough to land strikes of his own. Larkan's ribs and stomach were bright red, mottled bruising already forming on his skin.

"You're good with bikes and a bow, man, but you can't hit for shit," Reaper taunted him.

Jesus, Reap. Just end it already, I pleaded silently.

I weaved through the crowd back to my first aid kit, unable to watch anymore. Just as I opened the case, a cheer went up with Reaper's name being chanted.

"Yay," I grumbled, pulling on my gloves and breaking two cold packs. Larkan didn't lose a lot of blood from what I saw, but the bruising would be intense and sore for a few weeks.

Someone had already thrown Larkan's arm around their shoulder and dragged him toward me, Noelle right on their heels.

"Sit him down. Noelle, support his head," I snapped in my bossiest nurse voice.

"Aye-aye, *Mariposita*," Jandro winked at me before removing Larkan's arm from around his shoulders.

Noelle sat next to me on the retaining wall, then Jandro gently lowered Larkan to sit on the ground against her legs. She cradled his head in her lap as she smoothed his hair out of his face.

"Make sure he stays conscious," I told her, handing her a cold pack. "Press this against any swelling you see."

"Reaper's gonna want you on his arm," Jandro said, his tone almost a warning. "Since he won the fight."

"Well, he's gonna have to wait." I wet a clean gauze pad with rubbing alcohol. "The only reason I'm here is to help those who need it."

I began wiping at the cut on Larkan's cheek. He hissed at the sting and tried to squirm away, but Noelle held him still.

"Shh, it's just Mari, baby. She's helping." Her red hair fell over both of their faces for a moment as she bent to kiss his forehead. "You fucking fool. I told you not to show up."

"He would've known," Larkan groaned. "And then he'd be able to call me a coward."

"Are you staying with Reaper tonight?" Jandro asked me.

"I guess. I told him I would." I didn't bother to hide the annoyance in my tone. He was pulling my focus away from my job. As I dabbed healing ointment onto a cut made by the first man I was sleeping with, while the second hovered over me for attention, I wasn't too thrilled with either of them in that moment.

"Don't be mad at Reaper for this," Jandro went on. "It's an expectation of him to smack around the new guy. The fact that he's with Noelle just makes it a more convenient reason."

"Okay, not really interested in club politics right now. I need to check his ribs."

Jandro finally seemed to get the hint, but he leaned in and snuck a kiss on my neck before walking away. I sighed the moment his presence left, feeling regret over lashing out at him.

"Fucking men, right?" Noelle grumbled. She held

the cold pack tenderly to Larkan's jaw, all the while stroking his hair with the other hand.

I bit back a smile as I knelt next to her man. She could grumble all she liked. It was plain as day how much she cared about him.

"Can you take a deep breath for me, Lark?" I asked. He followed my instructions as I felt along both sides. "Nothing's broken," I reported. "You're going to be sore as hell for a couple of weeks, so just take it easy. Any pain reliever will do."

"Think I can manage that." He gazed straight up at Noelle like she was the only person that existed. "I got my pain relief right here."

"Oh my God, stop. He obviously didn't hit you hard enough to quit with the cheesy lines," Noelle laughed as she leaned over him again.

I gathered up my stuff to give them privacy just as the crowd's volume went up again. Another fight was about to start.

"Can you see who it is?" Noelle craned her neck.

"No, don't really care."

The sound of glass crashing made us both jump and silenced the spectators.

"Big G! Get your ass out here and fight me!" The words slurred and carried a dark animosity I'd never heard before.

"Oh God..."

The crowd thinned just enough for me to see Gunner, swaying drunkenly in the middle of the circle as he searched for his opponent.

SEVENTEEN

MARIPOSA

"That man is toasted." Noelle astutely noticed.

I looked at her. "They can't let him fight that drunk, can they? He can barely stand up!"

She shrugged and met my gaze with a sad shake of her head. "Nothing in the rules says you can't fight when shitfaced."

"He's gonna bleed all over the street with one hit."

"Then it's a good thing you're here." She gave me a playful nudge with her foot. "You're sweet on him too, aren't you? Why do you look so mortified about tending to him?"

I didn't want to get into the fact that he'd been ignoring me for days, nor did I want to admit how much his silent treatment hurt me. And why the hell did he get so drunk? His crystal blue eyes looked out over everyone, glazed and unfocused. They paused on me for several long seconds. Only a commotion from another part of the crowd pulled his attention away. Big G had emerged.

The size difference between them was staggering. Big G was, well, *big*. His cut and shirt came away to reveal a broad barrel chest and belly that started to hang over his pants. The guy clearly liked to eat and drink, but he was broad and looked strong. What made things worse for Gunner was that he also looked stone-cold sober.

Tall and lean, with long arms and slender muscles, Gunner would have owned this fight if he could keep control of his body. But he swayed unsteadily like a tree branch, while Big G was as solid as a rock. He would have to get lucky to land anything, while all his opponent had to do was flatten him.

"Jesus, Gunner. What are you doing?" I whispered.

"On what grounds do you challenge me, captain?" Big G asked with a casual cross of his tree trunk arms. He thought he had this in the bag. I prayed he stayed cocky like that and that it would cost him.

"On the grounds of you being a punk-ass bitch." Laughter and applause rose up from the crowd, but Gunner's face showed how seriously he took this. "You tried to pin me as a traitor to this club. But you can't even stay loyal to your own fucking wife."

A low murmur of, "Ohhhh" rose up from the crowd, making Gunner wheel around unsteadily to address them.

"Fuck all of you!" he yelled. "Most of you can't stay loyal to your women either! You pass them around and it's fucking shameful!"

Oh no... My heart dropped like a stone into my stomach. Jandro and Reaper exchanged wary glances but said nothing. *Please stop this fight*, I pleaded, but knew they wouldn't.

A cold, wet nose nudging my hand brought my attention down. Hades whined and licked my palm, deciding I was the one who needed comfort now. Stroking his ears and head with a shaky smile, I looked back up at the fight circle.

Big G didn't deny any of Gunner's claims. His smug, arm-crossed posture remained the same as he watched the captain of the guard sway on his feet. Finally, he held his hands out, beckoning Gunner toward him.

"Let's go then, captain." He sounded like he was mocking Gunner and I hated him for it.

Gunner brought his fists up in a defensive position, widening his feet. Despite his drunken unsteadiness, he was still light and agile, bouncing on the balls of his feet like a boxer moving in toward his opponent. A part of me hoped he was just faking being drunk to bring Big G's guard down, though that didn't seem likely. He wouldn't resort to being dirty and deceptive like that.

Big G held his fists up near his face, eyes locked on Gunner moving in. The crowd went completely silent, only the fighters' breathing and Gunner's shoes made any noise. They seemed to circle and watch each other for a full minute before the first strike landed.

Gunner aimed low, sinking a rapid pummeling of fists into Big G's gut. But the big guy barely moved. Because Gunner was so tall, hitting that low put his face in dangerously close proximity to Big G's fists, who took full advantage of his position.

I saw it in slow motion—large, hairy knuckles

crashing against an angelic face. It only took one hit for Gunner's head to snap to the side, his hair flying out from the momentum before the rest of his body spun to follow his head.

"Ohhhh!" the crowd shouted like a single organism when Gunner fell to the ground.

My eyes went to Jandro and Reaper again, pleading for them to stop this now, but they remained motionless. Neither of them cheered with the crowd. They just watched, tight-lipped.

Gunner climbed shakily to his feet. Blood coated one side of his face, dripping down his neck and torso in long, dark lines. His abs flexed with effort as he drew in ragged breaths. I couldn't believe I found anything sexy about him bloodied, hurt, and intoxicated, but a small, primal part of me did.

Big G at least had the decency to wait until he stood up before coming at him again. He wasn't fast, but unfortunately slow was still faster than Gunner. His meaty fist swung into Gunner's gut so hard, it almost lifted him off his feet. I covered my mouth to hold back my scream as the beautiful, bloodied man doubled over with a breathless groan of pain, then received another blow to the face that sent a spray of blood through the air like a morbid fountain. He went down again, and this time I knew he wouldn't stand up.

"Enough!"

At least twenty pairs of eyes were now on me. I didn't realize I yelled or jumped to my feet, but instinct took over as I ran to the center of the circle. Big G stood over his crumpled form like he might kick him, so I made sure to cover his body with mine.

"Gunner? Gunner, can you hear me?"

"Mawwh…"

"Don't talk, I'm just making sure you're awake. I'm going to turn you over now. Can you hold your head up for me?"

"I dun…"

Two more figures stepped up and loomed over us as I pulled Gunner up to a sitting position. Blood was everywhere, dripping from his mouth and at least one cut on his cheekbone that I could see. One eye was already swelling shut. He turned his head and spit out another full mouthful of blood.

"You shouldn't have interfered, sugar. We would've called it," Reaper's voice said from somewhere above me.

"You might have been too late," I snapped back. "He wasn't getting up. Big G could've killed him with one kick to the head."

Jandro handed me a towel. "Why the fuck is he bleeding so much?"

"Because he's drunk, you idiot," I growled, using the towel to wipe at Gunner's chest. "Alcohol makes your blood thinner."

"All right, I didn't know that." I didn't miss the hurt in his voice, but couldn't be bothered to tend to his feelings now. Gunner needed a lot more than a first aid kit.

"Help me get him up," I instructed my two men who just continued to stand there. "I need to take him to my office."

They each kneeled and grabbed one of Gunner's arms to throw over their shoulders. "Don't let his head fall back," I instructed when they lifted him up and started walking. "I don't want him to choke on blood. He might've bitten his tongue."

I jogged ahead to get the room ready while the guys dragged Gunner between them. By the time all three of their big, sweaty bodies filled up my tiny office, I had propped up the exam table so Gunner wouldn't have to recline, set out my suture kit, clean towels, and antibacterial ointment, and just ripped open a fresh box of gloves.

"Put him there." I nodded at the exam table while scrubbing my hands vigorously with hot water and soap. "Thanks. I'll grab you two later to take him home."

Again, Reaper and Jandro hesitated, making the already-tiny space even more crowded.

"The fights are done for tonight," Reaper informed me. "No one else has anything they need to settle."

"Good. It'll be an early night for me then." I snapped on my gloves and wet one of the towels with warm water. They still hovered as I proceeded to wipe the blood from Gunner's chest and stomach.

"I'll see you at home then?" Reaper asked.

"Yeah, I might just go straight to bed though." I spared him a glance as I began to dab the towel carefully around Gunner's neck and jaw. "I'm feeling a little crowded."

"All right." He sounded defeated, exhausted, rather than angry, as he turned toward the door. "Tomorrow is Python's judgement day."

I paused, then set the bloodied towel in the sink. "Okay. I just need some peace and quiet after I'm done tonight."

He nodded before leaving the room, Jandro following on his heels. I turned back to Gunner with a sigh. Reaper was trying to say he needed me before a difficult day tomorrow, but I could only be stretched so thin. Gunner needed me more, and even still, I couldn't keep giving everything to these men and have nothing left for myself. I needed one quiet night to recharge, and hopefully he understood that.

"Mareh…" Gunner sat up painstakingly, turning to me. "Need to shpit…"

"Here, love. You can spit in this." I handed him a paper cup, my pulse skyrocketing at the pet name that slipped out. "Try not to talk. Since your blood is thin right now, it'll take longer to clot. Just relax for me."

He leaned back, silent except for the wheezing breaths he took. Every so often he spat a small amount of blood into the cup.

"Do you want some water?" Hell, *I* needed some. Cleaning the excess blood off his long, taut body stretched out in front of me had me hot and flustered. That was wrong of me and not fair to him. I never got turned on with a patient before. It wasn't professional.

I turned to the sink without waiting for an answer and poured two fresh cups. The water wouldn't get very cold, but it would have to do. When I turned back to him, he seemed more lucid than I'd seen him all that evening.

"Cheers," he joked, tapping his water cup against mine before drinking deeply.

I chose to soothe my own parched throat rather than chastise him for talking again.

"Why did you drink so much before fighting?" I ran my fingertips lightly over the bruise forming on his stomach, trying with all my might not to be indulgent with my touch. This was about his well-being, nothing else.

"I messed up, baby girl." His slurred speech was now due to the swelling in his mouth rather than his drunkenness. "Fuck, I *am* messed up."

"What makes you say that?" I moved my hands up to his face, dabbing around the cut on his cheekbone with an alcohol-soaked gauze pad. It would need a few stitches but not many. "I need to sew you up a little. This might hurt."

He appeared unfazed as I got my needle and thread ready. "I've always been able to get what I want. Whether for me or other people. I had money growing up, but I wasn't spoiled. I was a crafty little shit, so I was always able to get stuff one way or another."

"And why does that make you messed up?" I carefully pulled the thread through his skin, mindful to keep the needle away from his eye.

"Because for the first time in my life, I want something I can't have."

I closed the cut with only three small stitches. The silence felt heavy around us. I didn't know how to respond. What were the odds of us thinking of the same thing? Of this weird tension between us? The potential future he *thought* we couldn't have?

When I went to put antibacterial ointment on his cheek wound, he grabbed my hand and held it. Gunner stared at me with his one beautiful, not-swollen eye in a way that was both intimate and uncomfortable.

"Are you happy, baby girl?" he asked in a soft voice, barely above a whisper.

"I don't like seeing you hurt." I pulled my hand out of his, continuing with my task of putting the ointment on his cheek. "I'm not terribly happy about a brotherhood that comes close to killing each other once a month."

"You know what I mean," he chastised gently. "Are you happy with *them?*"

The silence after his question pressed in on us like an invisible, oppressive force. I didn't know what kind of answer he was looking for, but I had a feeling he only wanted to confirm what he already believed. He wouldn't listen to any other answer.

"Is my answer going to change anything?" I shot back. "Are you going to keep ignoring me if I tell you yes? Or will you try to swoop in and rescue me if you hear what you want to hear?"

He blew out a long breath, turning his face away from me. "So you really like having your variety, huh?"

"So what if I do?" I challenged. "You don't want to be my friend if that's the case? Am I too slutty now for you to hang out with?"

"Don't," he snarled, looking back at me with now a narrowed eye. "I didn't say any of that. Of course I like you, I just…don't like the situation. It feels like they're using you."

"That's not what it is. They care about me, Gunner," I said. "And I care about them. It's confusing and weird, but I'm figuring it out because both of them are worth it to me."

"What about *your* worth? I don't mean it like that." He raised a road rash covered hand in a defensive posture in response to my glare. "I'm just saying you could be one man's whole world, and you deserve that. Instead, you're taking on two men part-time. Don't you want someone who wants all of you?"

"What are we really talking about here?" I snapped off my gloves and crossed my arms. "Why does any of this even matter to you? I'm still the same person, no matter who, or how many guys I'm fucking. But *you've* changed, Gunner. Ever since you came back from Colorado, you haven't treated me the same. Why? Tell me, because," I drew in a shaky breath, "it fucking hurts."

His gaze dropped, looking defeatedly at his blood-stained hands in his lap. "Because I can't just be friends with you, baby girl. But I'll never share you, either. All I can do is distance myself and hope what I'm feeling goes away. I'm sorry."

I nodded like I understood, but that was far from the truth. I knew the meanings of the words he said, but I couldn't understand *why*. Ironic, considering that just days ago, I felt utterly clueless about being with two men.

And it wasn't like Jandro and Reaper weren't enough for me. They just weren't Gunner—the sweet, beautiful man who just dashed my hopes of anything between us, even a friendship.

"Can you get yourself home?" I asked as flatly as I could muster.

"Yeah—"

The word was barely out of his mouth before I turned and left the office.

EIGHTEEN

MARIPOSA

The smell of coffee nearly dragged me downstairs before I became fully conscious. I pulled on a robe haphazardly, just noticing as I went out the door that I woke up in an empty bed. Reaper's clove cigarette smoke reached my nostrils as I descended the stairs, mixing with the coffee aroma in an oddly pleasant way.

That smell was of him, I realized. The Steel Demons president, sitting at his massive kitchen table with his back turned to me. Steam and smoke circled around his head like an aura. My hands reached his shoulders and I bent to place a kiss on his cheek.

"Thanks for making coffee." He didn't respond right away, but those green eyes watched my every move as I poured myself a cup from the French press and took a seat next to him. "And for giving me space last night," I added.

His chin lowered in the slightest hint of a nod. "Are you upset about what I did to Larkan?"

I sighed and took a sip of my coffee while thinking of the right words to convey my thoughts. "I don't like it, but I can understand why you did it. You're protective of Noelle and want her man to show you respect. I was more frustrated at you and Jandro vying for my attention while I was with patients. When I'm working, I need to focus on those whose lives are in my hands. I can't be your arm candy and do my job at the same time."

"Hmm." A smirk pulled at his lips, eyes shining through the smoke as he dragged on the cigarette.

"What?"

"Nothing, sugar. I just love that you're so straight with me." He reached over to place a hand on my knee, making sure to touch my bare skin under my robe. "And that you care about what you do so much."

I covered the back of his hand with my palm, sliding my fingers through his. "We're lucky last night's injuries weren't any worse. But it could become a life or death situation in a matter of seconds. I need you to understand that."

"I get it, babe. I do. Thank you for telling me."

A smile tugged at my own lips that not even my coffee cup could hide. "I think we're getting better at avoiding this fighting thing."

He ashed his cigarette butt in his tray with a throaty laugh. "Can't say I wasn't tempted to go there." His eyebrow popped up at me. "I hate being ignored, and we have such good sex after we fight."

"I'm sure you can find a way to provoke me when the mood strikes you."

"Maybe." He leaned toward me, his hand creeping up my thigh. "Being a happy fucking bastard has its perks too, though."

"Yeah?" I molded my hand to the side of his neck, angling my head for the kiss. "You're happy with me?"

"As a fucking clam." His mouth met mine with equal roughness and sweetness, teeth dragging across my lips with his signature bite. Tasting him was such a treat after not kissing him for over a full day. It was over too soon. He pulled away with a sigh. "I'll be a lot fucking happier in general once this execution is over with."

I moved our clasped hands to his lap in a small gesture of support. "Can you make it happen quickly?"

He shook his head regretfully. "No, it needs to be just the opposite. I have to drag it out, make it a public spectacle. I need to use him as an example so that no one betrays the Steel Demons again."

Reaper's shoulders hunched forward as if carrying out this man's sentence was a true, physical burden on him. My hands circled his thick, corded forearm, drawing myself closer to place my chin on his shoulder.

How quickly times changed. Over a month ago, I wrote him off as a heartless murderer when I saw him slit a man's throat right in front of me. Now the lines etched in his face and the faraway look in his eye told me clearly—he did not take killing lightly.

Back then I also would have done anything to save a person's life, no matter who that person was or what their crimes were. But now, my sympathy laid with the man who held the reaper's scythe. If allowed to live, people who endangered others and abused the trust of their community would continue to do so. By taking Python's life, Reaper secured a safer future for his men who had been loyal, their wives, and their children.

And for us.

"Sugar," Reaper nudged his forehead against mine, "would you believe me if I told you I *knew* I was doing the right thing? Not because I *feel* it is, but something bigger than me has told me their lives had to end? And it had to be by my hand?"

"Bigger than you?" I repeated. "You mean like someone above you is giving orders on who to kill?"

"Kind of." His eyes shifted to where Hades snoozed on the floor by his feet. "Not another person, though. Something…bigger than humanity."

"Like what, some kind of spirit? A god?"

He huffed out a sigh, rubbing his eyes. "It sounds fucking nuts, I know. But I swear to you, every life I've ever taken has been for a good reason. Tom and Liza abused that girl you worked with. Razorwire attacked us. People have tried to kill me first, or hurt my sister. The only one that makes no sense to me is—"

"Daren," I finished for him, cupping his stubbled cheek. "You didn't kill your brother, my love."

"I let him die. That's close enough."

"There was nothing you could do." I stroked my thumb across his face. "Human life is fragile. Weapons and wars aren't what kill us most often, it's those tiny, single-celled organisms designed to destroy us from inside."

Reaper turned his head toward my hand to kiss my palm. "Do you believe me, though?"

"That something bigger is at play, instructing you on which lives to take?" I lifted one shoulder. "If I've learned one thing from being around you and this guy," I nudged Hades with my foot, "it's that anything is possible."

NINETEEN

REAPER

I left him at the kitchen table, the man Mari had been kissing, holding, reassuring. Only she could see that side of me—still wrought with guilt over my brother's death. Still coming to terms with being…*something*'s instrument of death. I wasn't sure if I could call it a god or something else. Noelle seemed convinced that was the case, if her supposed dreams from Daren had any merit.

But I left it all behind, downing the rest of my coffee and rising from the table as Death personified. A man awaited my justice and that was the last he would know of me—the instrument that took his life and sent his soul to whatever bleak underworld awaited him.

Hades woke instantly, his four paws tapping over the marble floor and then the sidewalk outside as if he'd been waiting for me to carry out this task.

Mari walked next to me on my other side. She didn't reach for my hand as she usually did. Perhaps she sensed the change within me.

We didn't have to go far. A platform made out of

repurposed wooden pallets had been set up in the court outside my house. Python hadn't arrived yet, but a crowd of onlookers had already gathered. I made attendance for this execution mandatory. Every man, woman and child living in Sheol needed to witness the consequences of a betrayal.

Tessa sat on a retaining wall just off of my lawn with Noelle next to her. They each held the hand of Tess's rambunctious boys that wanted to run around and play. Tess talked nervously to Noelle, her free hand rubbing nonstop over her belly. She'd be ready to pop soon, a new life to replace the one I was about to take.

On the other side of the platform, Heather was already crying and wailing dramatically, sometimes into Bones's shoulder, other times to no one in particular. He rubbed her back, but otherwise looked like he had no desire to be there. Jandro and Gunner had been breathing down my neck about what we should do with them, and I honestly wasn't sure. My explicit instructions were to not take their lives, so I ruled out their guilt based on that alone. But I couldn't exactly tell anyone that.

After surveying my citizens coming out to bear witness, my gaze landed on Mari at my side. "Are you going to sit with Tessa?" I asked her.

"I will. But I'll stay with you until you need to go up there." She glanced up at me. "I should tell you something."

"Might have to wait, sugar." Down the street, Dallas and Big G escorted Python toward us, each of them holding one of his arms. "We're about to get this show on the road."

"It's about Python."

"What about him?"

"The last two times I checked his vitals, he tried to convince me to escape with him."

"Really." I couldn't bring myself to be surprised. That slimy bastard.

"The last time, he grabbed my shoulders. Dallas got him off me and never took his eyes off of him after that."

"Good to know." I watched Dallas and Big G tie the traitor to the sawed-off telephone pole erected in the middle of the platform. "You can sit with Tessa now, Mari."

She went without a word, leaving only me and Hades together. What she just told me ensured that this execution would drag on even longer than I originally thought. But she gave me a gift.

She took away the burden of my guilt.

When my men secured him and stepped off the platform, everyone went silent as Hades and I approached. Python stared at me as I took slow, measured steps toward him. His skin was slick with sweat. He strained against his bonds with heavy, ragged breaths, but he looked too stricken with fear to struggle for his life. Maybe touching my woman and trying to rope her into his scheming was his last resort. Too bad it would only prolong his suffering.

I turned to face everyone who gathered, Hades mirroring my movement.

"The Steel Demons do not take prisoners," I began. "This man has already received more kindness than he deserves by being kept alive this long."

"Reaper…" Python choked weakly from behind me.

I didn't spare him a glance. By trying to beg now, he was only digging himself further into a hole of pain with no relief.

"This man was a brother of ours," I continued, ignoring him. "Sworn to uphold the SDMC laws and to follow my leadership without question. Instead, he took it upon himself to conspire with an enemy who tried to have us killed."

I paced across the platform, making sure to meet everyone's eyes as I spoke. This speech was for every individual person, even Jandro, Shadow, and Gunner, who stood solemnly at attention with their arms crossed. Because everyone watching me, I trusted. And I would not make the mistake of trusting the wrong person again.

"Lying to me will not be tolerated." I made sure to carry my voice to ensure it reached everyone. "Conspiring against the club will not be tolerated. Putting your hands on *my* woman," I turned to face the prisoner, his face white, "will absolutely not be tolerated."

My hand lifted to my belt, where I grabbed the small pocketknife and switched it open.

"Reaper, please! I didn't touch her like that! I didn't mean, oh no—"

I ignored him as I grabbed the front of his shirt and sliced up the middle with my knife. With a clean rip, his shirt hung open in the front. Each side flapped in the breeze until I pulled them back, tucking each side behind his shoulders so everyone could see him bare-chested. And most importantly, the grinning horned skull of the Steel Demons emblem tattooed across his torso.

Like me, he went big on the ink. The tips of the horns touched his collarbones while the base of them met the skull at his sternum. The full design ended just past his ribs at the top of his stomach.

"Shadow?" I called out.

The large, silent man was at the edge of the platform in an instant, holding up a blow torch to me. I accepted it, switched it on, and meandered back to a horrified Python as I adjusted the flame.

"Only a sworn, loyal patched-in member can wear the Steel Demon," I announced. Then to Python, "You are defacing that symbol by wearing it on your skin."

"Reaper, please..." he whimpered.

"Other clubs have a history of giving a choice to their former members of how the emblem will be removed." I held my knife's blade up to the flame until it glowed. "And I was prepared to give you that choice as a final act of kindness. That is until," I lowered the blow torch, examining my freshly heated knife in the air, "I found out you tried to lull Mariposa into your cowardly fucking escape plan."

He continued to whimper and plead with meaningless cries. A dark spot spread rapidly on the front of his jeans as the smell of urine assaulted me.

"Your choice has been taken from you, Python." I ignored his accident as I moved closer to him, standing to the side so everyone could see. "And no matter how much you beg, you'll never escape the the blade of the reaper."

I held the red-hot blade within an inch of inked skin as he continued to whimper and cry. He could feel the heat from it, but I didn't touch him. I just let it hover over him while he braced himself, waiting for the burn. But I wasn't about to give him anything he wanted.

I flipped my grip on the handle, pointing the blade away from me while I pulled out another knife. A dull, jagged-edged thing that I chose just for this occasion. I sank it into the right horn of the tattoo before he could see me coming, but he felt every jagged rip of flesh from my steel.

His scream pierced my ears but I worked diligently. The knife didn't go deep but I had to use sawing motions to cut through him. A bloodbath covered both of us in seconds. I heard some people shriek and cry, then my men yelling at them to watch. No one was permitted to look away.

I took my sweet, painstaking time to cut a diagonal line across Python's torso, dying half of the tattoo a dark red. Pocketing my jagged knife, I switched to the heated blade and dug the tip into the opposite tattooed horn. Yeah, he forgot about that little guy. I could see it through his pain-stricken face as I began a second diagonal line in the opposite direction.

I got halfway through cutting my X on his body when Python passed out. Shadow tossed me the smelling salts and we were back in business within a minute.

Python woke up so hard, the back of his head bounced off the pole he was tied to.

"I'm sorry. Am I boring you?" I twirled the knife handle through my fingers. "I was just getting started."

"I'm sorry…I'm sorry…I won't…again…"

"Should've said that sooner." I picked up where I left off, continuing my diagonal line to create a huge, morbid X through his tattoo. "Not that it would've done you any good. The timing just would have been better."

My X was finished. But I still wasn't done.

As I picked up the blow torch and began re-heating the blade, my eyes lifted across the crowd. Expressions were grim. Some people looked green and covered their mouths. Good. They wouldn't forget this. When I looked for Mari's gaze, her eyes met mine with steadfast determination. She was the calm in this storm that raged just under the surface.

The urge was strong to make this execution quick, like she asked. I didn't enjoy humiliating a man, cutting into him like an animal for dinner. Every instinct in me wanted to pull my knife across Python's throat, or sink it into his chest to end his misery. But I had a responsibility in this execution, and that was to ensure no one fucked with the Steel Demons again.

I never said the words, but Mari and I both knew—I didn't know if I had the strength to do this, to make someone's death a horror show in order to send a message. Looking at her reminded me that I could. She stood strong and tall like a president's old lady should. And I, as her man and the club's president, had to hold up my end of the deal and do what I signed up for.

So I set down the blow torch and spun around with my freshly-heated blade. I pressed the flat of it against the word STEEL inked onto Python's stomach. His screams made my ears ring and burning flesh filled my nostrils. I pulled the blade away, leaving a grotesque red burn with no readable tattoo left. I flipped the blade and pressed it to his skin again, this time to the word DEMONS.

He passed out again, and we woke him up again. I made sure not a single readable letter was still on his body before tossing the burned blade away and retrieving my jagged one.

"I made a promise in church, Python," I said as I undid the top button of his pants and yanked his zipper down. "You were there. Do you remember what that was?"

He let out a pained, wheezing breath. I wasn't sure if he could hear me anymore and didn't entirely care. I just wanted him conscious. I wanted to own every bit of his pain.

As I cut away his soiled underwear and had him naked from the waist down, it seemed to jog his memory.

"No, no, no, no…"

"Unlike you, Python," I tapped my knife against his hip. "When I make promises, I keep them. It doesn't matter how small, I won't ever go back on my word to this club I would die to protect." My blade dragged inward toward the base of his dick. "What promise did I make?"

"My…balls…your dog…"

"Good enough. Hades?" I whistled over my shoulder and my furry beast's ears perked up as he trotted forward. Turning back to Python, I cupped his sack and tugged, stretching out the thin skin attaching his balls to his body.

"I hope you enjoy this and take a long, good look at me." I brought the edge of the blade right to the taut skin above my hand. "I'm the last person that'll ever touch you here." Then I drew the knife in one swift motion.

A river of blood followed and I tossed Python's family jewels over my shoulder. Hades jumped in the air to catch them like he was catching a frisbee.

The ringing in my ears hit a new pitch, and it wasn't because of Python screaming. Something, either externally or in my own head, was blocking out all sounds for the voice. *His* voice.

Even as Hades gobbled down on his meal, those dark eyes held me and gave me the command.

His life is yours to take. Reap him now.

"Gunner!" I yelled, disoriented like I was coming out of a daydream. The crowd was in chaos below me, stunned and horrified, but my captain of the guard pulled himself up to the platform, nearly slipping in blood coating the wood.

"What do you need?" he asked.

I pulled a handgun out of his holster, turned to Python, and shot him in the chest.

TWENTY

MARIPOSA

Reaper retreated into the house moments after he put Python out of his misery. People worked quickly to break down the platform and move the body. With the show over, everyone started dispersing to their own homes and workplaces. They all wore the same shocked, harrowed expressions. This event would stay in people's memories for a long time afterward.

In that regard, hopefully Reaper accomplished what he intended.

Heather swam against the current of people leaving, crying and wailing, to get to Python's body.

"What will they do with his body?" I asked no one in particular.

"Wrap it in a sheet and dump it just outside of Razor Wire's turf." The answer came from Jandro, who I didn't realize had come to stand next to me. "They'll see what we did to their informant and send the message up to General Tash. Hopefully he'll think twice about fucking with us again."

"I need to lay down," Tessa announced suddenly, pushing herself to stand.

"I'll walk you home," Noelle muttered, taking her elbow.

"Need me for anything?" I asked.

"No. Thank you, Mari." She gave me a strained smile. "I'll see you for my next appointment, if not sooner."

I nodded, giving her a wave goodbye as she walked off, Noelle holding one arm and her oldest boy holding the other. Everyone had to be in a state of shock. We all acted like we gathered for some routine announcement and didn't know how to process what we just saw. I wasn't affected by the blood and gore itself, but still needed to come to terms with what I just witnessed.

That, and the fact that Reaper was the one who did it.

"You okay?" Concern etched through Jandro's features as his hand caressed over my lower back.

"Yeah, I think so." I leaned into him slightly as I looked up. "I'm a little worried about Reaper, though."

"Yeah, I wouldn't try to see him right away." He looked toward the house as he pulled me tighter against him in a protective embrace. "He needs some time too. Everyone does."

I rested my cheek on his chest, leaning into his solidness and warmth as he brushed a kiss along my forehead.

"You hungry?"

"Are you kidding me?" I barked out a harsh laugh.

"Yeah, me neither."

The platform had been broken down and disassembled as we watched. Python's blood that had run off into the street left behind dark puddles that started to congeal and stick to people's shoes.

"Is there any way to clean the blood off the street?"

"It's not worth wasting the water," Jandro replied with a shake of his head. "We never know when we'll see rain again, so we have to keep our water stores for us." His fingers created gentle, soothing pressure on my back. "It'll be gone in a few weeks. The wind, sand, and wildlife will make sure of that."

I knew he was right. The dark stains on the ground, the only evidence of what happened here, would break down and dissolve into nothing over time. Python's screams and the grotesque imagery of his mutilation would soon fade from our minds in much the same way. It just felt so permanent now. My ears rang and the dark blood soaked into the ground like a tattoo. But every second that passed moved us further away from this event.

Python, his pain, and his crimes would eventually be forgotten. Someone else would betray their community in a similar way. History had a tendency to repeat itself. What did that mean for the message Reaper wanted to send? Hell, what did it mean for post-Collapse life in general? Were we stuck in a hamster wheel, never making any strides toward progress?

I wasn't sure what got me on this train of thought. Python's death didn't exactly sadden me, but it got me thinking. Not long ago, an execution like this would be considered barbaric. But if the past was what put us on the hamster wheel, we had to do something different to stop it, right?

"I want to check on Reaper." Slowly, I pulled myself out of Jandro's embrace.

He allowed it, but closed a firm grip around my hands. "I'm coming with you," he insisted. "Just in case he's, I dunno, not really himself."

We took off our blood-soaked shoes before stepping into what felt like an empty house. Reaper had left his own bloody boots by the front door, but was otherwise nowhere to be seen.

"Reaper?" I called, my voice echoing against the high, vaulted ceiling. Then I tried, "Hades?"

A soft bark floated down from the second level. Jandro and I took the stairs together, following the sound toward Reaper's bedroom.

"Hey, boy." I kneeled to greet Hades, guarding outside the door like a loyal sentry. "How's our human, huh?"

His fur was wet when I pet him, but not with blood. Jandro leaned down over us and took a small sniff.

"I think Reap gave him a shower. He's as fresh as a daisy."

"I bet you're right." I stroked over the handsome Doberman's ears and scratched down his neck. "Can we check on your master? Huh?"

Hades licked my cheek and stretched his front legs out on the floor until he was lying on his belly. As if he understood my question, he tilted his head toward the door as if to say, *you may proceed.*

"That dog freaks me the hell out sometimes," Jandro

muttered as he followed me through the door. "You ever seen how fast he runs next to the bikes too? It's unreal."

"Yeah." I stole a glance back at the dog, looking as proud and regal as a sphynx with his front paws crossed in front of him and his ears straight up in the air. I wondered how much Jandro knew about his special abilities, including how fast he healed from the shrapnel wound. "He's something special."

We found Reaper sitting on the edge of the bed, naked except for a towel wrapped around his waist. Water droplets still hung off the tips of his hair from his shower. His skin looked red and scratched on some parts of his arms and back, like he turned the water on to a scalding temperature and scrubbed vigorously to get the blood off.

Or to scrub away what he did to a man he once called a brother.

"Reaper?" I took a few steps toward him, but Jandro caught my wrist to hold me back.

"Reap," he called out. "It's Mari and Jandro."

His elbows on his knees, Reaper's head turned slowly to look at us. "I haven't gone deaf or blind in the last ten minutes, so I dunno why the fuck you're acting so squirrelly."

I wrenched my arm out of Jandro's grip and went to kneel on the floor in front of my first lover. "Let me see your eyes." I didn't wait for him to comply, but took his hands away from his jaw and pulled back his eyelids myself.

"Sugar, what are you doing?"

"Checking to see if you're in shock."

His pupils looked normal. Next I pressed two fingers to his pulse and flattened my palm against his chest. His pulse was elevated slightly, but at normal strength. And his skin was warm from the shower, not cold or clammy with sweat.

"Do you feel lightheaded?" I asked him. "Dizzy? Nauseous?"

"No to all of the above."

"Good." I lowered my hands to his towel-covered knees. "So you're fine."

He glanced up at Jandro, then covered my hands with his before looking back at me. "Honestly, I wasn't. Not until you two came up."

"Why?" Jandro remained standing at the far edge of the bed, arms crossed and brow furrowed with concern.

"I can't—" Reaper cut himself off, seeming to look past Jandro toward Hades on the other side of the door. "I can't do that again. I can kill a hundred men in a day if necessary, but…not like that."

"I don't think you'll have to," Jandro assured him. "No one's gonna forget that for a long time. You got the message across, now Gunner's men are handling the body."

I ran my fingers over his palms, trailing up over his wrists and to his forearms. "It's over now. You did what you set out to do, for the good of your club." My mouth lifted toward his. "And I'm proud of you, President."

"Sugar," he said in a strained whisper. "I found my strength in you out there. I've never been so glad to find a woman who doesn't faint at the sight of blood."

"I'll always support you." I rose to my feet, intending

to sit next to him on the bed, but his hands closed around my upper arms and he pulled me straight into his chest.

"Don't stop touching me like that," he pleaded. "Only the way *you* look at me makes me feel like a man and not a monster."

"I don't give a fuck even if you are a monster." I placed my knees outside of his thighs on the mattress. "You're *my* monster."

"Really, Mari?" He stared at me as he breathed the question, as if he couldn't believe it. "Even after seeing what I just did, you're not afraid of me?"

"My love," I stroked the back of my fingers down his cheek. "You make me feel like I don't have to be afraid of anything. With you, I'm fearless."

"My God, woman." His voice grew thick and husky with desire. An erection already began tenting his towel as he pawed at me. "How are you so perfect for me? How are you always exactly what I need?" He searched for the answer in my throat with his tongue.

"Um." Jandro cleared his throat. "Should I leave?"

"No," Reaper and I protested in unison. We wore matching smiles as our foreheads nudged against each other. "Stay, Jandro."

MARIPOSA

M y heart crashed so hard in my chest, I was certain both of them could hear it. Jandro looked a little dumbfounded, like he didn't believe what he just heard.

"You're sure?" His eyes bounced from me to Reaper.

Reaper pulled my shirt over my head as he answered. "Shut the door all the way, or else Hades will think he's invited to this party."

While Jandro did that, my top and bra were discarded on the floor. I slid off Reaper's lap to stand while he pulled my jeans down. He was more attentive with my lower half, kneeling on the floor to pull the fabric down from my hips all the way to my ankles. I used his shoulders for balance as I stepped out of them. His spot on the floor put him right at eye level with my panties, and he took full advantage of it.

He placed a slow, smoldering kiss on the crest of my hip bone, hands inching up my ankles to my calves, where his fingers rolled into my flesh. Kneading the muscles with his skilled hands, his mouth ghosted a trail over my lower belly until his lips met my opposite hip. There, he used more teeth, sucking a hard kiss on the skin before soothing it with the flat of his tongue.

His breath through the fabric of my panties sent a shiver up my spine. My fingers curled into his hair with impatience. I wanted no barriers between that mouth and my skin. As his hands moved to the back of my thighs, Jandro approached us slowly.

"Where do you want me, *Mariposita?*" His voice was tight with restraint, like he had to hold back from just inviting himself in. Even though that was exactly what I wanted him to do.

"Right here." I held an arm out to him.

He grabbed my palm and kissed it sweetly before moving in close enough for me to really touch him. His eyes stayed locked on mine as my arm wrapped around those thick shoulders. Always wanting to read me, to watch me. But I didn't want him to pull back anymore, so I took his hand and placed it on my bare breast.

Jandro needed no further instruction. With a groan, his mouth fell to mine. I slid his cut off of his shoulders, then tugged up on the back of his shirt. We only separated at the mouth for him to take his shirt off, then he filled his palms with my breasts. He moved to stand behind me, rolling my nipples between the rough pads of his calloused fingers while moving his kisses to my neck. When I arched into him, he traced every curve, gliding his hands over me while the warm, soft pressure of his lips lit up every sensitive nerve like a match.

He had me so delirious and needy for his touch, I

barely noticed Reaper had pulled my panties down my legs until I felt the rough stubble of his face on my inner thigh. When I looked down at him, he shot me a wry grin and smacked one side of my ass as if to say, *remember me down here?*

A jolt of panic hit me. Sure, I knew my way around a man's body, but two at the same time? Even when I started to get a handle on loving two men, pleasing them both in bed seemed like a monumental task when there was only one of me.

Jandro must have sensed how my body stiffened up, because he wrapped an arm around my waist and turned my head to one side so he could kiss me.

"We're here for *you*," he said as he molded the full length of his body against my back. "Don't worry about anything you *think* you have to do. Let *us* please you."

Reaper murmured his agreement as he nudged my legs apart, inching his burning kisses closer to my center. My knees were already weak, and I was all but certain my pussy would start dripping onto his face.

"Let me taste you," he moaned greedily, pulling me forward with his hands on my ass until I was practically sitting on his face. Right where he wanted me.

I gasped at the heat of his mouth on my sensitive flesh, rising on my tiptoes to ease the pressure a little, but he was having none of that. He devoured me like I was his last meal, holding me in place with his unforgiving grip. He sucked me into his mouth, alternating between teasing nibbles and deep strokes of his tongue inside me.

I found a rhythm, rolling over his mouth as Jandro supported my upper body. His arms wrapped around me, somehow helping to hold me up while also setting me on fire. He moved with me, his torso following my writhing as I rode Reaper's face. Jandro's erection rubbed against my ass, reminding me of his own need as a counterpoint to mine.

No matter what they told me, I couldn't bring myself to lay back and be selfish. To only take and not give. Part of my own pleasure was in giving, to hear those sexy masculine moans and watch them shudder as they lost control. And I wanted to ensure I gave to them just as much as they gave me.

With one hand still in Reaper's hair, I reached behind me to stroke Jandro's length through his pants. He hurried out of them quickly, all the while keeping one hand splayed on my belly to support me. When the hot, rigid flesh met the cleft of my ass, I wrapped a hand around the base and stroked upward. His pre-come already coated my palm, aiding in my gliding up and down to the rhythm of his tight breaths.

Reaper chose then to stop teasing me. Releasing my tender lips, his mouth dragged up to the tiny bundle of nerves that had been begging to be touched for ages. He stilled my squirming with a large hand on my hip, aided by Jandro's forearm against my lower belly. I was no match for all the sensory overload—not Jandro's mouth on my neck, his relentless torture of my nipples, nor Reaper's mouth sealing over my clit or his fingers pressing inside me to curl against my contracting walls. Those fingers beckoned me once, twice. On the third time, I shattered.

My feet left the floor and I was weightless, held up

by four strong hands I knew would never drop me. My vision danced with stars and my pulse thumped like my whole body was a giant drum. I felt it throbbing between my legs and every point of contact my men had on me. Someone cradled my head. Another set of hands supported my ankles.

I found myself lying on my back in a familiar bed, looking up at Reaper's hooded green eyes instead of down.

"Welcome back, sugar," he purred, stroking a hand down my side. "I think you blacked out for a second."

"Show-off," Jandro muttered from somewhere else.

I lifted my head to look around for him, finding the Vice President looking fucking delicious seated between my thighs. His cock pointed straight at me, thick and stiff. When he ran his palms up my thighs, his length flexed, bouncing once. I could watch this gorgeous naked man all day if I didn't need him inside me so badly.

Pushing up to my elbows, I noticed Reaper had discarded his towel at some point. He leaned against the headboard, his own erection pointing straight up in the air. I watched him stroke it absently, heat pooling in my belly.

He shot me a cocky smirk, seeing the desire in my eyes. "You want it, beautiful?"

"Yes."

"Tell me where."

I turned on my side, scooting closer to him. Further down the bed, Jandro followed me. I figured I'd just show Reaper where I wanted him, wrapping my hand around the stiff base, but he cupped my chin just as I was about to taste him.

"Tell me where you want me, sugar," he repeated. "And tell Jandro where you want him."

Heat burned my face. I didn't want to talk, I just wanted to feel. I wanted to lose myself in how incredible both of these men made me feel. But one thing I loved about Reaper was his dominance. Sex with him was the perfect mixture of dirty and intimate. And he knew exactly how to toy with me before we even got started.

"I want you in my mouth," I whispered, receiving a pleased hum from him. When I looked back at Jandro, he leaned over me on all fours, the silky head of his cock trailing over my hip and outer thigh. "I want you in my pussy," I told him, shyness making my voice small.

He leaned forward with a grin, closing the distance between us with a deep kiss full of warmth and sensuality.

"I'll take you anywhere you'll have me." His kiss trailed to my neck, then my shoulder. Those incredibly soft lips never lost contact as they skimmed down my ribs and waist like gentle rain.

Turning back to Reaper, I kept my gaze on his lust-filled eyes until the final moment my lips slid over the crown of his dick. His moan was a deep rumbling above me as I felt Jandro lift my leg and open me wide. He placed my ankle on his shoulder and the bed moved underneath all of us as he got into position.

Reaper gathered up my hair and held it in his fist,

allowing me to look back at his best friend stroking more pre-come up and down his shaft. The president's cock was halfway down my throat when Jandro's head kissed the opening between my thighs. He held my leg steady against his chest as he pressed forward, guiding himself in with the other hand.

The fullness in my mouth and my pussy at the same time was almost too much. Too good. Each man approached sex so differently, and having them together was simply everything. Reaper held my head still by my hair as he began to thrust into my mouth, curses and growls fluttering out under his breath as he fought to keep under control. Jandro's fingers dug into my thigh against his abs as he pressed into me in deep, fluid strokes.

"God damn." Reaper released me off his cock, giving me a moment to breathe. Too bad each of my breaths were stolen every time Jandro filled me up, his free hand still caressing me everywhere he reached.

"You're fucking incredible." Reaper cupped my face and leaned down for a kiss.

Our current position would only allow for a quick peck, but I wanted more. I wanted my lover's tight clutch of teeth and tongue, his all-consuming kisses. My leg slid off Jandro's shoulder as I rolled to all fours, causing him to slip out of me. While Reaper's and my tongues made love, a sharp unexpected slap on my ass made me yelp.

"Damn right, she's incredible," Jandro panted with a grin, smoothing his palm over the flesh of my ass where he spanked me.

I looked apologetically over my shoulder. "Sorry, I didn't mean to make you stop."

"Don't be." He seemed mesmerized by me, hands running up and down my sides to fill his palms with my curves. His eyes remained glued to my pussy, lifted and on display for him. "I don't want to leave the party too early."

"I'd give you shit and call you a minute-man," Reaper teased, filling his own palms with my breasts, "but I know exactly where you're coming from."

"Puns in the bedroom. I can see why your girl spent the night with me," Jandro shot back, laughing.

"Shut it. She just likes your window up there."

Chuckling, Jandro slid a hand between my legs, cupping my whole core with delicious pressure that had me arching and writhing. Those strong fingers teased a circle around my clit, and then his tongue probed and kissed at my slit. Any witty comeback I could add to their pissing contest was lost as all conscious thought went out the window. I needed more of that tongue, more of both of them.

Reaper cupped my face in his hands, steadying my writhing, squirming neediness with his green gaze.

"Put that beautiful mouth back on my cock," he ordered.

I obeyed, sliding my lips over steel wrapped in velvety skin. He growled when I took him deeper, fingers curling into my hair. Taking him down my throat on all fours was much easier than while lying on my side.

When Jandro's mouth and hands pulled away from me, leaving me unsatisfied and empty, I moaned around

Reaper's dick, arching my back higher with need. Over my sucking and slurping, I thought I heard an amused chuckle behind me. Then he slammed into me and I screamed at the sudden fullness, my mouth still stuffed.

"Oh yeah, fuck her like that. She loves it." Reaper brought a hand down to my breasts, pinching one nipple in place as Jandro rocked me back and forth with his thrusts.

He wasn't sweet and romantic anymore. He held my hips and fucked me hard, grunting like an animal with the occasional slap to my ass. He was nothing like this our first night together. I'd never seen this side of Jandro before and didn't know it existed. And Reaper was right. I fucking loved it.

Tingles turned to sparks inside me, climbing higher at a pace too fast for me to catch up. When Reaper stiffened and spilled his salty release in my mouth with a heavy groan, his pleasure sent me hurtling over my own peak.

Sparks roared into a blazing inferno, electricity and heat wringing through me in release so hard I could barely breathe. Jandro slammed into me with a final deep thrust, following my crash with his own.

When the world came slowly back into focus, I was sandwiched between two hard, spent bodies. All three of us were slick with sweat but no one seemed to care. I ended up on my side, my head nuzzled in the center of Jandro's chest. Reaper brushed a kiss along my back and spooned me from behind.

A smile grew on my face. These guys were the type

to talk shit, tease and rib each other, compare dick sizes, all of that. And yet they snuggled and sighed contently in the same bed, the same cuddle pile. I just loved how normal and safe it felt.

TWENTY-TWO

JANDRO

I brushed a piece of hair out of Mari's face, utterly helpless to stop myself from looking at her. She drifted off to sleep for a moment, but Reaper and I remained alert. We had to leave for church soon.

He propped himself up on his elbow on the other side of her, hand resting on Mari's side while I touched her hair.

"You can use my shower if you want," he grunted out. "I made sure all the blood washed off the tile."

I huffed out a soft laugh. "Thanks, bro. I appreciate you not kicking me straight out of your bed."

"Why would I?" His gaze flicked down to the sleeping woman between us. "Look at her. She'd be so fucking pissed if I kicked you out."

That was what I had to remember. The only reason I was in his bed at all was because of this gorgeous woman who somehow captured his heart and mine. Not only that, she cared enough not to crush those beating organs in her adorable little fists. This was all for her.

Reaper and I were two completely different men and yet we found one person perfect for both of us.

Finding one partner to spend your life with was rare enough. Adding in more people and having it just feel *right* between everyone? The odds had to be astronomical. Being involved with Reaper and Mari like this made me appreciate what I saw between Reap's parents when we were kids.

His mom was openly affectionate with all three of his fathers. It weirded me out a little back then, but nowhere near as much as my Catholic aunt. We'd be leaving the flea market after she bought jewelry from Reaper's mom, who we witnessed kissing three men one right after the other, and Tia Ana would pull out her rosary and start mumbling prayers. She thought the poor woman had been lured into sin by the devil, but little did she know that Reaper's mom had the lion's share of the power in the relationship.

Reaper explained more of it to me later as we got older, but nothing could've prepared me for experiencing this myself. It felt...oddly normal. We were just two guys who wanted to make one woman happy, because she made *us* happy.

"Fuck," I breathed, tracing a finger lightly over Mari's cheek.

"Hm?" Reaper grunted.

"This is just...nice, dude." I kept my voice low to avoid waking her.

Reaper made a sound like he was about to bust my balls for being sappy, but he stretched his arm out instead and let his head flop down to the pillow.

"I've never had anything like this with anyone," he muttered, running his fingers lightly over her waist. "Everything about her is just so damn good…I'm scared to death of something bad happening."

I looked at him, surprised. It was probably the first time I heard Reaper admit to being scared of anything.

"We won't let anything happen," I told him. "If you drop the ball, I pick it up and vice versa. That's how we've always been, Reap. Nothing will happen as long as she's got us. And," I looked back down at her with a sigh, "who knows how many more poor bastards she'll put under her spell. She could end up with a whole army to defend her."

"Two more," Reaper muttered. "Four total."

"Yeah? Not a bad guess."

He didn't respond to that. The next sound came from a pair of lips brushing against my chest.

"Please keep talking. I'm loving this conversation."

"You little shit." Reaper slapped Mari's ass hard, making her shriek. "How long have you been awake?"

"Ow! First off, you two aren't as quiet as you think you are. And secondly, you both keep touching me. It's not like you're whispering in another room."

"Sneaky, smart-mouthed little…" Reaper tickled her aggressively, gritting his teeth, but smiling. He tried to pin her down and kiss her, but her squirming and flailing escaped his grip.

"Save me, Jandro!" she yelped, burrowing into my chest.

I wrapped her in a bear hug and flipped us over to the sound of her laughter. "Sorry, *Mariposita*." I began my own tickle attack across her ribs. "You're not safe anywhere."

"Nooo!" she howled dramatically until she was breathless from laughter.

"Now this is not something I had considered," Reaper mumbled behind me.

"What?"

"Having to stare at your ass instead of hers."

"Better get used to it, buddy." I wiggled my hips and backed up towards him. "You never know when we might end up spooning in the middle of the night."

"Get that nasty thing away from me. I'll shove my foot straight up there."

I planted a final kiss on a giggling Mari before I stretched and crawled off the bed. "I'll take that shower now. Thanks, Reap. I definitely *won't* rub my dick and balls all over your nice tile work."

His groan was the last thing I heard before I turned the water on.

———

WHEN I GOT OUT, one of Reaper's towels wrapped snugly around my waist, he had already left and Mari was reclining alone in the still unmade bed.

"What do you have going on today?" I sat on the edge and leaned over, resisting the urge to ditch the towel and make the most of our precious alone time.

"Not much," she admitted, rolling onto her back to look at me upside down. "I'm getting low on medical supplies and already out of a lot of stuff, so I've been pushing back appointments with people."

"I'll make sure Gunner knows," I promised her, noticing how her face changed when I said his name. "What did he do?"

"Nothing."

"Mari," I warned. "It's obviously *not* nothing. What's going on?"

She chewed her lip, scooting across the bed until her head rested in my lap. "We talked a little after you guys dropped him off last night. I pretty much confronted him on how he's been acting."

"And what did he have to say?"

"Essentially that he's going to keep ignoring me because we can't be just friends. And he doesn't want to be a part of," she drew a circle in the air with her finger, "you know, this."

"That's his fucking loss then." I gripped her slender shoulder and started to rub. "If he can't see that this is good and working for us, it's his own damn fault."

"It just…sucks," she frowned. "I miss him. He was one of the first ones who made me feel welcome here, besides you. I understand if this isn't his thing, but to not even be friendly with me? I feel like I did something wrong."

A flash of anger hit me like a bolt of lightning. Fucking Gunner. "You didn't do anything wrong, *bonita*. You followed your heart and trusted us. Don't ever feel like being happy is wrong."

"I pretty much told him that. I just wish I could make him understand. But then again," she slid a hand up my abs toward my chest, "I didn't really understand it until this morning."

"Nothing like multiple orgasms from multiple dudes, huh?"

"Stop." She smacked me playfully, returning my smile. "I mean, that's kind of it, but it's more than that. It's hard to explain, other than it just feels right. I think you know what I mean."

"I do." I brought her palm to my lips and kissed it. "I was always fine with sharing in theory, but yeah. Like you, I didn't really understand it until today."

"Executions and threesomes," Mari sighed. "So much excitement already."

"You know the best part about this, though?" I leaned down to her, cradling her face.

She tilted her lips up to me. "Hmm?"

I kissed them and whispered, "rubbing my ass crack all over Reaper's shower."

"Oh my God, Jandro! You did not!"

"Seriously, I had to do handstands to get those hard-to-reach spots."

"You are…the absolute…worst!" she choked out in a fit of laughter.

"Not when I can get you to laugh like this." I kissed her again and released a sigh with my forehead on hers. "I have to get going, but I will tell Gunner to make your supplies a priority. And to stop being a fucking dipshit."

"You don't have to do that second part." She rolled up to sit. "I have a feeling Reaper gave him a piece of his mind, and that's why he was so drunk at the fight. If he doesn't want this, we shouldn't push him."

"I won't get on him about being with us, just about treating you with the same respect as any other member of this club." I pushed her hair behind her shoulder for one last look at those perfect tits. "Which you are, by the way. We're gonna need to tattoo you soon."

"Tattoo?" Her eyes widened. "You mean *that* tattoo?" She pointed at the horned skull running across my ribs.

"That's the one," I smirked. "It's in the rules, *bonita*. Everyone gets it as a symbol of commitment to the club."

"Does it have to be that big?" She tilted her head to peer at mine more closely. "And where would it go?"

"It should be big enough to see all the details. Mine's a little smaller than Reaper's, and Shadow's is probably the smallest of everyone's."

I paused for a moment to swallow. I'd forgotten that she'd seen Shadow's, because she fucked him. I was a little jealous before, but she was mine now. I had no reason to feel that way. Still, the recollection left me with a small, weird feeling. Like learning a detail of your lover's past that you didn't really care to know.

"As for placement," I went on, "that's up to you, as long as all the details can be visible. I'm partial to right here, personally." I dragged a finger from her collarbone down over the swells of her breasts, continuing down through the valley between them.

She smacked my hand away. "I'm not getting a giant skull on my chest as my first tattoo."

"There is also the classy, under-breast corset style." I touched her again, this time running my fingers over the sensitive underside of her flesh. "Lots of women like ink there. Tattooing over the ribs is painful, though."

Her lip curled in distaste. "What else?"

"Slightly less classy, you have the lower back area, affectionately known as the tramp stamp. Noelle had hers done there. Hers looks a little wonky because we had to go to an outside artist." I drummed my fingers on her thigh. "We'll probably have to do the same with you, unfortunately."

Mari's brow furrowed. "Why?"

"Because," I paused for a moment that stretched on too long. "Our resident tattoo artist is Shadow."

TWENTY-THREE

GUNNER

y face fucking hurt. The swelling went down a little around my eye, but I could still barely see out of it. I knew what I should've done—swallowed my pride and marched down to the medic's office with an apology. But now, sober and with enough regret to last a lifetime, I wasn't ready to see her yet.

Horus and I weren't alone in the conference room long. Shadow came in a few minutes later, followed by Reaper and Hades. Our president greeted me with his cursory nod and grunt, like this was any other day. Like he didn't filet a man alive this morning. None of the men slowly filing in acted like they just witnessed a brutal execution. Big G had the balls to shoot me a smug look. Whatever. I purposely turned my chair to face away from him. I burned one bridge already. Why stop there?

Jandro was one of the last ones to arrive, slipping in quickly to take his seat next to Reaper. They bent their heads toward each other and started whispering,

Jandro's face immediately taking on a huge grin. I rolled my one good eye and ignored them too. I didn't even want to speculate on what they were talking about.

"We all here?" Reaper asked the room when the last man shut the door behind him. "Good. Church is in session." He slammed the gavel down with a definitive blow, then folded his hands on the table. "Today I did something that I hope never to repeat."

A deafening silence filled the room. Hardly anyone dared to breathe.

"In fact," Reaper stroked his jaw, "I'll go ahead and say I will *never* repeat what happened today. Because no true Steel Demon is stupid enough to go behind my back. Do I make myself absolutely clear?"

"Yes, president," came the resounding chorus.

"Python was a trusted member among us, and that was my mistake," he went on. "I failed you as a president because I trusted a man who didn't deserve it. I will not make the same mistake twice." He paused, his gaze resting on a small chip in the wooden center of the table. "We're shocked at what we saw. Some of us are grieving, mourning a loss. But this had to happen. And now that it's over, we must move on. Remember, but don't dwell. I kept my word and I expect nothing less from the rest of you."

His eyes scanned the room. "Would anyone else like to bring up a matter of business to discuss?"

I cleared my throat.

"Yes, Gunner?"

I ignored the way his brow furrowed at me and addressed the room. "There's a traveling market setting up next weekend on the Navajo Flats, just an hour's ride from here. While I'm still trying to secure a long-term trade partner, the market's vendors should have enough goods to keep us well-stocked in the meantime. I suggest several of us ride out, to maximize our load."

Dallas raised a hand.

"Yeah?"

"The wife's been begging to spend some time outside of Sheol. You think this market will be safe for women?"

"I don't see why not," I shrugged. "Many of the vendors are women offering clothes, jewelry, crafty shit. If Andrea don't mind carrying her own stuff, she can make it a shopping trip."

"Great, now she's gonna tell my sister," Reaper grumbled.

"Will there be medical supplies?" Jandro asked. "Mari's running low on some things she needs."

"Might be a lot of those weird snake oil remedies, but there should be legit vendors there too."

"Who wants to ride to the market?" Reaper asked the room. Nearly every hand shot up and our surly president groaned. "Some of you fuckers need to stay here to defend this place."

"I'll stay, President," Shadow volunteered. "I have no need for anything at the market."

We all knew the big guy hated big crowds of people, but no one was about to point that out.

"Thank you, Shadow. I'll need a few more. You all can draw straws or whatever the fuck you do. Anyone else have business to bring up?"

Jandro raised a hand. "I want to propose patching in the prospect Stephan as a full member of the SDMC. He earned my respect when he stepped up to fight me last month, and he's had my back while I've been working overtime on everyone's bikes. I trust the kid. He'll go to war with us on a single word from Reaper. Of that I have no doubt."

"You think he's ready?" Dallas stroked his beard with a frown.

"He's young. He hasn't proven himself yet," Brick pointed out.

"Let's bring him on the market ride with us," Reaper suggested. "He'll bring up the rear, where Shadow usually is. If shit gets hairy, we'll see how well he does. If he impresses me, then we can patch him in."

Jandro nodded, accepting that solution.

All other church topics were mundane stuff—the status of our solar panels, water treatment systems, food rations, blah blah blah. I was itching to get out of my seat and go for a solo ride, maybe fly over some canyons while looking through Horus. Of course I wouldn't be allowed to leave that easily.

When Reaper banged his gavel, signaling the end of church, the next thing I heard was, "Hold up, Gunner."

Jandro, naturally. Reaper hadn't succeeded in bringing me into their weird, hippie love triangle, so now his tag-team partner was trying his shot.

"What's up?" I propped my elbow on the table as everyone else filed out of the room.

Jandro moved to a seat closer to me, mimicking my posture. "What's going on, Gun?"

I shrugged, regarding him with a bored expression. "Nothin'."

"Yeah?" He cocked his head. "Why did you get shit-faced right before fighting Big G?"

"Why the fuck does it matter?" I demanded. "And while we're at it, why is everyone grilling me about shit that's none of their fucking business?"

"Because it's not like you to set yourself up to lose." Jandro leaned back in his seat. "Come on, dude. I'm coming to you as your friend, not your VP. Everyone knows you can hold your own against Big G, but you put yourself out there intentionally to send a completely different message. Why?"

"It wasn't intentional. I meant to just have a couple to get warmed up. I drank too much. I fucked up, okay? You think I *wanted* to embarrass myself like that?"

"I think you wanted someone to see you in a different light." He gave me a hard look. "Someone who hasn't seen you fight before, who wouldn't know you well enough yet to see how out of character this is."

"Jesus Christ." I dropped my forehead to my hand.

"You didn't expect her to care," he went on. "You thought she'd just shake her head at the drunk captain acting like a fool. But instead, she got between you and Big G's kick that could've broken your jaw, or worse."

My spine shot up straight like a bolt of lightning struck me. "Did he hurt her?"

"No," Jandro said coolly. "And if he had, *we* would've taken care of it. You were in no shape to be outside your own goddamn front yard, let alone fighting or defending someone else."

"Huh. *We*, you say." I spat the word out. "Like you and Reaper are her knights in fucking shining armor. Give me a break."

"I don't give a fuck what you call it," Jandro shrugged. "Didn't expect that either, did you? That she chose this? That she actually *wants* to be with Reaper and me? Blows your little golden boy mind, doesn't it?"

"Your peacocking is not fucking impressing me," I shot back. "Don't act like your intentions with her are so noble and pure."

"And yours are?"

"Fuck off, Jandro." I stood abruptly, causing Horus's talons to dig into my shoulder. "Next time you or Reaper get in my face about this shit, I won't wait for Fight Night. You'll get my fist right in your fucking teeth."

"You're the only one that's hurting her here," he called after me. "And yourself. All because you won't get out of your own way."

I slammed the conference room door behind me and headed for my garage. I needed to ride. I needed to fly until none of these people could touch me.

Especially her.

TWENTY-FOUR

SHADOW

I sat on my bed, which was little more than a worn-out mattress and box spring. A crude table served as my nightstand. It had been broken and repaired more times than I could count. On top of it stood the small, orange container, now empty. Last week, the woman—Mariposa—gave me seven tablets to see if they would help me sleep better.

I almost didn't take any. I considered throwing them away. But my current regimen had been losing effectiveness for years. Alcohol numbed me to a certain point, which slipped further out of reach the more my tolerance grew. I didn't know of any other options for relief. Neither did Jandro. So after staying up half the night debating with myself, I took one pill.

I never slept so well in my life.

For seven nights in a row, always after I took a tablet right before bed, I woke up still *in* bed. Not sprawled out on the floor. No cold sweats drenching my body. No sore knuckles or pounding headache. Not even a single piece of furniture turned over.

I went to sleep. And then I woke up feeling… refreshed. At ease. It was hard to believe this was how normal people experienced sleep.

But now the container was empty.

She said I could just try them to see if they worked, then go see her for more. It sounded like an easy enough solution when she was right there, holding the pills out to me in my own home. Staring at the empty bottle now, no task ever seemed so daunting.

I would have to go to her office. Talk to her again. Think of the right words to say and not fuck it up like I did before.

The memory of her hands on me, her parted lips and the sounds she made, the silky heat and pressure of her gliding around my shaft, flashed through my mind faster than I could push it away.

"Fuck."

My cock throbbed and flexed on its own accord. I stood up and started pacing around my room, giving my dick a few tugs to ease the pressure it ached for.

She didn't want that. She didn't enjoy it. I was wrong to do what I did. She wasn't available to touch and never would be to me. I couldn't think of her like that. But it was difficult not to when that was the most pleasurable experience I ever had with a woman. And I couldn't just avoid her.

I saw her a few more times here at my house in the past week. Talking to her was getting easier, but only when she started it by saying hello or how are you. Thinking of a mundane question to ask her was like pulling teeth for me. Jandro and Reaper kept all of her attention anyway. She would smile and greet me, then forget I was there long before Jandro took her up to his bedroom.

I used to wish she would forget me like everyone else did. Her presence threw me off-balance and made me uneasy. She disrupted the almost-peaceful routine I had established in this club. Now, for some reason I couldn't place, I *wanted* her to see me. To remember I was here.

"Yo, Shadow!" Jandro called from his end of the hall, booted footsteps approaching quickly. "We're heading out. You got everything you need?" He paused in my open doorway, wearing mirrored sunglasses on his head and all his riding gear.

Thankfully, my semi-erection had subsided. "Yes, I'll be fine. See you when you get back."

"Cool. I'll get you a churro. See ya." He moved as if he was about to go downstairs, then swiftly backpedalled. His eyes fell on the pill bottle next to my bed.

"Where did you get that?" I couldn't place his tone. It didn't sound good, but there was no point in lying.

"From Mariposa. She gave me something to see if it would help me sleep."

He slid his hard gaze to me. "When did this happen?"

"Last week. The day after the first night she spent here. She came over while you were at the shop." I lifted my hands, anxiety clutching me like a fist in my chest. "I didn't do anything, Jandro. I swear to you, I didn't touch her. I know better now. She gave me a week's worth just to try because of my nightmares."

"Relax, bro." His palms lifted to mirror mine, taking a few steps into my room toward me. "I'm not mad, I know you wouldn't do anything. I'm just surprised, that's all. Neither one of you said anything to me."

"I didn't think to tell you. I'm sorry."

"No, don't worry. It's all right. Again, just surprised." He rubbed his chin, looking back at the bottle. "So they worked for you okay?"

"Yes." I ran a hand back through my hair. He was the only one who didn't flinch at seeing my face fully uncovered. "I've slept better than I had in…ever."

"And you were okay with, you know," he paused, "accepting medication from her?"

I knew what he was referring to. The mental health ward in the prison we met had primarily female nurses and orderlies. While in prison, the doctors diagnosed me with a whole slew of mental disorders and prescribed me handfuls of pills to take every day.

I tried to explain I didn't want any females near me or giving me anything. When that didn't work, Jandro tried to explain on my behalf. That resulted in him being assigned to a new post far away from me. Without my only friend, and constantly having to be restrained so women could force pills and water down my throat, I snapped.

The next thing I remembered was waking up in the solitary holding unit, permanently restrained with cuffs around my wrists, ankles, and neck. Jandro told me what the report said—I had assaulted my whole nursing team.

They suffered concussions and broken bones, and intended to press charges.

"Yes," I said, bringing my awareness back to the present. "Mariposa has always been kind to me. And she gave me the option of refusing if I didn't want to try them. It was nothing like before."

He rubbed the back of his neck, looking away from me. "I know you wouldn't hurt her, man. You gave them plenty of warning back then, and as far as I'm concerned, you acted in self-defense. I'm sorry I had to ask, but I just," he blew out a long breath. "I care about her. Fuck, what am I saying? I love her."

I nodded, like I understood anything about what that felt like.

"Hey, while we're on this topic. Um." He clapped his hands together. "Can I ask you to think about something?"

"Okay?"

"Mari needs her tattoo—"

"No," I cut him off with an abrupt shake of my head. "I can't, Jandro."

"Just think about it is all I'm asking. You've made tremendous progress since she's been here, dude. And she's the president's old lady, for fuck's sake. She deserves a damn good tattoo, not one from some junkie with a guitar string."

"Jandro." I rubbed my forehead, my throat already closing up. The thought of drawing the demon on her skin and making it permanent was both exhilarating and terrifying. "I would have to *touch* her."

He cocked his head, eyebrows lifting. "That ship's already sailed *way* off into the sunset, my friend."

"And it never should have happened. I know that. She's yours too, now. So I don't understand why you'd want me to—"

"Bro, I said think about it, not overthink it, okay?" He clapped a hand on my arm. "Just think of her as a blank canvas, like every other tattoo you've done. I trust you, dude. You don't have to make it all weird just because she's female."

"What?" I barked out in frustration. "Have we met before?"

He burst out laughing, practically falling into me. "Fuck me, man. You've got a sense of humor now too! She really is rubbing off on you."

TEN MINUTES later I was on the rooftop balcony of the clubhouse with a rifle across my lap. Motorcycles shot out of the gate with a roar, dark shadows racing across a pale, sun-bleached landscape.

Reaper rode up front, leading the pack as usual. Hades raced at his side, long legs stretching out and fearsome jaws open with a smile. And clinging to our president's cut, Mariposa sat behind him. Her hair flew out behind her like the tail of a dark comet. Our club followed them, off to the traveling market where they would spend most of the day. Me and a skeleton crew stayed behind to guard our home and valuables.

Gunner's men had dropped off Python's body at the

front gate of Razor Wire's clubhouse four days ago. We heard no response and hopefully that was good news, but we could never be too careful.

Eventually the bikes disappeared into the horizon and the sound of roaring engines with them. The occasional screech of some bird of prey became the only sound cutting through the breeze. I lifted my face toward the sky, closing my eyes against the bright mid-morning sun.

Gunner's bird never did come close to me again since that one time we were both up here. Even if it was the same bird that gave me my sight, it didn't matter. I had no bond with any animal. Although I often wondered how I was able to hear that first bird speak, and why it chose to bestow me with the gift of my sight.

There were so many things I didn't understand, things I just never learned as I was growing up. One of the first men temporarily caged with me taught me how to read and write. He was surprised I knew how to talk. I'd heard people speak all my life. I just rarely had someone to talk to.

Another man who took the place of the first, taught me basic math and science principles. I must have been in my teens when I learned to add, subtract, and divide. I learned about the concepts of gravity and dividing time into seconds, minutes, hours, and days. He told me how the sun made plants grow, and that it nourished people too.

I became obsessed with sunlight and the sky after that. Feeling a sliver of sunlight on my face felt like a huge act of rebellion. The women would come in, cut me, and leave me bleeding, never noticing that I dared to soak up all the sunlight I could through the cracks in those dungeon walls.

The other men came and went while I was the only constant. They all taught me various things with one overarching concept becoming clearer as I got older—men were good and women were evil.

My time in prison was the start of me unlearning that idea. The male guards harassed and abused me. Jandro was the only male staff member that was kind to me. The female workers were afraid of me. That was the pattern I noticed after spending time out in the real world. I had feared women all my life and now I was the stuff of *their* nightmares.

Jandro kept telling me there was another side to them. Sometimes they smiled and laughed. They would talk softly and listen when I had something to say. If I was lucky, they'd sit in my lap and touch me. The mere idea used to send me into an anxiety attack, but Jandro assured me it was a good thing.

Regardless, none of those things ever happened to me. Even my sexual experiences happened with a sense of dread and fear hanging over me and the woman involved. I didn't know how to make them feel less afraid, so I just got it over with as quickly as possible for both our sakes.

Once I was with Mariposa, it was like everything Jandro told me had finally clicked. I liked seeing her smile and hearing her laugh, even when it wasn't directed at me. I realized being with a woman could be enjoyable beyond the fleeting pleasure of an orgasm. Sometimes it just took a while to find that person.

"No. Fuck."

I set the rifle down the moment I felt my dick begin to swell, and began pacing back and forth on the roof. "God damn it," I muttered to myself. "Stop this. Stop it. I need to stop."

There was no way I could tattoo her. Not if I couldn't stop thinking of that moment every time I heard her name or my mind drifted. I would fuck up somehow if I actually touched her. I always did. Maybe Jandro trusted me, but I sure as fuck didn't trust myself.

A sudden buzzing sound on the breeze had me cocking my head. It sounded like a bee colony looking for a new hive. I picked up the rifle again, scanning the horizon for the telltale swarm, but saw nothing but blue sky.

My grip tightened on the gun barrel as the buzzing grew increasingly louder. I blew a short, high-pitched whistle between my teeth, signaling to the other guards to stay alert.

A black spot hovering in front of the mountainside in the distance made me squint. It looked like a bird at first, casting a shadow on the ground below, but the shape was wrong. As it got closer I saw the flying, buzzing thing had four limbs connected to a single body in the middle, with the buzzing sound coming from a small propeller on each of the limbs.

The realization made me suck in a breath and bring the rifle butt against my shoulder. I waited until my shot was all but guaranteed before I fired.

My shot hit one of the limbs, sending it flipping over into a tailspin hurtling toward the ground. It crashed with a small plume of smoke just a few hundred feet outside of the gate.

"Someone go retrieve that and bring it to me!" I yelled to the men below. I wasn't a natural leader, but Reaper left me in charge. Next to him, Jandro and Gunner, I was the most senior SDMC member. The younger members would be smart to obey my orders without question.

The gate slowly opened and two dirt bikes zipped out, zooming across the desert to the crash site. I paced on the roof as I waited. The others wouldn't be back until tonight. What was I supposed to do in the meantime? I didn't make these decisions. Reaper did.

The guys retrieved the object and brought it back within minutes. I didn't want to leave my post in case I saw more, so I had them bring it up to me on the roof.

"Do you know what it is?" I asked Benji, who held the flying piece of machinery out to me. It looked vaguely like a small helicopter.

"I'm pretty sure it's a drone," he answered, turning it over in his hands. "You can use it to spy, drop off packages, stuff like that. See this?" He pointed at a small black circle on the central body. "That's a camera lens."

My blood turned to ice. I remembered a church meeting where Gunner brought up that General Tash had been looking to buy drones from us, before we found out he was working against us.

"So someone was controlling this remotely?" I asked.

"Yeah. Probably not too far away either. These things don't work over really long distances."

"Destroy it now," I barked. "The camera inside, the navigation system, whatever could send information back. I want every piece of this thing turned to dust."

Benji hesitated. "You sure? I'm not super techy, but someone here could probably get information off the chips and find out who it belongs to."

"Did I fucking stutter?" Reaper used that phrase when he got tired of repeating himself. "I already know who it belongs to."

Benji's wide eyes showed that I got the point across. "Yes, Shadow. Right away." He scampered off the roof with the drone under his arm.

Absently, I watched him and the other guys wrecking it in the street below. They took turns shooting at it, slamming it into the ground, and running over it with their bikes. I checked my rifle and returned my gaze to the sky, wondering how I would tell Reaper about this.

My hands squeezed around my weapon, ever vigilant. I silently hoped that whoever controlled the drone never got the information they were looking for.

TWENTY-FIVE

MARIPOSA

"Property of?" I glared at the jackets Noelle was holding up.

She rolled her eyes as she tossed one to me. "Don't get all high and mighty on me. It's an MC thing. If you're someone's old lady, you are considered property of that club. It means we protect you and it lets other clubs know you're off limits. Don't take it too literally, 'kay?"

I ran my fingers over the letters embroidered above the SDMC patch that all the guys wore on their cuts. An unexpected giddy feeling bubbled up in my chest. I was honestly excited to wear the demon on my back, even if I wasn't fond of the words "Property of" centered above it. Reaper and Jandro were the heart and soul of the SDMC and I was proud to display that I belonged to them. I just hoped my tattoo wouldn't require those words.

The leather jacket was already well-worn with lines and creases telling the story of its previous owners. It still fit like a glove when I slid it on, wrapping me in a new kind of armor. The type of armor that told onlookers I found safety in the arms of the most dangerous men in the Southwest.

"Why the fuck do you always look so good in my shit?" Noelle grumbled as I turned to look at the back of the jacket in her mirror.

"Don't worry," I laughed. "I'm done borrowing your stuff. I'm getting all my own clothes at the market today."

"Keep the jacket. It really does look good on you, and I don't need an extra," she told me with a wave of her hand. "What are you bringing to trade for goods?"

"Drugs, of course." I shot her a wry smile. "They're what got me here from East Texas. Pain pills, sedatives, amphetamines, you name it. If you want to feel something, there's a pill for it."

"Look at you, little dope slinger." She swatted my hip playfully. "Makes sense, considering you survived on your own this long. I don't think that's a market Gunner ever tapped into. He just doesn't have the knowledge you do."

Hearing his name brought on a twisting sensation in my stomach. He still hadn't said a word to me since after he fought, and Jandro never told me how their talk went. We could avoid each other easily enough, but nearly a week later, the pangs of missing him refused to go away.

I shook my head at Noelle, bringing my thoughts back to our conversation. "I only slung pills when I needed to pay for travel, or if real medical services weren't needed. My main priority is helping people, not profiting off of addictions."

"I know, babe. It's just interesting to know that about you." Noelle ran her tongue across her teeth. "You did dirty work to survive, but didn't backstab anyone in the process. You were a Steel Demon girl before my brother ever set eyes on you."

"Yeah, right." I blushed at the remark. "I wasn't nearly badass enough to fit in with all of you."

"Well, you're stuck with us now." She squeezed my shoulder through the worn leather jacket. "You might have noticed this already, but we're more than just a club. We're family."

"Even fighting like family members," I mumbled.

"Exactly. Now let's go shopping!" With an excited squeal, she pulled me down the stairs by the hand, practically skipping out the front door.

She wasn't the only one excited. Under the idle rumbling of engines outside, everyone was abuzz about this traveling market. Apparently it only came through the area sporadically, once a year at best since the Collapse. Because more people were nomadic these days, the market's vendors followed population density, which changed with the seasons. Most of the time, from what Reaper told me, it depended on whether a certain area was in a war zone or not.

Thanks to the Steel Demons keeping order and making agreements with local businesses, our section of the Arizona territory was considered relatively peaceful. It meant people felt safer living here, and made trading goods profitable.

The major border wars had shifted eastward, with conflict growing between the New Mexico and West Texas territories. When I passed through those areas on my journey west, the conflicts had been scattered and unorganized, run by small-time gangs with little resources or connections. General Tash, the central power in New Mexico, was highly organized and well-stocked with trained soldiers and heavy artillery, the latter of which was mostly supplied by the Steel Demons, before the general betrayed them.

Reaper and Jandro ranted at each other for half a night, fueled by whiskey and añejo tequila, about the many border conflicts surrounding us and their predictions on the generals' moves. I tried to follow and keep up, but with the booze making me drowsy and the orgasms they gave me earlier, I couldn't stay awake. But I still woke up cozy in bed and sandwiched between them, which was becoming our new routine.

"Mmm, I love that jacket on you," Jandro's honeyed voice murmured in my ear as a hug wrapped around me from behind. "When we get back, I want to get you completely naked except for the jacket."

Grinning, I looked over my shoulder for a kiss, covering his hands with mine at my waist. "If you promise to be a good boy."

"I'll be anything you want me to." His kisses moved to my neck, affectionate and sweet. "Who you riding with today?"

"Reaper on the way over." I kissed his pouting bottom lip. "You on the way back."

"Saving the best for last, I see," he smirked, then

kissed me deeply before slowly untangling himself from me. "I'll see you there, *Mariposita*."

I somehow made it over to Reaper and Hades on wobbly legs. Jandro never failed to have me swooning on my feet.

"Is that smile for me?" Reaper handed me a small mug of coffee, green eyes twinkling. Even he was in a great mood today.

"Always." I stood on tiptoes to reach his lips. "Jandro just put it there first this morning."

"That motherfucker," he growled in jest before his mouth descended on mine.

I had kissed both of them seconds apart for days now, and the contrast of Jandro's softness with Reaper's roughness never failed to send my nerves tingling. The thrill of it went straight down to my toes, concentrating in my core. Neither one was better than the other. My body craved each man for the unique pleasure he gave me.

We finished kissing and I drained the coffee before handing the mug back to him.

"Ready, sugar?" He screwed the mug back on the thermos cup and handed me my helmet.

"I still think you should wear one of these," I said, pulling it over my hair.

"I'll buy one today," he grinned.

Liar.

———

AFTER AN HOUR of riding through an uninhabited desert, colors and movement began to appear on the horizon. I popped up my visor and squinted over Reaper's shoulder. The colors expanded outward in both directions. I started to see tents and canopies, and what looked like metal shining in the sun.

By the time Reaper slowed, the club was pulling up to what resembled a bright and lively downtown district. This market was a whole lot more than just a few vendors selling things at tables. A pair of musicians played on a guitar and drums while children danced. One stall roasted a huge pig over a bonfire, turning it slowly on a spit. A repurposed taco truck advertised wood-fired pizza. The cute little cart next to it said, "Fresh-baked cookies!"

Every kind of food imaginable was here, and hundreds of other vendors on top of that. Just scanning from the bike I saw jewelry, clothes, furniture, books, teas, and candles. I began to see why everyone was so excited about coming here. It was a feast for the eyes. and one that made it easy to part with your goods to trade.

When Reaper pulled up to park at the crudely erected gate just outside the market, I only then noticed the other motorcycles parked in the area across from us.

"Reaper."

"I know, sugar. Other clubs are here to do business too, but they're nothing to worry about." He swung a leg off the bike, then picked me up by the waist to set me on the ground. "Just keep this jacket on at all times. Got it?"

"Yes, president," I teased.

"Fuck, you just had to call me that while wearing a *property* jacket." He stroked a thumb across my cheek. "You're so fuckin' hot, you know that?"

"Aww, thanks Rory." I grabbed his belt loops and pulled him closer. Somewhere behind me, Jandro cracked up laughing.

"And boner ruined," Reaper grumbled.

"There's pills for that, you know."

"Shut your damn mouth." Capturing my face between his palms, the kiss he gave me prevented me from doing just that. "Don't wander too far," he whispered against my lips. "Stay with Noelle, or anyone else in the club. And remember—"

"Keep the jacket on, I know."

"Good girl." A final kiss. "Love you." He sent me off with a swat on the ass to Noelle, who waited for me at the market entrance.

"He sent you away fast." She narrowed her eyes in suspicion at her brother as we started walking through a narrow path between colorful stalls. "I thought he'd want you glued to his side."

"What, you think he's up to something?" I looked back briefly. He was just digging into his saddle bags like the rest of the guys.

"You never know with him. Nothing bad, of course," she assured me at my wide-eyed expression. "You keep his dick locked in a cage as far as he's concerned. He's not going anywhere in that sense."

Now that she pointed it out, I was going to keep thinking about it if I didn't have a distraction.

"Let's find something for Tessa," I said. "Not for the baby, but a gift just for her."

Noelle grabbed my arm with an excited squeak. "That's a great idea! The poor thing probably hasn't gotten a nice non-baby related gift in years. Let's see, she loves anything to do with flowers…"

Noelle ended up picking out a hand-painted sunflower wall hanging and I got Tess a candle that smelled like roses. I couldn't read the foreign writing on the label, but the candle had a picture of a motorcycle on the tin, which seemed fitting.

We stuffed our faces with street food and meandered for hours. The market seemed to stretch on forever! I still hadn't found much clothing in my style, so while Noelle paused to look at garden statues, I moved on to a shop with lots of pretty fabrics billowing nearby.

The garments were lightweight and decorated in every color and pattern imaginable. A few mannequins showed their versatility—wrapped around the body to make a halter dress, a long skirt, or around the head for a scarf. It seemed like a great solution to keep the sand out of my hair while riding.

I flipped through the selections on the table when a tiny, elderly woman emerged from under her canopy and gave me a wide, toothless smile.

"Ohh, you!" She pointed at me. "So beautiful! You must try on, yes? Please try!"

I smiled back, taking note of her broken English and heavy accent. "*Español?*" I was still rusty at the language, but Jandro had recently started teaching me more. Might as well practice it out in the wild.

"Oh no." The woman waved her hands and shook her head. "No, no, no. Is okay! Please just try!" She snatched the length of fabric I was holding with surprising strength and moved behind me, holding it out as if to put it around my shoulders.

"Oh, you don't have to do that." I turned around and held out my hand to take it back from her. "But thank you."

Undeterred, she waved the fabric at me. "You try on! So beautiful! I give you so cheap! Please!"

Deciding to humor her, I relented, turning around and lowering to her level so she could put the scarf on me. Rather than putting it over my shoulders like I thought she would, she proceeded to tug at my jacket collar.

"Take off. You must try on."

"Hey, hey, take it easy!" The jacket slid to my elbows with how insistently she tugged at it. I was already thoroughly turned off from buying anything from her, but didn't want to cause a scene in a crowded market. I'd try on the scarf, take it off, and politely tell her I wasn't interested.

I allowed her to peel the jacket from my arms, intending to hold it or tie it around my waist, but she suddenly turned and ran behind her stall with it.

"Hey, what the fuck!" I took off after her, mad as hell. "Give that back, you fucking thief!" I pushed fabrics out of the way, chasing her at full speed and crashed into a wall.

No, not a wall. Just a very solidly-built man. Tree-trunk sized arms came around me, crushing me against an unyielding chest.

"She the one?" A gruff voice above me asked.

Someone else lifted the back of my shirt, prompting me to kick and flail with all my strength, which wasn't much against the man restraining me.

"Don't touch me!" I shrieked. "Ugh, let me go!"

A bony hand grabbed my face and turned my head cruelly to look at one of my captors. His face was dark and lined with years of harsh sun exposure. I saw myself frozen with fear in his harsh, dark eyes. Who were these men? And what did they want with me?

"You got any club ink?" the face-grabber asked me. "Think carefully. I got no problem stripping you down and finding out myself."

I knew he wasn't lying. If he would just get out of my face so I could see one of my men…

"N-no," I answered. "But I had a property jacket. I'm with the Steel Demons and you assholes are *so* fucked!"

Both of them chuckled at my false bravado. "I don't see any jacket. Nor any of them pussy Demon fuckwads anywhere."

"They're here!" I insisted at the top of my lungs, though my voice barely carried over the hustle and bustle of the market. "And when they find out I'm missing, you're in for a world of hurt."

"How about you shut up and let that cunt do the talking?" He grabbed between my legs and I felt the first real jolt of terror wrack my body. These men were probably looking for unclaimed women at the market to sell.

What did they give that old lady so she could take my jacket away?

Thankfully the chaps over my jeans provided an extra barrier between me and his groping hand. Still, my stomach roiled and tears sprang to my eyes. No, this couldn't be happening. After all this time wandering alone, then finding love and safety in the last place I expected it, and this was it? Meeting my end by getting tricked in a marketplace? Because I would rather die than endure what these men would put me through.

"Get her on the truck." The groper finally pulled his hand away from my crotch and wrapped it around my throat. "If you keep quiet, I won't hafta cut your tongue out. You understand?"

I gave a shaky nod with my head and allowed myself to be dragged away.

TWENTY-SIX

GUNNER

Too many people. Too many weird smells. Too much bullshit.

This market was seriously lacking compared to the other ones I'd been to. Or maybe it was just my sour mood.

Nothing brought me out of my funk, no matter how much flying, riding, or swimming I did. Only seeing *her* lifted my spirits. Mari. She didn't need to kiss my wounds, just her voice and her soft touch was healing enough. Even I had to admit she seemed much happier in the past week than when we first brought her home. I always knew she belonged in the club, whether or not she was with me.

Then Jandro or Reaper would kiss her, sometimes they both did at the same time, and my mood took another fucking nosedive. If three was a crowd, four would be downright suffocating. I guess for them it made some sense. Jandro and Reaper were already best friends when I met them. They did everything together. I never saw it, but certainly wouldn't be surprised if they shared a woman before.

It wasn't just that they both had her, but how easily the three of them seemed to connect as a single unit. Mari and Jandro would share a joke at Reaper's expense, he'd grumble about it, then she turned around and was all cute and silly with him. They acted like this three-way relationship was completely normal, natural even.

But it wasn't. And after some time, they would see that. The whole thing would come crashing down and I refused to be caught in the middle when that happened. I refused to be a reason Mari got hurt.

You're hurting her right now, douchebag. You saw those fucking tears in her eyes when she left you in her office.

I shook my head as if to clear away the dissenting thoughts and threw back another beer. I found the brewer's stall right away and had been parked here for a good hour, but I was nowhere near as fucked up as the night I fought Big G. That was a mistake. An even bigger mistake was letting Jandro see right through me. I didn't know how he caught onto that, but that fucker was nothing if not perceptive.

Shutting my eyes, I let my consciousness slip in Horus's. He was sitting on a cactus just behind the market, watching for rabbits and ground squirrels. A sound rattled through his mind and my own, pulling me back into my own body with confusion. It was hard to make out over all the noise in the market, but I cocked my head and listened again.

"Gunn…!"

I swore I heard my name being shouted but something wasn't…

"…rus! Gunner! Help me!"

"Fuck, Mari!"

I ejected off of the barstool and started running, slipping into Horus again to use his eyesight. There she was, being dragged off by two slimy-looking fuckers toward a box truck.

"Stop them, Horus!" I pumped my arms and legs as fast as they would carry me, but no animal on earth was faster than a peregrine falcon diving for an attack.

He came down like a bullet just as I turned a corner and saw them with my own eyes. The big guy carrying her got a neck full of talon from my loyal bird, forcing him to release Mari with a bloodcurdling scream.

"Gunner!"

"Come here, baby girl! I got you!" I held my arm out to her while drawing one of my guns with the other. She curled into me, trembling as she clutched at my cut. I wrapped a protective arm around her back while scoping out what I was up against with a sinking feeling of dread.

The other guy had a gun on me, standing over his big friend, who was still bleeding profusely from the neck. Horus was nowhere to be seen, but he'd done his job. The big fucker was growing pale and would be dead within an hour. But more of their crew started coming out of the woodwork—from behind the truck and hiding places between crowded stalls. All of them armed.

Fucking sex traffickers. They must have been

scouting this place for fresh merchandise. I had no idea how they managed to touch Mari and get her jacket off, but it was too late to dwell on that now. My only hope for her safety was to convince these shitbags she was already my property.

Literally.

"Sorry for what I'm about to say," I mumbled into her hair before raising my head to address the men closing in on me. "This woman belongs to me!" I declared, keeping my shooting arm outstretched. "None of you had a right to touch her."

"She's not tatted, Demon," the scrawny guy with a gun on me snarled. "Where's your proof?"

"She's a new purchase, so I haven't inked her yet, but I have a receipt. It's on my bike."

"What, and let your club gut us? No, thanks."

Damn it. Mari must have told them we were all here. They weren't buying it and my hope started to dwindle. Thankfully, she caught on and made a convincing actress.

"It's true!" She peeked back fearfully at the trafficker as she molded her body to mine. I clenched my teeth against the sensations of her hips and and hands on me. This was the wrong time to enjoy it. "This is my master. My body is his."

"Prove it," the dipshit said again while a dozen guns cocked. Mari flinched at the sound and glanced up at me with terror in her eyes.

"I'm sorry," she whispered, bringing a trembling finger to my jaw. "I know you don't want this, but—"

Her lips tilted up to mine with the softest ghost of

contact. How I wanted to savor the warmth of her breath on my mouth, to taste her slowly and explore her kiss properly. To do so with no one else around us, just me and her learning about each other this way. But our very lives were on the line, and I had to play the part of a callous slave owner.

So I grabbed the back of her head and claimed her mouth roughly, choking off her gasp with my tongue. She went along with it, wrapping her arms around my neck and digging her fingers into my ponytail. Her leg lifted to wrap around my hip, drawing me tighter into her body. I couldn't figure out whether to be sorry or glad this wasn't real. I never would've kissed her for the first time like this. But I may also never get a chance to kiss her again.

"Quit fuckin' around!" the small guy with a gun roared. "This bullshit proves fuck-all."

"Well, what do you want?" I demanded. "I told you my receipt is on my bike!"

His mouth twisted into a cruel smile.

"Describe her pussy *in detail*. I'm talking size, shape, color, and any marks she's got down there. Then we'll check to make sure you're right."

Fuck.

"Her tits too," one of his homeboys added.

"She's not yours to inspect," I growled. "You're not touching my property and lowering her value."

"Think of it as verification," he said smugly. "Which you conveniently can't seem to do."

Shit, shit, shit. My eyes darted around, looking for any possible way out. We'd be shot before I could squeeze my trigger. Reaper and Jandro had gone off to a completely different side of the market and no one else was around. I purposely went off by myself because I was tired of getting the third degree from everyone.

And it was a good thing I did. Otherwise Mari would've been captured and completely alone. I stayed away from her enough in the past two weeks. I wasn't about to leave her now.

My arm tightened around her shoulders as my gun hand lowered slowly. "I don't give a fuck who you all are. She's mine and I'm not letting her go."

"Suit yourself," the scrawny guy shrugged. "You're almost pretty enough to pass for a bitch." He jerked his head toward the box truck. "Get in."

His gang moved in, took my gun, and patted me down for the rest of my weapons. When they succeeded in fully disarming me, they ushered us into the back of the truck. The big guy bleeding from the neck was shoved, then dragged, out of the way. He was completely motionless and must have died minutes ago.

Just before they pulled the door down to seal us in darkness, I saw my falcon diving across the sky.

JANDRO

"Nah, nah, nah, man," I waved my hand at the auto parts vendor. "Your prices and your parts are bullshit. Don't be trying to hawk this cheap shit at me. I know you got Harley branded clutches. Where they at?"

The guy switched to Spanish to pretend like he didn't understand me, then looked like a damn fool when I told him off in a rapid string of insults that would've earned me one hell of a beatdown from my aunt.

He finally quit trying to swindle me and I got an alright deal on the parts I needed. This whole bartering system wore me out. I didn't have Gunner's patience for getting the best deal I could. Maybe one day we'd have a national currency and fixed prices again, but I wasn't holding my breath.

I made my way over to Reaper and Hades emerging from one of the metalsmith stalls. Hades' nose immediately went to my pants pocket, sniffing aggressively at the brown paper bag I had stashed in there.

"Okay, pooch." I held up an index finger. "*One* doughnut hole. That's all you get, all right?"

He licked his lips and stared up at me expectantly. I pulled the snack from my pocket and tossed it in the air so he could catch it in his mouth. Reaper shook his head disapprovingly.

"You're gonna fatten him up like a Christmas ham."

"Nah, he'll run those calories off on the way back." I nodded at the small drawstring bag in his hand. "You get what you need?"

"Yeah. Will you tell me what you think of this?" He glanced up at me as he opened the bag, and I dare say he looked nervous.

Inside the bag was a velvet ring box. He popped it open and carefully lifted the ring from the cushion to show me.

"Damn, dude." I accepted it carefully, turning it over to see the light catch the stone. "You did good."

Polished to a high shine, the stone in the center shifted from pink to green depending on which way the light hit it. Ridges and formations within the stone made it look like a tiny landscape full of depth. A microscopic world of canyons, valleys, and meadows.

The setting was a simple silver bezel, sitting on top of a band that twined around like a length of rope. The letter R was stamped on one side of the band, and the letter M on the other.

"You think she'll like it?" Reaper asked with more than a hint of eagerness.

"She'll love it, bro. She's gonna flip." I grinned as I handed the ring back to him. "What kind of rock is that?"

"Watermelon tourmaline," he said softly, examining it one last time before returning it to the box. "It was one of my mom's stones. The setting was hers too. I just needed to find a smith that could put it together."

"Awww, look at you, Reap!" I gave him a good-natured punch to the shoulder. "Make sure you tell her that. Girls love that sentimental shit. When are you giving it to her?"

"I dunno, not today." He wrapped the drawstring bag around the ring box and slid it into the inner pocket of his cut. "When it feels right."

I rubbed the back of my neck. "I uh, might've gotten her something too. Not all sentimental like yours, but something I thought she'd like."

"Yeah?" His eyebrows lifted. "Let's see it, Romeo."

I dug through my pack, reaching for the pocket I carefully sectioned off from my tools and bike parts, and produced the slender, shallow box.

Reaper took it from me and carefully pulled off the lid, looking up at me with wide eyes and a grin when he saw the necklace laying on the tissue paper.

"Jandro, are you fucking serious?"

"Please don't tell me it's lame," I begged. "I traded a set of perfectly good spark plugs for it."

"No, dude. This is really nice." He lifted the pendant, a monarch butterfly, and carefully ran his thumb over the surface. "What is this, iron and stained glass?"

"Yeah. She said the wings were made from windows in a cathedral. Probably a bunch of bullshit, but it made me think of Mari when I saw it, so—"

"She'll love it." He replaced the box lid and handed it back to me just as a low growl emitted from Hades' throat.

"Oh, you don't think so, pooch?" I slipped the necklace back into my pack. "Should I give Mari the rest of your doughnut holes instead?"

"Something's wrong," Reaper muttered, his fingertips drifting over Hades' raised hackles. "Where *is* Mari?"

"She went off with Noelle last I saw." I pointed in the general direction, but Hades was already taking off in a completely different direction. He cut straight through the center of the market, heading for the back side.

Reaper and I followed him without a moment's hesitation, dodging shoppers and vendors alike. When the dog broke into a full-on sprint, my hand drifted to the gun in my holster. Reaper did the same, hand-gun already drawn as we hurried to keep Hades in our sight. He started barking his head off, which helped to get people out of our way.

We reached the last row of stalls and pushed through, with only the barren desert to greet us. It wasn't too windy but a fair amount of dust had kicked up and stung the hell out of my eyes.

"Look!" I grabbed Reaper's shoulder and pointed to someone laying motionless in the dirt.

It wasn't Mari, but a big dude who had bled out

from a serious injury from the looks of it. We turned him over and found that his neck had been shredded, like someone started decapitating him with a rusty saw and abruptly stopped.

"What the fuck?" Reaper whispered in disbelief.

"Your guess is as good as mine." I began searching his pockets, lifting up his shirt for any tattoos or signs of who this guy might be. "He hasn't been dead long, that's for sure."

"Look," Reaper pointed. "Tire tracks."

My heart nearly collapsed in on itself like a black hole. "Those are big tires. Some kind of truck."

"Oh God…" Reaper tipped his head back, grabbing a chunk of hair in his fist. I knew we were both thinking the worst—human traffickers.

"No time to worry. Let's round up the Demons," I slapped his shoulder hard to make him focus. "And follow those fuckin' tracks. Where's Gunner?"

Our answer came in the form of a screech and a fast-moving shadow above our heads. Hades stood on his hind legs, barking at the falcon who clutched something in his talons.

"Shit." The color drained from Reaper's face. "They got Gunner too?"

Horus screeched again and released what he was holding--a scrap of the property patch from Mari's jacket.

I couldn't tell how he knew, but Reaper somehow understood what this animal communicated to him. His expression contorted into one of pure hatred. Not even when we caught Python did he look this pissed.

"Horus can see the truck from over a mile away," he said with an eerie calm. "They couldn't have gotten far. Hell, they're probably not even a mile away right now."

"We can be on 'em in minutes, then," I said, my blood simmering. Python got it easy compared to what these scumbags were in for. Snatching women from a public market was bad enough, but to rip *our* patch off of our woman and not think there would be retribution for it? The entire Arizona territory would hear about this. Fuck, the entire Southwest would. I hoped our revenge would reach General Tash's ears and make him shiver just a little.

"Hades, follow those tracks. We'll catch up." The dog took off, following Reaper's orders. Horus soared high, following Hades from above. If I wasn't so messed up with worry about Mari, it would've weirded me out how humanlike the animals' responses were. Not that it was that different from how they usually acted, but this time was particularly obvious.

Reaper then turned to me, his face hard and determined. "Round up the Demons. We're getting our girl back."

TWENTY-EIGHT

MARIPOSA

Gunner never let go of me. The walls he set up between us over the past two weeks collapsed into nothing the moment he saw I was in trouble. From that moment at the market to our dark, musty prison in the back of the truck, he held me as tightly as either of my men would.

"They're coming to get us, baby girl," he assured me, lips against my forehead. "Reaper and Jandro already found the body. Horus is right above us and Hades isn't far behind. Our people will be on these fuckers like flies on shit."

Somewhere in the back of my mind I remembered Reaper telling me of Gunner's otherworldly ability to see through his falcon's eyes, but his words didn't register. I was in some state of shock. Either by pure, dumb luck or something else altogether, I had never gotten this close to being truly kidnapped. The Steel Demons taking me out of Old Phoenix didn't count, as they technically rescued me from people who would have pimped me out. I just didn't know it at the time.

My hands groped in the darkness, feeling for Gunner's hands, his face, his hair. Anything to paint a full picture of him in my mind and confirm he was really here.

"I'm so sorry you ended up here with me—"

"Stop." His thumb caressed over my lips, halting the guilt bubbling out of me. "Don't apologize. You think I'd let you get taken on your own? Not a chance. You're safer with me."

I tucked my head under his chin, seeking comfort in the space next to his neck. He smoothed out my hair in a gentle, repetitive motion. Being near him was always calming in a hypnotic way, just like when he taught me to float on my back.

"What are they gonna do?" I asked, my lips pressed to his throat.

"Strip us down. Appraise us like cattle to determine how much value we have," he said matter-of-factly. "They won't hurt us. We're merchandise to them and our value will decrease if we're injured. The club will reach us before they find buyers. We just have to sit tight, baby girl."

He sounded so sure, so confident. Not a single tremor in his voice or his hands soothing me. I wished I could soak up his fearlessness and wrap it around me like a shield. The Steel Demons had a reputation for power and no mercy to their enemies, but what if these people were their match? This world was filled with predators, each bigger and hungrier than the last. Even

Reaper had to know he wouldn't stay at the top of the food chain forever. There was always someone bigger.

I had no sense of time in the darkness of that truck. We could have driven for twenty minutes or two hours, for all I knew. Once we stopped, a fresh burst of fear spread throughout my chest. I heard the truck cab's doors opening and slamming shut, then the quick footsteps of the scrawny guy walking around to the back.

Light flooded in as the door rolled up. I shielded my eyes with Gunner's chest while his arms tightened around me.

"Get up." Cruel, bony fingers grabbed my arm and pulled me roughly to my feet. Scrawny guy was surprisingly strong for his size.

"Hey, take it easy!" Gunner glared as he sprang up from the floor. "She's still mine, despite this bullshit charade. Don't leave bruises on my property."

I didn't know why he was still keeping up the act. It was clear they didn't care.

Three more guys walked up the ramp to grab him, their holstered weapons clearly on display. Even with an unarmed Steel Demon, they weren't taking any chances. Together, they walked us out of the truck.

With a few quick blinks I realized we weren't out in the desert in direct sun, but somewhere shaded. Large rock formations loomed all around us. The ground felt cool for a change, and had quite a bit more grass and vegetation growing due to the lack of harsh sun.

As we walked through, I saw that the rock formations contained dozens of caves and small alcoves within them. Supplies and personal items sat within the grooves of several walls like shelves. If I wasn't so terrified, it would have been fascinating to see how these people turned this natural formation into a permanent home. It made sense—this place provided strong shelter that didn't succumb to harsh wind or rain, and the caves gave a sense of privacy.

Our captors led us through a short tunnel that opened to a large, open room. I couldn't call it a cave because it had no ceiling. The sun illuminated a flat area in the center like a spotlight. We were shoved directly to that spotlight, where dark iron chains and manacles had been hammered into the rocky ground.

I wondered, through the numb fear in my mind, how many people had stood here before. One manacle clapped around my ankle, the other around Gunner's. How many frightened women, children, and even men had been bound here in such a dehumanizing way?

Without another word our captors retreated into the tunnels, leaving us alone. The chains didn't give us much movement, only about three feet or so around the spike anchoring it to the ground. But we were still close enough to hold each other. Just like in the truck, we sat together on the floor, me wrapped up in him.

Gunner gave a few tugs to his spike with no result. Next, he tried sliding one of the chain links under the head to use leverage to pull it up. No dice. After giving up on his own chain, he tried to do the same with mine.

"Stop." I took his hands away from the iron and brought them clasped between us. "I'm sure they'll punish you for trying to escape."

"Good. It'll distract them from paying attention to

you." But he didn't go back to testing the chains. Instead he brought my hands to his lips and pressed soothing kisses to my knuckles.

"You picked a hell of a time to start being sweet to me." Despite the dire situation, my insides fluttered at the warmth of his lips.

He raised those gorgeous blue eyes to me, sadness and regret pooling in them. "I'm sorry, Mari. I'm just trying to make you feel safer. I'm not thinking about before or what'll happen once we're back. Maybe it's selfish, but I'm taking this one second at a time, and I'm all you got right now. So I'm going to be what you need."

We were already so close, it was impossible to tell who leaned in first. In the next moment, we were simply kissing. It was nothing like the rough, possessive grab in the market. Gunner was warm and sweet, but still kissed me with a sense of urgency, like we would be ripped away from each other at any second.

I wound my fingers through his hair, gliding my tongue across his to deepen the kiss. I didn't want this to be the last time, but the first of many more to come. This didn't have to be just because I was afraid and didn't have anyone else to lean on. I desperately wanted him to see that, to know I'd been wanting this for weeks, if not the past month. My feelings for him were real, they always had been. And being in love with two other men didn't diminish them in the least.

"Gunner."

"Shh." He sipped another sweet kiss from me,

cradling my face in his hands. "Don't say anything, baby girl. Don't remind me that you're not really mine."

"Gunner…" His name came out in a choked plea that time, my throat already closing up with heartache.

What was the point of all this if he was just going to return me back to my men and ignore me all over again? My heart couldn't take this yanking around from him. I'd rather deal with Reaper's cold shoulder over this.

A series of footsteps echoed throughout our stone prison before I could say any more. The guys who captured us returned, solemnly leading another person through the tunnels toward us. As they fanned out to the sides of our open room, I was shocked to see a woman walking straight toward the flat area where we were shackled.

She was attractive in a cold, bitchy way. I estimated her to be in her late thirties or early forties. Pale blonde hair was pulled back in a French braid, the length of it falling over the front of her shoulder. Icy blue eyes peered at us shrewdly. She was dressed like a soldier, in a camo jumpsuit with black laced-up boots. Just by the way she walked, I could tell the uniform wasn't just for show. By the men's stiff spines and sharp eyes at attention, all signs pointed to this woman running the operation.

"I had to see for myself to believe it," she mused, her footsteps halting just out of reach of our chains. "A Steel Demon, and one who came willingly." She all but ignored me, her eyes resting on Gunner appreciatively.

Turning to her men, she asked, "Did someone search him for a tattoo to be sure?"

Silence answered her. A few of them swallowed nervously.

"THEN WHAT THE FUCK ARE YOU WAITING FOR!"

Her shout came so loud and suddenly, even Gunner flinched. The sound echoed off the stone walls, repeating her wrath down to the men who rushed at us to fulfill her order.

Three of her minions wrenched Gunner away from me, two of them holding him still while the others stripped off his cut and then his T-shirt. Both clothing items discarded in the dirt, they victoriously turned him around to show the proud, grinning demon inked onto his upper back.

"So it is true," the woman purred. "And what role do you play in your little biker gang, handsome?"

He turned back around to face her, wrenching his arms out of the grips of the men who held him.

"My title is the arms dealer," he answered flatly. "But I oversee all the major exchanges of goods into the club."

"I see." The woman began a slow walk around us, eyes feasting on Gunner like he was the main course of a five-star meal. He ignored her and drew me back into his chest. Despite trying to hide in his embrace, the woman seemed to notice me for the first time. "And who is this?"

"My woman. I purchased her." He threw a glare at the men surrounding us. "Your goons were trying to steal her, then ignored me when I offered to show them my receipt! Once I'm outta here, I'll make damn sure no one buys skin from you, lady! What kind of business are you running here, trying to poach what's already owned?"

"Firstly, my name is Corinne. Remember it. You'll be moaning my name tonight." She paused in her appraisal of his body to give a cruel smirk. "And secondly, I know for a fact that you're lying. It's common knowledge that the Steel Demons don't deal in flesh. Fortunately for us, that makes the trade far less competitive. And keeps you out of the loop."

Gunner's hands on me stiffened, pulling me into him ever so slightly with protective determination. Corinne continued walking her circle around us, sizing him up as she probably fantasized all the ways she wanted him.

"Now that we've established the girl is not owned by you, I frankly don't care who or what she is." Her gaze leveled on me, heavy with loathing and disdain. "Females are always in demand, so she'll go with the rest of them. As long as you have functioning holes for cocks, sweetie, you'll have purpose here."

I never saw a smile so evil in my life. What happened to this woman, what twisted her mind up in such a way that she treated fellow women, let alone any human beings, in such a way?

"As for you." Her voice took on a more wistful tone as she returned to looking at Gunner. "You put me in a predicament, Demon. Your body is an exquisite specimen to be sure, but male flesh is a harder sell."

"A hole's a hole," Gunner shrugged. "Throw me to

your buyers, not her. If the only requirement is a hole to stick cocks in, why does male or female matter?"

"Gunner!" I hissed in a whisper. It was bad enough that he got dragged along with me at all. I was *not* going to let him be sold off in my place.

"Just further proof you know nothing about the subtleties of this industry," Corinne said. "Ultimately it comes down to a hole, yes, but what I'm selling are fantasies. A buyer comes to me with an image of a perfect bedroom companion already in his mind. My job is to match that description with an actual body. Rarely are my buyers women. And they're even pickier in their fantasies than the men."

She motioned at one of her men, who pulled me away from Gunner. "Stop! What are you doing?" I demanded but there was no use fighting. He dragged me back until the iron cuff bit into my ankle. I could only watch in horror and rage as Corinne approached Gunner and ran a finger just above the waistline of his pants.

He shoved her hand away with a snarl. "Don't fucking touch me."

"Elric?" she chirped.

The scrawny man who snatched me at the market walked up with a satisfied smirk. He flipped his gun around to hold it backwards, then slammed the stock into Gunner's stomach.

"No!" I tried to run to him, but my feet wheeled in midair. My guard held me back like I was weightless as I watched helplessly.

Gunner doubled over, choking on ragged, pained

breaths. Corinne grabbed his shoulders to make him stand upright again, then ran a hand sensually over his chest and abs. This time, he didn't push her hand away.

"You are exactly what my female clientele is looking for," she drawled with huskiness in her voice. "Good skin. Nice muscles. A handsome face." Her hand slid into his pants, groping unabashedly as he winced and squirmed, but her guards held him in place. "Nicely-sized dick too. Although there's still the question of whether you know how to use it." She looked over her shoulder at me, utterly nonplussed at my horrified face. "What do you think, sweetheart? You want to take a test drive to see if he provides a satisfying experience?" Her hand slid back up his body all the way to his neck, where she grabbed his jaw with a rough hand. "If he knows how to make a woman come, I just might have to keep him for myself."

"Why are you doing this?" I demanded, tears springing to my eyes. Watching her grope and grab him was too fucking much. His eyes had gone vacant, his mind off somewhere else while she made her dehumanizing assessment of him.

Corinne turned back to face me, her carefully drawn eyebrows raised in smug indignation. "I do this because no one says I can't." A manicured hand went to her hip. "Because it's what I'm good at. Because we all had to resort to extremes in order to survive the Collapse. And because if I didn't," she lifted her chin at me, "it could've been me chained up for sale and you lording over me, touching a man I love."

I shook my head, the tears falling freely now and

making dark spots on the ground at my feet. "I'd never subject another woman to this. I'd never treat *anyone* like this."

She tilted her head at me with a pitying, patronizing look. "That's why you're chained to a rock and I run an empire, sweetheart."

REAPER

My tires flew over the sand like I barely touched the earth at all. Hades sprinted about twenty feet ahead of me, his paws also barely on the ground. At my back, my club rode in a tight formation with Jandro just over my right shoulder and Dallas on my left. Usually an easygoing smiling pair, each of them wore solemn grimaces as we rode hard.

Dallas wasn't in love with Mari, but they had grown close and he considered her family. Every man behind me did. We were going to war for her.

I never got eyes on the truck that had taken Mari and Gunner, and judging by Hades' running pace, that was intentional. Seeing them meant they could see us, or worse, hear us. We could've caught up quickly, but since we were going in blind to our enemies, it was better to keep them unaware.

Hades veered us toward a large outcropping of sedimentary rock. He didn't use words, never unless he told me who to kill, but I understood his meaning all the same, and signaled to my men.

We pulled up the shady side and parked the bikes, cutting off the engines quickly. I swung a leg off just before coming to a complete stop. "Where is she?" I demanded the dog who had run up to my side. "Where's our girl, Hades?"

He looked at the rock towering over us, placed his front paws against it, and whined. I looked up the steep rock face, as tall as a three-story building, and saw nothing but…rock. I scratched his ears, looking into those deep, dark eyes.

"I don't understand. Is she up there?"

His head fell back in a long howl that morphed into a bark. The next thing I felt was my ear getting pierced.

"Ow, fuck!"

Horus nipped at my ear again with that crazy sharp beak. Making soft chirps, he released the chunk of rock wall and set those talons into my shoulder.

"Jesus fucking Christ! How does Gunner walk around with you like this all the fucking time?"

"They want you to climb to the top, Reap," Jandro observed, craning his neck. "I don't think anything's up there, but maybe you can see where they're keeping her."

"Are you fucking kidding me?" I stared up at the sheer rock face in front of me going straight up to the sky. "Maybe you two missed the memo," I said to the animals, "but I don't have wings, or claws, or four fucking legs."

"There's footholds and edges to grab." Jandro

wedged his foot into a little nook in the rock, then pulled himself up a few feet, arms and legs out to the side like a gecko.

"You coming with me then?"

"Better if only one of us fell and broke our neck than two, don'tcha think?"

"Fuck, we don't have time for this." I went to my saddlebags and pulled out a set of riding gloves with the fingers cut off. After pulling them over my wrists, I stretched my fingers out and got to climbing.

The first twenty feet or so wasn't so bad. I made it about halfway up before my dumbass decided to look down.

"Jesus." I never had an issue with heights, but I now knew why some people did. It was a long, rocky way back down to the bottom. I didn't even think about how I'd get back down.

The wind up here also felt much stronger than on the ground. I felt it pushing me around like a leaf on a tree branch, only my fingers were far less likely to stay connected.

I pushed on, with Horus occasionally hovering around me and chirping like a small, feathered cheerleader. The gloves were a good idea, but the soft leather was quickly getting shredded by the sharp rocks. The rock wall started biting into my palms, and not even my thick calluses could protect me. I ignored the trickle of blood running down my forearm. I was too close to stop now.

"Ah, fuck!"

One of my footholds tumbled loose and I found

myself scrambling for a hold. My knees crashed into the rock face as my hands cramped painfully to bear my entire weight. A small shower of pebbles rained down, quickly going silent as they hurtled toward the earth. I never wanted to be a tiny rock so badly before now. If I fell I'd bounce and be unharmed, rather than raw meat splattered all over the place.

I took a breath. And then another. And one more.

I was still here, clinging to this cliff face for fuck knows what reason.

A harsh laugh escaped my lungs at the sheer absurdity of it all. I followed my dog and a bird to this wall, and was only climbing it because they indicated I should. If Mari was here, she'd be trying to make me see how impossible and unscientific this was.

But she's not here. The whole reason you're doing this is because she's not here.

Hades had been silent in my head ever since Python's execution, but I swore my bond to him only grew stronger since Mariposa came into our lives. That first night she spent with Jandro, he wasn't sleeping at the foot of my bed like usual. When I got up to take a piss in the middle of the night, I didn't see him anywhere. Stumbling around my house half-asleep, I finally found him sitting at a window, looking toward Jandro's house.

When he growled in the market right before he started running, I felt *his* fear and rage separate from my own. It was like I could feel him in some compartmentalized part of myself that I never knew was there. I couldn't even place if I felt him in my body or somewhere in my mind. All I knew was we felt the same thing, in the same space, but separately.

Whatever he was—dog, god, or something else—I trusted him. He cared about Mari and sought to protect her. And I knew that without him, my girl would be long gone.

Looking up, the top of the rock wall was only a few feet above me. Two more pulls and I'd be there. My hands were a bloody mess, but I couldn't let that stop me. I gritted my teeth against the pain of my torn-open palms as I secured new handholds. *One, two, three, pull up—*

"No!"

The rock I grabbed came loose and my arms were windmilling. My hands held nothing. Everything slowed down as I teetered backwards, the rock wall getting further and further away as I tried desperately to grab for it. Only my heel remained connected as sorrow filled me and the open, endless sky filled my vision.

I love you, Mari. I'm so sorry...

Pain sliced through the top of my back. I didn't expect to hit the ground so fast. Eyes closed, I waited for pain to wrack the rest of my mangled body and for death to take me.

Except it never came.

"Screeeeech!"

Horus cried out right next to my ear, but why...

I cracked one eye open, then the other to find myself staring at the rock face with my foot still connected.

And something holding onto the back of my cut.

"Horus?" I twisted my neck around trying to figure out how I was hovering with all but one foot in midair.

Another piercing screech filled my head, then the sound of cloth ripping as I dropped a few inches. I scrambled for the wall, leaning my weight forward. Only when I was secure did Horus's talons unhook from the back of my shirt.

"No fucking way…"

The falcon, no bigger than a raven, flew to perch at the very top of the rock only a few inches away from my hands. He looked at me, tilting his head in a way that was eerily human. I never heard Horus speak like Hades, but if he was saying anything, it had to be something like, *Yeah, I weigh two pounds and I just saved your ass, motherfucker. Now you gonna finish what you started, or what?*

My hands reached the edge. All the pain was gone, either from the adrenaline or the sheer disbelief at being alive. I hauled myself up, placed one boot on solid ground, and then the other. I could've kissed the ground beneath my feet, but I wasn't done yet.

"All right. I'm up here," I said to the bird. "Now what?"

He turned and walked on those wickedly curved talons toward the far edge of the rock. It wasn't completely flat up here, so I carefully sidestepped boulders and ridges to follow him. The moment I saw what was on the horizon, I dropped down out of sight, peering around a boulder.

Not five hundred feet from here was another huge rock formation, at least ten times the size of this one. Formed by millions of years of erosion from wind and rain, dozens of tunnels and caves had been carved into the stone. And parked outside one of the caves, surrounded by armed guards, was a box truck.

"Bingo," I whispered, all the pieces clicking into place.

Had we rode up any closer, they would have been alerted to the sounds of our motorcycles. But from what I could see, the guards were at ease, if even bored.

I turned to Horus. "You know exactly where they are, huh?"

A screech and a few head bobs were my answer.

"And if Hades doesn't already know, I bet he can smell them." A plan began forming in my head.

I stayed up there at least ten more minutes, trying to memorize the layout of the rock formation and the guards' movement. By then, the bleeding of my palms had slowed considerably. I shrugged off my cut and pulled my T-shirt over my head, tearing open the jagged holes Horus's talons had made. When my shirt was nothing but strips, I wrapped them around my hands and tied them securely.

Mari would be fretting about infection and nerve damage probably, but they would have to do for now. Despite the new hand protection, my white T-shirt bandages were stained dark red by the time I made it back to the bottom.

"So?" Jandro wasted no time when my feet touched down. "What'd you see?"

"I can see where they've got them." I pressed my thumbs into each of my aching palms. "We've got to go on foot, a small team of us. Everyone else wait here for a signal."

"And the animals?"

I grinned, stretching my fingers out. "They're going in first."

THIRTY

MARIPOSA

I winced as the needle jabbed cruelly in Gunner's arm and quickly filled the attached tube with blood.

"What are you doing with that?" I demanded through gritted teeth.

It was beyond infuriating what Corinne was doing to him. Touching him, poking, prodding, and now taking his blood without permission. She hadn't done anything extreme yet, considering the world we lived in, but she was still taking away his agency. Not giving him the option to consent or refuse. She was violating him and I never hated anyone so much.

"Running tests," she answered snippily. "For diseases."

"Hope you find a whole cocktail of 'em," Gunner hissed at her. "Everything under the sun, 'cause God knows I've been everywhere."

"I doubt that very much, Demon," she purred. "Any idiot can see how you touch and look at this woman." Her head snapped over to me. "You treat her like no other woman exists, but my men tell me you haven't slept with her. You're holding out for some reason, waiting for her."

His jaw tensed, Adam's apple bobbing as he swallowed. The clever-tongued Demon was speechless for once.

"It's a fascinating love story, I'm sure," Corinne sighed. "But I have no time for it, as I have profits to make. Still," she ran a finger along his jaw, her men restraining him against leaning away from her, "I'm not above petty victories. Maybe I'll let the little female watch when I tie you to my bed tonight."

"Fuck you," he spat. "You'll never have this."

"I already do," she chuckled. "Once your blood tests come back clear, you are mine to do with as I please. There is another test I must conduct however, and you'll see I'm not completely heartless."

She turned to me, smirking gleefully.

"You can have him first. It's the one and only time you'll get with him, so make it count."

I stared at her in complete disbelief. "What?"

"You two are going to fuck. Right here. Right now." She waved away her men holding us and stepped off the flat slab of rock we were chained to. Someone brought out a metal folding chair and she took a seat less than ten feet away from us.

Without anyone to hold us apart, Gunner and I found each other again. He pulled me into his chest and my finger immediately went to apply pressure to the puncture wound in his elbow from the needle.

"What's taking them so long?" I whispered, hiding my face in his hair.

He squeezed my nape, lowering his forehead to mine. "I don't know, baby girl. Maybe something happened."

"Get on with it already," Corinne demanded from the sidelines. "I don't have all day."

I glared at her, somehow feeling safer behind the barrier of Gunner's arm. "Why do you want us to...?"

"Like I said before," she rolled her eyes at me, "A nice body and big dick mean nothing if he doesn't know how to use them. I want to see how well he pleases you before taking him for myself."

"Fucking hell." Gunner sucked in a breath, his arms sliding protectively around me.

I kept my eyes trained on her, my hand wrapped around his bicep with my forehead on his shoulder. "You can't force us to do anything."

She gave the tiniest jerk of her head and the scrawny guy, Elric, quickly shouldered his weapon. He fired one shot toward our feet, making us both jump back with a cry as sparks flew from the round's impact.

"Actually, I can," Corinne retorted. "I'm well-practiced in forcing my merchandise to do anything and everything I want. So I suggest you get started before I use more...*serious* methods."

My hold on him now trembled, my body otherwise frozen in fear. This bitch wasn't just on some power trip, fulfilling a mission to topple everyone who got in her way. No, she was certifiably insane.

"Mari..." Gunner's lips tickled my ear, his hands

sliding up to caress my neck. While fear froze me, threatening to make me shatter, the beautiful golden man held strong like a fortress wrapped around me.

The kiss he pressed to the edge of my jaw was tantalizingly slow, his lips open as the tip of his tongue danced along my skin.

"Gunner, no," I whispered, the tears threatening to return. "Not like this."

"I didn't want it like this either, baby girl, but what choice do we have?" He held my face with one hand, pulling my hip forward with the other. "I won't let them hurt you."

"But what about you?" My breaths came out ragged and choked. "She's going to—"

"Don't worry about me. I'll only give her what she wants as long as she guarantees no harm will come to you."

"Reaper and the others," I argued desperately. "The club. They wouldn't leave us. They have to be coming."

He released a sad sigh. "I don't hear any motorcycles. Do you?"

"It can't be—"

"Shh." His kiss was achingly sweet, full of sadness and apology. "Remember what I said when I first touched you?"

How could I forget? He was the first one of them who touched me with real desire. His body pressed to mine in the kitchen at Old Phoenix. I was so scared he would assault me back then, but now I knew that was the last thing he would ever do.

"You said you'd make it good for me."

His eyes bore into mine like two glittering swimming pools—full of depth, regret, and unabashed want.

"I meant it back then," he whispered. "And I still mean it now."

This time, when his mouth swept across mine, I let him in.

His tongue flicked over mine in a soft, but insistent caress. When his hands fell to my waist and pulled me flush to him, I let him. No more complaints and threats came from our audience, so I figured we were doing well enough. My eyes closed as my fingers dove through his blonde hair, filling my senses up with him as I shut out the rest of the world surrounding us.

He skimmed those long fingers under the hem of my shirt, then molded his palms to the curves of my sides. His thumbs grazed the edges of my breasts but didn't move higher, nor did he attempt to take my top off.

"I don't want them to see you," he murmured into my ear. "They don't get to enjoy you like I do."

"Gunner…" My head leaned back as his mouth moved down my neck. There was so much I wanted to tell him, so much I wanted to say. If this was truly our last moment together, it should have come pouring out of me. But every word was stuck. Blocked by the tight fist of despair in my chest.

And this gorgeous, infuriating man kept shushing me whenever I said his name, like he didn't want to hear any of it. Maybe it was better that way. Better to not know what was never able to happen.

He took my hand from his shoulder, kissing my palm once before bringing it down his body to press against the front of his jeans. My throat tightened up, choking off all of my air. He was hard, forming such a sexy outline of his length through his clothes.

But I couldn't bring myself to touch him. None of this was right. It was so wrong, my stomach contorted into knots. This should only be happening with his full consent, because he *wanted* to be with me, alongside Reaper and Jandro. Not because we had guns pointed at us.

"Gunner, I can't—"

"It's okay, Mari. Please." His voice held a tinge of desperation. "I want this. I want *you*. Fuck the circumstances. I've always wanted you." His palm cupped the back of my neck, holding me in place for another deep kiss full of longing. "If this is the only way I can have you, so fucking be it."

"Elric. Make them hurry it up."

Corinne's voice snapped me out of it like ice injected into my spine. A gun cocked, the barrel pointed at Gunner's legs. "Pants off. Now." Gunner obeyed without hesitation, unzipping and shoving the worn denim down his thighs while leaving his boxer briefs in place. "And you," the barrel swung to point in my direction. "Top off. Let's see those pretty tits."

"No," Gunner bit out, moving to stand in front of me. He glared directly at Corinne. "You want to see how good I am? She doesn't need to be naked for that. And you're not gonna find out anything by rushing us. As a woman, you should know it takes time to get warmed up."

"There's a difference between warming up and

stalling," she retorted. "And I don't appreciate you wasting my time. In any case, I think I've seen enough. Unchain him, Elric, and bring him to my personal slave pen."

"No!" Now it was me fighting to get in front of Gunner, trying as hard as I could in vain to prevent them from taking him.

But his body went impossibly stiff, rigid like a block of stone.

"Gunner?" I looked up to see his eyes had rolled back so only the whites were visible. His brow and eyelids twitched, his mouth slack and open.

"What's going on with him?" Corinne demanded. "Is he fucking epileptic? Oh, that won't do at all…"

I used to think the same thing, but when my eyes caught sight of the bird circling above us, my heart dared to soar with hope where there had been none before.

"Horus!"

It had to be. And Gunner must have been seeing through his falcon's eyes right at that moment. He was right about no motorcycles being nearby, but the club *had* to be here if Gunner's falcon was.

The bird circled so high, it became a barely visible speck. Gunner seemed unsteady on his feet, so I wrapped my arms around his waist to support him.

"Shoot him," Corinne ordered with disdain in her voice, seemingly oblivious to her impending peril. "The last thing I need is a twitching, drooling idiot in my bed or on the market."

"No!"

I covered as much of Gunner's body as I could with mine just as Elric took aim. He squeezed his trigger with an evil smirk, and I shut my eyes as the shot rang out.

"Aghhh, fuck!"

Something hit me, but it wasn't a bullet. It was wet and warm. Blood.

I cracked my eyes open to see Elric clutching at his neck, blood spurting between his fingers with each beat of his heart. He fell to his knees, on death's doorstep already.

"Elric—what?" For the first time, Corinne showed emotion besides smug superiority. Her eyes widened in fear as she watched the life drain from her favorite henchman.

Above and behind her, dark feathers clung to a chunk of rock wall. It was clear from her and everyone else's reaction that no one saw Horus shred Elric's neck open.

"Madam, we seem to be under attack—"

"NO FUCKING SHIT, WE'RE UNDER ATTACK!" she roared at her guard. "Secure the perimeter! Find out who—ahhh!"

A dark blur moved like lightning throughout the room, going so fast it seemed to defy the laws of physics. An image flashed in my mind's eye--the rough shape of a man whose face I couldn't see. The man from my dream who claimed to be Hades. A voice rang out so loud, it should've echoed off the stone walls. But it seemed to come from within my head.

Their lives are ours to take. We will reap what has been sown.

Gunner had come to at some point and wrapped me

in a protective embrace as we observed the carnage around us.

Corinne and all her men were on the ground, wailing, screaming, crawling. Blood dripped from their ankles as though a major tendon had been severed. And Hades, muscles sleek and rippling, walked between the bodies with his lips pulled back and teeth stained red.

His dark predatory eyes met mine and once again, I got a flash of the faceless man who sat at the end of Jandro's bed.

"Mari! Are you hurt?"

Hands covered in bloody bandages grabbed my shoulders and spun me around. I choked out a sob at the sight of the familiar handsome face and green eyes.

"Reaper!" I didn't even hear him run up to us. "I'm fine. What happened to your hands?"

"I'll tell you later, sugar. We're getting you home." He kissed me deeply, full of relief and longing. "These fuckers have keys, right?"

"Too bad Shadow's not here. He'd smash those locks in two seconds."

"Jandro!"

"Oh, baby." He yanked me out of Reaper's arms and crushed me to his chest. "Don't you ever scare me like that again."

"Not planning on it," I murmured, wanting to burrow in the scent and safety of him.

Reaper pulled the keys from Elric's lifeless body and unlocked both of us. The moment we were free, he whistled and Hades came running to him.

"Now, boy." He gave the dog an affectionate ear stroke. "Call the Demons here."

Hades trotted to the center of the flat stone where Gunner and I had been chained, then threw his head back and let out the most haunting howl I ever heard.

"Don't worry, sugar." Reaper caressed the nape of my neck. "They're going to pay for this. All of them."

THIRTY-ONE

MARIPOSA

"My poor baby." Jandro lifted my foot and brushed a kiss against the red line where I'd been chained. "I'm never letting you out of my sight again."

"That's fine, but stop kissing me there." I wiggled my toes at his face. "I don't want more germs on your lips."

Expecting a silly comeback, Jandro's solemn face stunned me as he moved up my body. He'd been so doting when we got home, parking me permanently on his couch with blankets and pillows, forbidding me from getting up except for bathroom breaks. Surrounded with warmth and softness, the guilt on his face still cut me deeply.

"What's wrong?" I held the sides of his face. "Don't tell me you blame yourself for this."

"No, it's just, when I realized you were actually gone, I—" his voice cracked. "I never got to tell you."

"Tell me what?"

His mouth slid over mine, stealing my breath. "*Te

amo, mi mariposita. I love you so fucking much. *Tu eres mi corazon.*"

"*Te amo tambien,*" I murmured in my clumsy Spanish in between breathless, needy, all-consuming kisses. "I love you too, Alejandro."

He broke away mid-kiss, reaching into his saddlebag next to the couch. "I got you something at the market."

My eyes widened. "Jandro, you didn't have to—"

"I know. I wanted to, though." He handed me a slender, clamshell style box. "Don't tell me if you don't like it. Save my pride and fake it for me."

"Don't say stuff like that," I chided as I lifted the lid.

There was no possible way I could fake my reaction to the butterfly pendant resting on white tissue paper. "Oh my God, Jandro. This is..."

I had no words because it was absolutely perfect.

The pendant felt heavy when I slid my fingers behind it to lift it out of the box. Light shone through the yellow-orange wings, a delicate contrast to the gray metal frame they were embedded in. The metal created the shape of the wings and the signature dark stripes of the monarch butterfly, while the colored glass accentuated the beauty and fragility of such an insect.

"Do you like it?" Jandro prodded gently.

"Are you kidding me? I *love* it!" The metal chain spilled over my fingers as I lifted the whole necklace from the box. I couldn't stop staring at it, nor sliding my fingers over the smooth glass. "I don't think anyone's ever gotten me a more perfect gift. Help me put it on?"

"Don't speak too soon," he chuckled, taking the

clasps from me as I moved my hair. "Someone else might've gotten you something special too."

"Oh?" I looked at him over my shoulder, touching the pendant now sitting just below my throat. "Are you going to tell me any more than that?"

"Nope." He kissed the crook of my neck, wrapping me in a delicious hug. "I'm glad you like the necklace."

"I love it so much." I leaned back against him and kissed his temple. "Thank you. I'm never taking it off."

"Mm, that's what I like to hear." He rained more kisses down on my neck and shoulder before slowly unwrapping from me. "I'm going to check on the food. Don't go anywhere."

I snorted. "Like I could if I tried."

He went to the kitchen, humming to himself as he stirred the tortilla soup. Traditionally the recipe called for chicken, but he couldn't bring himself to kill any of his girls. He was tempted with Foghorn, but needed him for future generations. So we were having a vegetarian version tonight.

I sank into the pillows, reminiscing on this crazy fucking day. Once the rest of the Steel Demons rode up to the caves, they thoroughly searched the entire place. No other slaves were to be seen, but they did find plenty more chains and shackles.

On Reaper's orders, they shackled one ankle of every trafficker still alive, even Corinne, and attached the other end to their bikes. We rode home, dragging them behind us until their bodies were unrecognizable.

Halfway to Sheol, we stopped to unhitch the dead weight. Reaper and Jandro heated up two brands with a blow torch and stamped the bodies with the Steel Demon emblem. If anyone found them before the vultures picked them clean, they'd know exactly who these people crossed.

Jandro's front door opened as I was lost in my macabre thoughts. I looked up to see Shadow's large form crossing the living room toward me.

"Hi, Shadow," I smiled at him.

"Hi, Mariposa." He stopped several feet away from the couch, hands clasped behind his back like a soldier standing at attention. "I'm glad to see you're unharmed after what happened today."

My smile grew wider. The statement sounded rehearsed, like he practiced saying it several times. But it didn't take away from the sentiment. I actually found it endearing. He was trying, and getting so much better with every baby step.

"Thank you. That's really sweet of you."

"Yo, big dude!" Jandro called from the kitchen. "Reaper let everyone go?"

"Yes, he'll be over soon. He's helping unload supplies." Shadow's eyes darted from me to the kitchen. "I have something to fill you in on later."

"Cool. We'll talk after Mari goes to bed."

Reaper called an emergency church meeting right when we got home to let everyone who stayed back know what happened. Only Jandro stayed glued to my side to look after me. From the way Shadow was acting, my guess was they saw their own share of action here while we were gone.

"Is Gunner helping with supplies too?" I asked

Shadow, wondering how much more conversation I could drag out of him before he retreated.

"No. He went home as far as I'm aware."

"Oh."

And just like that, my mood spiraled. After everything, he still went back to avoiding me. Did he not mean everything he said while we were chained up together? Did he touch me, kiss me, protect me all that time, just out of a sense of duty to his club and president?

It took a few moments of racing thoughts for me to realize Shadow was still there. And to my complete shock, he came closer until he took a cautious seat on the arm of the couch. We were still a good six feet away from each other, but his presence was so large and overwhelming, he might as well have been sitting on top of me.

"Is everything okay, Shadow?" I noticed his distressed expression.

His odd-colored eyes flicked up to mine and I felt that familiar heat rush through me whenever he looked at me.

"Reaper gave me orders to tattoo you as soon as you feel up to it." He swallowed thickly, looking massively uncomfortable. "To prevent something like this from happening again."

"Oh. Okay." I folded my hands on top of the blanket covering my legs. "And would you be comfortable doing that?"

He raised a hand as if to run it through his hair, then seemingly changed his mind and dropped it back to his lap. "I've never tattooed a woman before but...I think I'm willing to try."

I offered him my biggest smile yet, beaming with pride. "I'm sure we'll both get through it when the time comes. From what I've seen, you do great work."

His lips twitched in what could've been the start of a smile. "Thank you." He jerked his gaze away from me abruptly and returned to standing. "I'll let you rest now. Just let me know when you're ready."

I nodded, watching as he retreated to his area of the house. "I will. Goodnight, Shadow."

"Goodnight, Mariposa."

IT TOOK NEARLY a half hour of convincing Jandro to let me stop by Gunner's house. I ate my weight in tortilla soup, demonstrated that I could walk just fine, and reminded him that double guards were posted around the perimeter that night. He begrudgingly accepted after I promised him I'd have just a quick chat with Gunner and come right back. I probably could have talked to him the next day, but my damned heart wouldn't let me wait that long.

And yet I found myself at his front door, just staring at the painted wood for minutes. My heartbeat wouldn't slow the hell down and one deep breath didn't feel like enough. Neither did five or ten.

Come on, Wilder. Time to be fearless. I raised my fist and knocked before the next thought could talk me out of it.

Of course, Gunner had to answer the door looking

so damn delicious in sweatpants and an unzipped hoodie with no shirt on underneath. His hair was freshly washed--still wet in some parts, fluffy and soft in others.

"Hey, Gun." Everything I wanted to say evaporated from my brain like a puddle on the street.

He pushed his sleeves up to his elbows, regarding me with a curious look. "Hey."

Not *hey, Mari*. Not *hey, baby girl*. Just hey.

"I, um." I fiddled with the sleeves of Jandro's sweater I borrowed. "Just wanted to see how you were doing."

"Probably about as well as you." He crossed his forearms, leaning against the door-jam like waiting for the real reason I came over.

I didn't miss the fact that he didn't invite me in. The fortress that had shut me out, that laid down its defenses when I got captured and kept me safe, was slowly closing itself off to me again.

And I'd had enough.

I'd scale those walls he was trying to put back in place. I'd take a battering ram to the doors that guarded his heart, whatever I needed to do. I got through to one man who hated being vulnerable, I could do it again. There was no undoing what had already been done.

As the silence dragged on between us, Gunner sighed and returned a hand to the doorknob.

"Well, thanks for checking on me—"

"We're not doing this again, Gunner Youngblood."

He froze, staring at me bewildered. "Doing wha—"

"This. You, shutting me out. Ignoring me. Ignoring everything we did and what was said today. I've tried to be patient with you, but I'm not playing this game anymore. If you want this to happen, just *try*." I sucked in a breath, realizing I hardly breathed at all as the words finally poured out of me. "Don't kill this before it has a chance to start."

His eyes were glued to the floor as I went on my tirade. When he looked up, I saw nothing but aching sincerity.

"You're right. About everything," he said almost too softly for me to hear. "I got the stupid idea to distance myself from you to save us both from pain. Even when Reaper and Jandro tried to talk sense into me, I was too fucking stubborn to change my behavior. I'm sorry, baby girl. I'm an idiot and I never wanted to hurt you."

Silence wrapped around us again. I was honestly floored by the sincerity of his apology. But the hurt he spoke of was still fresh.

"Okay. Well, that's a start," I mused.

He gripped the edges of his door frame as if stopping himself from reaching out to touch me.

"For what it's worth, I meant every word I said to you in that cave. To this very second, everything I said remains true. It's just..." He ran a hand through his hair, fluffing up the golden locks as he trailed off.

"The sharing aspect," I filled in for him.

"Yeah," he sighed. "That."

My mind raced with assurances to tell him, although nothing felt quite right enough to reach my mouth. They all sounded like excuses, really. Sneaky methods to coerce him into this situation he wasn't thrilled about. And the last thing I wanted to do was drag him into an arrangement if he really didn't want to be there. The truth of the matter was, what Reaper, Jandro, and I had wasn't for everyone. And it was entirely possible and fair that such a relationship was just not right for Gunner.

No matter how badly I wanted it to be.

"Can I just," his hand flopped out of his hair, "have some time to think about it? Get used to the idea first, maybe ease myself into it? I'm not saying no, I just… don't want to make any promises I can't keep."

"Y-yes!" I stammered in disbelief. "Of course!" Then more coolly, "And if you're worried about anything, or just have questions, you can ask me anything. This only works as long as I'm an open book with everybody. But you can ask Reaper and Jandro too."

Finally a heart-melting smile cracked the solemn facade. "I'm sure I'll have them. It's a starting point, I guess." He sighed. "If I'm going to do this, I have to go in with the right mindset. And I know I already got started on the wrong foot. Now I have to backtrack and start all over." His hands scrubbed down his face with a laugh. "My brain is so fucking fried, I don't even know what I'm saying anymore."

"We'll take it one day at a time," I assured him. "So, I'll see you tomorrow?"

"'Course you will." He finally released the door-jam and reached for me. "Come here."

Warm skin pressed against me as he held me tightly. A kiss dropped to my forehead like gentle rain. For some reason, that kiss unwound everything I'd been holding back and a shuddering sigh escaped me.

"Thank you," I whispered shakily into his throat.

"For being there today. For giving this a chance. For being you. For *everything*."

Another kiss, this time at the corner of my eye to catch the tear that threatened to fall.

"I'll always be here, baby girl."

Epilogue

MARIPOSA

After leaving Gunner's house, I caught up with Reaper and Hades just as they were leaving the clubhouse.

"What're you doing out here, sugar?" He tucked me into his side with Hades falling into a walk beside me on my other side. "I thought Jandro wasn't going to let you out of his sight."

"I talked him into letting me see Gunner for a minute. Alone."

Reaper gave me a knowing look. "Things happened while you two were locked up there, huh?"

I swallowed, giving myself the conscious reminder that it didn't bother him. He didn't see it as cheating. I had nothing to be ashamed of, nor did I do anything wrong. I knew it well now, but sometimes old thinking patterns cropped up.

"We kissed…kind of a lot. Most of the time, he was just holding me or shielding me. But they almost forced us to—"

"Mari, you don't need to confess every little detail to me." He chuckled as he stroked a thumb along the back of my neck. "In fact, I'd probably prefer you didn't. But is he going to join the fold or not? There's no in-between. He either has you and us, or he doesn't have you at all. That's the deal."

"He's…going to think about it."

Reaper made a disapproving sound as he stuck a cigarette in his mouth.

"Don't," I warned him. "This is weird to him. Hell, it was weird to me. The whole reason you didn't tell me right away was because you thought I wouldn't want to be shared, right?"

"But then I explained it to you," he retorted. "Gunner knows the deal. I've known him half my life. He's seen how my family worked. He should know how he feels about you. In my humble fuckin' opinion, he needs to shit or get off the pot."

"Just give him a little time." Feeling impulsive, I snatched the cigarette from his hand and took a long drag before returning it back to him. "To get used to the idea."

"Mm," Reaper chuckled amusedly, running his tongue along the filter. "I'm never throwing this one away, knowing your lips were on it."

"Gross, Rory."

"I'll give him time, only because you said to." He ignored my use of his real name. "But I don't have infinite amounts of patience. And as you know," he squeezed the back of my neck with light pressure, "I have zero tolerance for anyone who hurts you."

Hades suddenly stopped.

And like a pair of hands sprung up from the sidewalk to hold me in place, my feet stopped too.

Both of us halted with no warning at all, Reaper continued walking a few steps before noticing.

"What's gotten into you two?"

Hades stared directly down the intersection we just passed. The next block up would be Jandro's house. Down that intersection was his shop.

I had to go there.

The same force that stopped me from walking pulled me toward Jandro's shop like a rope around my waist. I couldn't explain it as anything other than a *need*. I had to go there. And I had to hurry.

"Mari?" Reaper called after me as I started down the street, Hades at my side.

"I don't know what's going on," I called back to him. "I just…need to see something."

The feeling grew stronger, more urgent, the closer I got. I bypassed the front of the duplex and went around the side. A wooden fence with a gate blocked my path to the backyard.

No, no, no. I stood on my tiptoes to reach over the fence with the latch, but wasn't tall enough. I was this close to climbing the damned thing to get to where I needed. Hades scratched at the wood and whined.

"Reaper, help me!"

Thankfully, he could see how serious I was and didn't dally.

"Mari, what do you need back there?" He reached over me and unlatched the gate with ease.

"I don't know, I just have to go there."

I ran through, following nothing but the feeling in my gut. It led to me to a large pile of debris. Ducts, hoses, chunks of drywall, concrete, and old motorcycle scraps piled nearly as tall as the fence itself. Some of it had to be from when Jandro tore down the walls between the duplex garages.

The feeling tugged me straight to that pile in a way that was almost painful. Oh no. I thought it was bad, but it was getting worse.

"Mari, what is it?" Reaper followed me, concern filling his voice.

"We have to hurry!" A desperate sense of urgency clenched my heart like a fist. I moved rocks and debris as fast as my hands could move, paying no attention to the cuts and scrapes on my hands.

This was life or death.

I could feel her life, fragile as a newborn baby, hanging in a delicate balance. I didn't know how I knew this presence was a her, but for some reason my instinct was to give her a female gender.

"Help me, Hades!" I begged as he came up next to me to sniff the rubble pile.

He barked once and immediately began digging. His front paws pulled away more dirt and sand than I ever hoped to with my bare hands. I helped him move the heavier stuff—slabs of rock, concrete, and piping.

"Wait a minute, boy. Stop," I told him.

I turned my head and leaned my ear down close to the pile when he paused. I thought I heard something but maybe…

"Meowww! Meowww! Meowww!"

"She's alive!" I cried. "Keep digging! We have to save her!"

At that point, Reaper snapped into action. He came up next to me without a word and picked up the heaviest pieces to toss over his shoulders. Hades dug out a small burrow just big enough for his head and front paws to fit through. He paused to stick his face in all the way, snorted out a nose full of dirt and kept digging.

"Please, please, please…"

I couldn't begin to understand this at all. Yes, a kitten was stuck under there, which was awful. But the idea of losing her wasn't normal sadness, it was devastatingly painful. Like I'd be losing a part of myself.

"This whole fucking thing is gonna collapse if you're not careful," Reaper warned.

"No, we can't let that happen!"

My vision grew blurry with tears. When I blinked them away, Hades reached into his burrow again, ears folded back carefully in the cramped space. When he scooted back out and turned to look at me, he held something in his jaws.

"You got her!" I gasped in relief, holding my hands out. "Is she…"

As gently as I'd ever seen him be, he placed a tiny, black saliva-soaked kitten into my awaiting palms. Her eyes still had that bluish color in very young kittens, and she barely weighed anything at all.

"Meowww!" she yelled at top of her tiny kitten lungs, squirming in my fists. "Meowww!"

She looked and acted just like a kitten, as far as I

could tell with my bodily senses. But there was something else I couldn't quite place. The feeling that pulled me to this scrap pile, the desperation and the need to dig her out had calmed, but the presence of it remained within me. It felt like something separate from me, and yet a part of me all at once.

Reaper looked at me knowingly as I held the tiny kitten to my chest.

"You were meant to find her," he breathed softly. "And nothing else in the world mattered until you did."

"Yes," I nodded. "That's exactly right."

"She chose you," Reaper added. "Like Hades chose me."

The dog sniffed the tiny, squirming ball of fur and gave her an affectionate lick. I didn't know what was happening, what this was. But right then I only saw Reaper's loyal companion. The strange, faceless man who shared the same name did not make an appearance in my head.

Reaper reached out one finger to stroke the top of the kitten's head. "Has she already told you her name?"

I nodded again, rubbing warmth into the tiny, helpless animal that I already knew was so much more.

"Her name is Freyja."

TO BE CONTINUED IN PAINLESS - STEEL DEMONS MC BOOK 4

PRE-ORDER PAINLESS BELOW!
BOOKS2READ.COM/SDMC4

Hello reader (yes, you!),

I wanted to take a moment to say thank you for coming this far on Mari and the Steel Demons' journey. These characters have not let me go since the moment I got hogtied to the motorcycle, much like Mari in Book 1! I would be writing this story whether I had zero readers or millions, because I simply *have* to. I'm eternally grateful that so many of you have come along for the ride as well. Hold on tight because it's far from over!

A few special people deserve some shout-outs: Izzy and Danielle for being the first true readers of the series, and the ones who really made me believe this little story had legs. Janet, my lovingly nitpicky beta reader who remembers *every* little thing I forget, helps keep my story straight, and breathes down my neck in the least creepy way ever. Telisha, my amazing editor who cleans up my WTF-typing and makes the story readable. This labor of love would be so much harder without these amazing ladies in my life!

And of course, a huge thank you to all the readers and authors who took a chance on me with this series and have helped spread the love via reviews, social media, or telling your friends. There are too many to name, but I appreciate every one of you!

If you'd like to hang out with me regularly, join my reader group, Crystal's Coven. We're a friendly bunch, and I'm always posting teasers and excerpts there before anywhere else online.

Group link: facebook.com/groups/crystalscoven

Thank you one last time for coming on the adventure this far! See you in the next book!

-Crystal

About the Author

Crystal Ash is a USA Today Bestselling Author from California. She loves writing steamy, heart-wrenching romance with tortured heroes, especially if they're in a reverse harem. Crystal's other loves include animals, mythology, and well-crafted alcohol, most of which can also be found in her stories.

When she's not writing, she's probably drinking craft beer with her husband or trying to coax her feral cat into accepting affection.

crystalashbooks.com

facebook.com/Crystal.Ash.Romance

instagram.com/crystalashbooks

amazon.com/author/crystalash

bookbub.com/profile/crystal-ash